RUN

MATTHEW BECKER

AETHON THRILLS

aethonbooks.com

RUN
©**2024 MATTHEW BECKER**

For Mom (1961-2022),

Thanks for instilling a lifelong love of mysteries and thrillers.

PROLOGUE

The off-duty Secret Service agent noticed the possible threat before anyone else in the square. He had been keeping an eye on the scrawny man in the big coat ever since he had gotten through the security check. The suspect was practically a kid, no more than mid-twenties. His dirty blond hair was styled in a deep fade, with a line shaved at the part, like those European soccer players. But his furtive movements and fierce, darting eyes gave him away.

The agent was just another person in the crowd today, there to see the president and a newly elected congressman speak to fawning supporters in Old Town Alexandria's Market Square. The Euro-haired kid didn't look at him once.

It was a smart move by the would-be assassin, wearing such a large puffy coat. The agent had to admit that. If he hadn't been looking with a trained eye, he wouldn't have been able to make out the gun-shaped bulge underneath. It was November, anyway, and no one would think twice about a coat that size with the chill they had been experiencing. How the suspect got it past the security, though, was another matter entirely. If the agent was right, there would be plenty of fallout and recrimination over how that had been allowed to happen.

The agent mirrored the possible shooter's steps, ten yards

behind. When the kid made it to the front of the crowd, the agent changed course and came up to the gate to the suspect's left, with only a few people between them.

The president was droning on about leadership, commitment, or integrity—who even knew at this point?—but the agent's eyes and ears were focused on the shooter, whose right arm was now tucked inside his unzipped coat. The move was coming, he could feel it. But not yet. The agent knew it wouldn't happen while the president was behind the podium. Too small a target to aim at with a handgun. The assassin would wait until the president and congressman were shaking hands, beside the podium. That would be the right time. That's what the agent would do if he were assassinating a president.

The president's speech ended, and the agent tensed, waiting for the movement he knew was coming, ready to leap into action as soon as the gun came out.

What he wasn't expecting was the shooter firing through the coat.

"Gun!" the agent yelled, a split second too late. The kid had already fired and people were screaming.

The crowd scattered as feathers exploded out of the assassin's coat.

Pop! Pop! Pop!

Euro Hair got off three more shots as the agent closed the distance. What was likely only a second felt like an eternity, like he was running through molasses. He finally threw himself on the assassin, pinning him down on the ground and knocking his gun away.

Breathing heavily, he looked up and set his eyes on a scene that would stay with him forever. The congressman lay gasping, an ever-widening circle of blood around his waist, while two Secret Service agents lay face down in front of him. Neither of them was moving, and from the pools of blood around their heads, it looked like they never would again.

The president, though. Where was he?

The agent swept his eyes around the square and saw two Secret Service agents rushing the president into his limo at the corner of Royal and King streets. Despite it all, he allowed himself a deep breath. The president was okay. The main target had escaped, unharmed.

He held down the shooter, who didn't struggle at all, his face surprisingly calm. Police officers rushed over, and Secret Service agents clapped him on the back, thanking him. It was only after the assassin had been taken away and ambulances had rushed the victims to the nearest hospital that the off-duty agent allowed himself to take stock.

He had done his duty. He'd saved the president.

CHAPTER 1
BEN
11 MONTHS LATER

Monday Night, October 20

"Hurry up, Ben!" Veronica Walsh called from down the stairs of their Old Town Alexandria townhouse. "We're going to miss the speeches!"

Ben Walsh hustled as he tucked his blue-and-white checkered shirt into his chinos. He flung a dark blue jacket over his broad shoulders. Tonight, they were off on a date to a special event at the Hungarian Embassy celebrating American and Hungarian relations. As the chief of staff for a rising political star, Ben often staffed his boss for such events. This night, though, was not about him or his boss, so he could just relax and enjoy the celebration. Veronica's good friend Dzsenifer—Jennie to her American friends—had invited the two of them to be her guests at the party. Jennie worked on all things political and military at the Hungarian Embassy and had been posted to Washington, DC, for almost two years.

Veronica stood impatiently by the door as Ben bounded down the stairs. He grinned when he saw her. She was wearing her green cocktail dress with the plunging neckline, his favorite. His grin faded, though, when he saw the gloves on her hands.

"Do you really need those?" he asked. "No one would make anything of it."

"Ben," Veronica cautioned. "Don't."

Ben sighed. He couldn't understand why she made such a big deal about always needing to hide it. No one would judge, and it would be an interesting story to tell. Or so he assumed, never having actually heard the tale of how it had happened.

The doorbell rang and Veronica opened the door to let the babysitter in. The last-minute invite had sent Ben scrambling to find one, and he was relieved when their wealthy neighbor Miranda Belle had been available and willing to watch the twins. She babysat the twins a few times before and always struck Ben as lonely and melancholic. He couldn't blame her, though. Despite only being twenty-six years old, she'd already experienced a tragic past. But she was reliable and caring, and the children loved her.

The rain that had pummeled Washington, DC, for the past week had stopped, so Ben and Veronica decided to enjoy the clear night and take the metro into the city. They exited the station and walked down Connecticut Avenue, doing their best to avoid soaking their shoes in the glistening puddles that remained. Ben took a deep breath and let the familiar post-storm scent fill his nostrils. Nothing beat that smell. He looked over and saw that Veronica was breathing in the fresh air too as she tucked a runaway strand of her blonde-highlighted hair behind her ear. Ben loved the contrast between her blonde streaks and her dark hair and olive skin. Getting those highlights had been a stroke of genius, he'd told her.

Ben's phone rang in his pocket. He looked at the screen, and the face of his best friend, Jeremy Wiles, stared back up at him. He glanced at Veronica, saw that she was watching him closely, and hit *ignore*.

"I can text or call him back later," he said. "This is a date night—my focus is on you."

Veronica smiled. "I appreciate it. With these calls for advice at all hours, I swear he considers you his unofficial campaign manager."

Ben nodded and squeezed her hand as he put his phone away. Having a best friend who was a presidential candidate was not something he'd ever thought he would experience. He still couldn't wrap his head around it.

"He hasn't exactly grasped that I declined that position, has he?" he asked. They turned onto Tilden Street and strolled toward the embassy. "I just couldn't leave what we're building here. But tonight's not about him. It's about us. When was the last time we got to dress up and go out on our own?"

"It's been too long." Veronica shot Ben a rueful smile as she looked out over the street. "You know this is my running route?"

"I didn't, actually." Ben gazed up and down the street imagining her running past every day.

"It's nice to just walk here and be able to look around. I'm normally zipping by, trying to get back before my next class starts."

"Humble brag about how fast a runner you are?"

"You bet." She bowed with the flourish of a Broadway star. "Did I ever tell you this is right where Jennie and I met?"

"Oh, really?"

"Yes. After running past her for several days and coveting her running shoes, I just had to find out where she got them."

"So that's where you got the inspiration to buy those shoes," he said.

"Yep. She had only been in the city for a few weeks. I think that's why she was so friendly. Can you imagine being sent overseas alone and trying to make friends while doing the amount of work she has to do? She was so eager to use her English—which was already better than mine was when I arrived here!" She laughed.

They passed the embassy of Kuwait on their right. Ben

always loved walking by the embassies in DC. Each one held so many stories, so much intrigue.

"You don't talk much about learning English," Ben said. "You don't talk much about your childhood at all, really." He cast a cautious glance at his wife, knowing he was dipping his foot into forbidden waters again.

Veronica's smile disappeared. "You know why," she said. "The peso crisis happened when I was young, and my family lost just about everything. I told you we lived in poverty until we finally were able to leave Guadalajara and come to the United States. Those are not happy memories I want to think about."

She stopped and turned toward Ben. "You know I don't like to talk about my past. Please don't keep bringing it up. I'll always tell you as much as I feel I can."

"I'm sorry." Ben looked away. Most of the time, Veronica was bubbly and outgoing. Nothing changed that positive demeanor as quickly as a mention of her past, though.

"I just don't understand why you keep prying," Veronica said.

Ben remained silent. He knew nothing he could say would help, but he couldn't shake the feeling that she was keeping secrets from him.

They walked in silence the rest of the way to the Hungarian Embassy.

"Veronica!" Jennie cried out when she saw the two of them enter. She hustled through the crowd. Barely over five feet tall, this was a harder task for her than most. Veronica gave her a hug when she finally made it over.

"I'm so happy you two could make it," she said, grinning. "Look at those gloves, they are stunning!"

"We wouldn't miss it, and thank you!" Veronica replied, holding her right hand playfully up at face level and wiggling her fingers. "You know me and germs." She gave a short self-deprecating chuckle.

Jennie led them around the room, introducing them to her embassy colleagues. They filled their plates with traditional Hungarian paprikash and kolbász and found a good spot to watch the speeches.

The keynote speaker was a Republican Senator with whom Ben's boss, Congresswoman Chamique Moore, had clashed several times, so Ben let his mind and eyes wander during the speech. He saw the Hungarian ambassador nodding along encouragingly. Nearby, a Democratic congressman, who had co-written several bills with Moore, was doing anything but. At least Veronica seemed to have forgiven him, catching his eye and rolling her own at a particularly egregious line.

After the speeches were over, Ben turned around and saw the food had all been replaced with desserts. He glanced at his wife, deep in conversation with an older man in a gray three-piece suit, and snuck over to check out the offerings.

"If you get one dessert, it needs to be that one."

He turned to see that he had not been as stealthy as he thought. Jennie pointed at a triangular piece of what looked to be a layered chocolate sponge cake. "Dobos torte. It's magical."

"Who did you leave my wife with?" Ben asked as he snagged a piece.

"A guy I work with. I told him she was a mathematician and he asked if she knew Paul Erdös, and the conversation went quickly above my head. When I saw you by the desserts, I escaped." She shrugged as she let her gaze pass over the table full of sweets.

Ben shook his head, smiling. Veronica could make friends and find connections anywhere. He glanced over Jennie's shoulder—easy enough to do when she was over a foot shorter than him—and saw his wife enthusiastically chatting with the old man. He grabbed a second piece of Dobos torte and headed back toward his wife, leaving Jennie to continue navigating her way through the dessert table.

"Ben, you have to meet Dominik," Veronica exclaimed as he

handed over her piece of cake. "He has an Erdös number of one. I've never met anyone with a one!"

"Ben Walsh, nice to meet you." Ben stuck out his hand and Dominik shook it with surprising vigor.

"How do you do? I am Dominik Puskás. No relation to the famous one," he added. "You have a lovely wife. How did you trick her into marrying you?"

Ben smiled politely and shared a look with Veronica. Her eyes told him to let the inherent sexism in that question go. "I ask myself that every day," he responded, pivoting quickly. "So, what exactly is an Erdös number?"

"I won't bore you with the details, but it's the math version of six degrees of Kevin Bacon," Dominik said. "We all keep track of how many degrees of separation we have between ourselves and Paul Erdös, based on our publications. He was prolific, you see."

"My Erdös number is four," Veronica said. "Not too bad, but not particularly impressive either. Although Bill Gates has a four too, so that's cool."

"I co-authored a paper with Paul Erdös and many others several decades ago, so my Erdös number is one." Dominik bowed his head. "May he rest in peace." He signaled one of the waiters. "My new friends look thirsty. Can you get us three shots of pálinka?" He saw Jennie returning from the desserts table. "Actually, make that four."

"Pálinka?" Jennie asked as she approached.

"Of course. I can't let this beautiful woman who knows of Paul Erdös get away without having our traditional drink."

"I think you'll love it," Jennie said to Veronica. In a whisper she added, "And if you don't, just pretend you do and give it to me."

The waiter reappeared, four shots of pálinka on his tray. They each took one.

"Now, if you're doing it right it should be sipped, but most people can't handle that, so take it as a shot," Dominik explained. He peered at each of them in turn. "We can all take it as shots together, to make sure no drop goes to waste."

"Let's do this. Bottoms up!" Veronica said, and all four drank their shot.

Ben squeezed his eyes shut as the liquid burned its way down his throat. "Oh, wow." He struggled to get the words out. "That is so intense." He looked over at Veronica, who was smiling away as if it had been apple juice. His face must have registered his disbelief because she winked, and Ben could have melted on the spot.

"It'd take a lot more than that to knock me off my stride," she scoffed with a playful roll of her eyes.

Dominik's face broke into a mischievous smile. "Now you are honorary Hungarians!"

———

Drunk on far too many shots of pálinka, Ben decided to take his chances again while they waited for an Uber. "Do you have a favorite memory from living in Mexico?"

Veronica flung her arms up. "Can't you just let it go, Ben? We've been married for almost a decade now, and yet how many times have you brought it up tonight alone?"

Ben grimaced, noticing that other departees were now watching them. He lowered his voice. "I'm sorry. I just don't get why you won't talk about it."

"Look," Veronica said as the Uber arrived, "it's not like I was some secret serial killer in a past life. I didn't have the best childhood, but I'm much tighter with my parents now, and that's all you need to know. You don't see me forcing you to answer uncomfortable questions about your relationship with your parents, do you?"

With that, she opened the door of the Uber, climbed in, and slammed it shut, forcing Ben to walk around the car to join her.

CHAPTER 2
FRANCISCO

Monday Night, October 20

From his vantage point on the roof, Francisco focused his binoculars on the two children playing in the living room of the townhouse across the street. The little boy, who was sitting on an oversized recliner with his legs dangling, cocked his head as if a thought had suddenly popped into his brain. The girl continued playing with her toy train set, bouncing the toys across the hardwood floors. Her eyes were glued to her Thomas the Tank Engine train, which was pulling all its cars back to the station. Neither seemed aware of the hidden presence outside, nor his plan that would turn their lives upside down.

Francisco wore a black hoodie and matching sweatpants, with a skintight top and leggings underneath, size small to fit his slender physique. His long black hair was hidden by a dark beanie. He glanced up and down the street, sweeping the area to make sure he hadn't been seen.

Francisco crouched down as low as he could on the slanted roof, waiting for a glimpse of his target. His slight stature belied a body built for a specific, often deadly, purpose. An accomplished marathon runner as well as a judoka, he had perfected both options of the "fight-or-flight" mentality that dictated much of his professional life. He preferred the flight—there was no thrill like distance running—but was experienced enough to know that sometimes he had to be ready to punch his way out of a situation. What he did enjoy were the looks on his beaten opponents' faces, the mixture of denial and shame after being humiliated by a man who appeared lighter than a feather.

After three weeks of searching and following, he was just one step away from completing his mission in the United States. He missed his family and friends back home in San Salvador. He even missed his boss, despite being the reason Francisco was so far from home, shivering on a foreign rooftop in late October.

Of course, the final step would be the hardest, so he was under no illusion he would be back home with his family anytime soon. He thought about his sister. In honest moments, he had to admit she was even more formidable than he was. She ran the judo studio he had warily stepped into several years ago after losing one too many fights. It was she who had taught him how to use his whole body in line with the judo principle of maximum efficiency, minimum effort.

She also understood when he had come to her after a session and asked if she could teach him how to make the art more streetwise.

The crisp air snaked its way down into his chest with each breath he took. *Why would anyone choose to live in a place where the October air feels like ice?* He hadn't considered this obstacle when seventy-degree weather greeted him weeks before. Living in a city that barely dropped below sixty in winter was much preferable to this. Not that it would affect the work. He was far too professional for that.

Francisco watched as the boy continued to peer around the living room, as if behind every object hid a great adventure. A young woman walked in. The babysitter, Francisco presumed, since her light hair and pale face could not have been further from the siblings' darker skin and black hair. It was difficult not to be distracted by her presence. She was the most beautiful woman Francisco had ever seen. Twice already he had *accidentally* bumped into her on the street. He stared for a couple long seconds before snapping out of it. There was a job at hand.

The two children had been the first sign that Francisco was looking in the right place. He had been briefed by those at the very top about what to expect, and the kids' presence convinced him he was in the right place.

He was about to deliver an almighty gift to his boss.

Francisco was here for one reason. He was well-known among his peers for the one skill he had perfected over all others. Better than anything else in his not-insignificant arsenal, Francisco could make a person disappear without a trace. Most importantly, he could do the deed in such a way as to allay any suspicion of his involvement. Though there were plenty as ruthless in the organization, none could match him for the specific job needed here in the United States.

The night sky continued to darken as he waited for his target to return. He'd been doing this a long time and knew patience was required in this sort of mission. He also knew, though, that the target had no idea he was this close and had no reason to behave erratically. So it was no surprise when the car drove up and dropped off an athletic Latin-American woman wearing a dark green dress and leather gloves. She carried a leather purse and an exhausted look. A tall White man in a smart coat with aviator glasses exited the other side of the car, but Francisco was not interested in his presence. This must be her. The woman for whom his boss had been searching for decades.

He just needed proof. He knew the gloves would obscure her hands outside and that the curtains would hide her while inside, so he only had a fleeting opportunity tonight. She had hidden her trail well. Her hair, once long and jet-black, fell just below her ears and was streaked with blonde highlights. The left pinky, though. That's what he knew to look for. That would tell for sure if she was his target.

The couple entered the house to the delighted screams of the two young children. The door closed and Francisco missed the reunion. He picked them up again as they moved through the house pulling the curtains shut. This was the moment he had been preparing for. Peering through his binoculars, he watched closely as the woman pulled the drapes together with her bare hands and disappeared from view.

With a deep breath, Francisco pulled out his phone, dialed, and spoke in a hushed tone. "This is it. I've found her."

CHAPTER 3
BEN

Wednesday Midday, October 22

If only they knew the true glamor of this life. Ben shook his head and chuckled as he walked down Constitution Avenue. Tourists and onlookers frantically snapped pictures on their phones as he, Congresswoman Chamique Moore, and the rest of her domestic policy experts walked from Capitol Hill.

"This is spectacular. I feel like a celebrity," Dwayne Bates, Ben's newest hire, said, looking around and waving.

Ben glanced over and down at Dwayne's grinning face. Standing well over six feet tall, Ben was used to looking at people from above, and he had six inches on Dwayne.

Ben knew the bystanders weren't really taking pictures of him or Dwayne, anyway. The Congresswoman was the star of this show.

Now thirty-eight years old, Chamique Moore was one of the youngest of a crop of progressive members of Congress who were elected together ten years previously. Born and raised in Revere, Massachusetts, just north of Boston, she continued to live there and represent her hometown.

"Piece of advice: if you want to make it in Congresswoman Moore's staff long-term, I'd suggest getting some better shoes to walk around in." Ben looked down at Dwayne's brown Oxfords, looking worse for wear and standing out in comparison to the running shoes the rest of the group were wearing. "We do a lot of walking on this team. See and be seen. Legislating shouldn't be done behind a veil."

The rain had come back with a vengeance on Tuesday but let up overnight, allowing them to make their outdoor trek. Ben chuckled as he watched Dwayne leap to avoid a large, glistening puddle.

Ben checked his phone as they walked. He was surprised to see a text from Veronica. She didn't normally reach out during the day unless it was a time-sensitive issue, and she knew he would always pick up the phone in that case. He read the first three words and felt a warmth grow inside him. *I love you.*

The rest of the message cooled him down. *I just need you to know that.*

He looked at the time stamp. It had been sent an hour or so ago, just after eleven. He read it again.

One more time.

Why would she send this? He knew she loved him—he didn't need a text reminder.

Ben didn't notice that the rest of the group had slowed, and he walked right into the back of Congresswoman Moore.

"What? Ben!" she scolded.

"I'm sorry, Congresswoman. I got distracted." She liked informality when with her staff, but in public they maintained a level of decorum. Bumping into the back of your boss in the middle of a busy street filled with tourists did not meet that standard.

"What's up?" she asked.

"I don't know, but I got a strange text from V."

"Call her. You'll be distracted either way, so go ahead and see if you're needed."

Ben moved away to place the call. He knew Veronica's schedule had her teaching morning classes this semester, so this wouldn't be in the middle of class.

No answer.

Nothing inherently odd about that, as she was often with colleagues or students and didn't like to interrupt those conversations. He put his phone away.

"No luck. I'll try again later," he said as he caught back up to the group.

———

Ben texted his wife a few more times in the afternoon but didn't get any response. He tried her office phone at Georgetown University, but it went to voicemail. Odd that she didn't even send a quick text back saying she was busy. He looked at his phone again and realized his texts to Veronica hadn't gone through. *Why would her phone be off?*

His afternoon was chalk-full of meetings and calls, and he appreciated the chance to get lost in politicking and crafting policy. At six-thirty, he finally finished up his final tasks for the day, checked on his staff, and gave a quick oral end-of-day report to Congresswoman Moore. He got home just before seven, bone-tired from the exertions of a full workday, which were exacerbated by the nagging worries that even busyness couldn't abate. He walked in and immediately noticed the silence. *Maybe Veronica is picking up Nico and Maria from the birthday party*, he thought, before realizing they wouldn't be ready to be picked up for another hour.

"V, are you here?" he called.

No response.

"Veronica?"

Nothing.

The worry morphed into a legitimate fear.

"What the fuck?" He looked around the empty entranceway.

He walked through the house, the fear growing as each room turned up empty.

Where could she be? Why send that text? Thoughts raced through his mind as he stood in their bedroom, his last hope of finding her at home gone. His heart thumped loudly against his chest.

Breathe, you've got to breathe, he told himself. Think logically. She went to campus this morning. Start there.

A sense of dread he couldn't put into words caused him instead to flip on the news.

"Breaking," the anchor declared. "Police continue to respond to the multiple-casualty shooting incident near Peirce Mill on Tilden Street in Rock Creek Park."

Ben froze.

No.

It couldn't be, could it?

He'd seen a news alert about a shooting in between meetings, but with the city having a homicide rate of well over two hundred victims per year, he hadn't even considered it might be connected to Veronica.

His worst thoughts were interrupted by his phone finally ringing. He scrambled it out of the pocket of his chinos, relief flooding through him.

It wasn't Veronica.

"Hey bud, just had a few quick questions I wanted your opinion on." Jeremy Wiles' voice was far too calm and normal for Ben.

Ben erupted. "No! Not now!"

"Whoa, what's wrong, my guy?" Jeremy's cool demeanor was a hit on the campaign trail, a major reason he was leading in every national poll, but Ben was not interested in it now.

"It's V. She isn't answering my calls, and they've been going straight to voicemail all day, so her phone must be off. I figured she must have just forgotten her charger, but, oh my God, this shooting."

"Wait, hold on one second," Jeremy said. "There's no reason she'd have been anywhere near whatever happened in Rock Creek Park."

"No, that's not … that's not true." Ben could barely get the words out. "That's her running route. She runs out the Western Ridge Trail by Rock Creek and turns around at Peirce Mill. Every day."

CHAPTER 4
JEREMY

Wednesday Night, October 22

"What was up with that strange call you got yesterday?"

Jeremy Wiles looked up from the computer to see his campaign manager, Ernest Brown, standing at the door.

"Which call?" Jeremy feigned ignorance.

"That one from the mysterious voice who would only talk directly to you."

"Ah, yeah, that guy."

"I wouldn't have let it cross your radar, but the man had such gravitas in his voice I felt compelled. He just kept saying, 'I've found what he's looking for,' until I patched him through."

Jeremy shook his head, smiling. "You should have trusted your instinct. It was just some crackpot, nothing of any importance."

"Wow, really? I wouldn't have thought that." Ernest shrugged.

Jeremy waved his hand dismissively. "What else have you got for me?"

"Latest polling. Marist. You're still plus three on anyone else in the Democratic field head-to-head and the only one ahead of President Leishear. Probably still down to your shared history."

"Not because of my solid recognition points?" Jeremy smiled. American history was riddled with pretty-boy politicians from the Northeast—Boston, in particular—and he was confident he was next in line. Not that he'd taken anything resembling a straight path to get to where he was.

"Hey look," he said. "I need you to take care of wrapping up tonight. I had a non-campaign thing come up that I have to deal with. Can you do that?"

Ernest raised a playful eyebrow. "A non-campaign thing? Like a date night with Natalia?"

Jeremy admonished him with a side-eye glare. "That'll be all. Thank you, Ernest."

"Have a good night, sir," Ernest said as he pulled the door shut. "But don't forget you promised me her autograph!"

———

"Ben." Jeremy put his phone on speaker as he drove down 14th Street toward the National Mall and Alexandria to its south. "I'm on my way over."

"I'd say you don't need to, but that's not true, and I'm glad you are."

Jeremy could hear the relief in Ben's voice, briefly poking through the wall of stress and worry.

"What do you need? I told Nat not to wait up, so I'm here for whatever."

"I don't know. I really just don't know what to do."

"Have you eaten?"

Ben's silence answered the question.

"Okay, let me grab something quick for us and I'll bring it over. You know you've got to eat, right?"

"Thanks, Jeremy. I can't even think about that right now."

"No problem," Jeremy said. "You don't want to get hangry." He needed Ben to stay upbeat and keep his wits about him.

"If I recall, you've never been in the firing line of my pre-meal wrath, have you?" Ben asked.

Jeremy smiled to himself as he drove across the 14th Street bridge and merged onto the George Washington Parkway. He could hear a bit of lightness in his best friend's voice. *Amusing choice of words, though—firing line—considering my profession before this last year,* he thought. "I was not. I knew when to stay out of sight."

Ben sighed, and Jeremy could tell his success at distracting his friend from ever-darkening thoughts had been short-lived.

"I just don't understand," Ben said, his voice so quiet Jeremy had to lean his head down to hear him through the phone speaker.

"Have you heard anything new?"

"No. I'm just watching the news, refreshing socials, waiting for something. And I keep checking my phone every two seconds, even though it's on high so I'd hear if she calls or texts."

"I'm going to voice what I think is going on in your mind. Stop me if I'm wrong," Jeremy said.

"Okay, go ahead."

"You're worried that Veronica was somewhere near the shooting and may be injured or worse, so you're watching the news just until you hear who the victims are."

"Yes."

"Here's my thought, and how I can help: I'm going to hang up with you, and I'm going to call the main hospitals, starting with George Washington, and see if I can find out anything. I'm sure you've already done it, but I can throw around my weight if I have to and see if I get anywhere. That sound good?"

"Please … yes."

CHAPTER 5
THE GIRL

saw my first dead body when I was only five years old. In hindsight I think I was too young to truly understand its magnitude. It certainly changed me, though.

How could I be the same after?

Especially since it was not the only body I was to see as a child. Not the only person in whose death I played a major role.

My father was something of an important figure in town, so my family lived in a large house with high walls surrounding the grounds. There were several smaller houses too, where all the people who worked for my father lived. At the time, I didn't fully understand the reasoning for the walls but loved being able to wander around the compound unsupervised. My favorite activity was playing on the swings with my ten-year-old brother. I would run in the house afterward, all sweaty, and my mother would always have an ice-cold glass of water waiting for me.

Mom was the sweetest woman I had ever known, and I idolized my brother and dad. I loved my little family and all the friends and relatives who lived near us.

I was out climbing in my favorite tree that morning. It had a special nook that was easy for me to reach, and I could sit there all day and watch all the goings-on in our compound. I saw one of Dad's friends come toward our house. I recognized him, although I didn't know his name. He had a large belly and wild unruly hair. He was wearing a Hawaiian shirt buttoned with only one button, showing off his gut as if he was proud of it. I didn't think he should be proud. I always wondered why Dad put up with him, let alone liked him. He walked up the stairs past the giant Corinthian columns. Mom told me once that those were the fanciest columns from Greece, and even though I didn't know where Greece was or how they got them from there, I loved their majesty. I thought this man should have to go around to the back. He shouldn't get to look at the fancy columns. I didn't think he should be allowed to live on the compound, even though he lived in the smallest house, far off in the corner.

He was only inside for a few minutes. He came back out the giant double doors with a large, overstuffed brown envelope. I knew the routine. I had seen this happen several times in the past when I'd been outside in my tree. I liked to watch from a distance and learn things about my father's business. Normally this guy left as quickly as he came, and I would hear his loud car rev as he sped off outside the gates, taking the envelope to who knows where.

I hated that sound.

This time, though, he turned right and crept along the wall to Dad's garage. I stared as he jimmied the door open and disappeared inside. He reappeared a minute later, but with two envelopes in his hands. He looked around, unaware that I could see him from the tree, and hurried away.

That evening, as the whole family sat together eating dinner, I asked my father, "Why did you let the man in the crazy shirt go into your garage? I thought that was your special place and no one was allowed in there."

The dining room went silent. Mom looked worriedly up at Dad, whose eyes were flashing.

"Who went into my garage?" he asked, his voice steady and calm. He placed his fork down, balancing it on the edge of the plate without a sound.

"The man with the envelope," I replied. "He went in with it but then had two when he came out."

I felt like his gaze could pierce right through me. I tried and failed to suppress a shudder.

"This is a serious accusation. I know you don't like him, but he's always been a good friend to me. Are you sure of this?"

I fell silent. How could I be sure? I glanced over at my brother, slopping his soup without a care in the world. No help there. I shot a hopeful look at my mother.

"We can check this ourselves." Relief flooded through me as Mom stepped in.

"Your father and I will take care of it. Don't you worry, little one," she said to me. I sat there, slinking lower in my chair, hoping I hadn't done anything wrong.

Don't get me wrong—I loved Dad, but there was something scary about him, and I did not want to make him mad.

———

The sound of raised voices woke me up late that night. I peeked out my window and saw Dad and his unlikeable friend arguing outside near the best swing, the one that swung so high it was almost parallel to the ground. Dad was furious. I could see his fists clenched tightly, the telltale sign I had learned early on. I snuck down the stairs and crept to the side door to hear better. As I chanced a glance out the screen door, I saw Dad raise a brown envelope in his hand, exactly like the one the man had taken from the garage.

"She saw you. There's no use lying to me. She saw." Dad wasn't one for using more words than necessary.

"No! She's a kid—she has no idea," the man protested. "I took the envelope to Mauricio, like always."

"You and I both know you took two envelopes. One to Mauricio, and I'd guess if I searched your house, I'd find the other one," Dad growled at him.

"I—"

"Were you going to hold onto those marked bills as an insurance policy, to try to blackmail me? Or were you going to go spend it? It doesn't matter. You disrespected me. You disrespected our arrange-ment. And you disrespect my daughter, calling her a liar," Dad said, each sentence terse and brimming with anger. "Look over at the door. She's standing here right now, listening."

I scampered back behind the wall, my heart thumping. How could he have possibly seen me? He was facing away from the house!

"Don't do that, my little squirrel. I heard you come down the stairs. Come on out." My father beckoned me out of the house as he spoke.

I paused and then stepped over the threshold.

"Angel here needs to apologize to you."

I walked slowly over to them.

Dad turned toward the man. "Say 'sorry' to my daughter."

Angel looked directly at me. "I am very sorry, child. I didn't mean to disrespect you." He looked hopefully back up at Dad. "Look, nothing happened, and I apologized to your daughter. Are we done here?"

Instead of replying, Dad turned to me and crouched down with a big smile. "This is a life lesson. Saying you're sorry is very important. But ..." He straightened, still smiling, and faced Angel. "When you do something bad, just saying sorry is not enough. Sometimes there needs to be a punishment."

Without changing his expression, he pulled out his gun and shot Angel in the forehead.

CHAPTER 6

BEN

Wednesday Night, October 22

Ben stood in his kitchen sipping a cup of herbal raspberry tea, trying to come up with other ways to calm himself down. The countertops were bare and gleaming, every glass and plate neatly hidden away in cabinets. *Control the things you can, right?*

He could barely contain the stress and nerves inside him. He was the guy who always had an answer, always knew what to do. If there was a problem, Ben could fix it. But not this. He couldn't just go and fix this.

He wanted to scream, to yell, to punch a wall. Anything for a release. *I'm always prepared for anything, so I should know what to do*, he thought. *But how do you plan for this?*

He knew this helpless feeling was the downfall of plenty of men and women like him, especially in this city. When a person is used to being in charge and in control, and that's taken away, the stress builds up inside until they explode.

Ben had picked up the kids from their friend's birthday party. Luckily, Nico and Maria were too tired to ask many questions. He hadn't wanted to lie to them, so was grateful when they accepted the half-truth that Mom hadn't come home from campus yet.

Jeremy reappeared after Ben tucked the kids in. He stood next to him, allowing Ben to process it all in the silence. The remnants of Ben's barely touched dinner bowl sat in stark contrast to Jeremy's bowl that could have come straight from the dishwasher.

"It's past ten o'clock, and we haven't heard anything. Something has happened." With the twins asleep upstairs, he put his fear into words. "She must have been there, Jeremy."

"Look, we've tried every hospital in the area, and none of them said she's there."

"Yes, but they didn't exactly deny it either, did they?"

"They just didn't comment, that's all. I know. This is really hard." Jeremy stared at Ben, conviction in his eyes. "But look, no news is good news right now. The police wouldn't tell me anything, but surely they're confirming victims and we haven't heard anything. The longer you aren't called, the better chance she wasn't involved."

As if on cue, the news anchor announced that the police had confirmed four victims dead at the scene, and one in critical condition being operated on at George Washington University Hospital. No names were announced yet, but this seemed to be a random attack. The shooter, one or more, was still at large.

That was it. A multiple homicide, with an unknown gunman, and it was given a few seconds of airtime. Local news only.

Ben listened, staring at the television, willing it to provide positive news, as the anchor listed off the other news of the day. It was the anniversary of a deadly hit and run near Potomac Yard with still no leads on the culprit; a Salvadoran crime boss had been spotted in Miami last week; and there were swirling rumors that the Chief Justice of the Supreme Court, Bartholomew Marsden, was preparing to retire. *How could they be focusing on anything else?* Ben thought. *None of this is at all significant right now.*

Jeremy suggested calling the Georgetown mathematics department, but Ben couldn't get any answer.

"I think we're going to have to wait until morning to get any word from them," Jeremy said.

"Okay. I need to talk through everything again."

Jeremy nodded, encouraging him.

"What I don't get is this text she sent me."

Jeremy looked at him, an eyebrow arched. "What do you mean?"

"She sent me this weird text telling me she loved me, and I need to remember that."

"Wait, when?"

"This morning. Definitely before noon. Hold on." Ben pulled his phone out of the pocket of his worn jeans and scrolled. "At 11:13 a.m."

Jeremy's eyes narrowed. "And when did they say on the news that the shooting happened?"

"The first 9-1-1 call was just before one in the afternoon."

"Weird. But okay, follow that thread," Jeremy said. "If you think those two things are connected, then what you're saying is that Veronica knew something about the shooting before it happened."

"I know. But otherwise, it's just a crazy coincidence?"

"Ben. Look. There are a million reasons why Veronica might want to tell you she loves you, and all but one mean something other than being involved in this."

Ben felt his face flush and his muscles tense up. "I just don't get how you can be so calm right now. I'm freaking out and you're trying to be rational. I don't like it."

Jeremy walked around the kitchen island and placed his hands on Ben's shoulders. "You know I'd be doing the exact same thing if we couldn't find Nat. That's why I'm here—to try to help you by being rational."

Ben stepped back and Jeremy's arms dropped. "All right, Mr. Rational. What now, then?"

"Let me ask you a question," Jeremy said. "And I want you to know I just need to ask this."

"Go ahead." Ben had an idea what was coming.

"I don't want to ask this …" Jeremy trailed off.

"Spit it out!" Ben said with more ferocity than he intended.

"Could she be with someone else?"

"No."

"Is it possible she's off with someone, and that was why she sent you that note and just hasn't heard about the shooting yet?"

"Absolutely not."

"And you're sure of this? I mean, kinda by default, isn't it true that you wouldn't know?"

"She wouldn't. I know her too well."

Jeremy shrugged.

"Anyway, she wouldn't do that to Nico and Maria. She would be home in time to see them before bed." Ben nodded to himself. That made sense. He felt sure she wasn't cheating on him. But wouldn't that be a better option than the alternative? She'd be safe, at least.

"If we really think this is true, then you've gotta call your in-laws."

Ben squeezed his eyes shut and bowed his head slightly.

"It's late," he said.

"I know," Jeremy responded. "But imagine their reaction if you waited."

"You're right. I'll do it now." Ben sighed and grabbed his phone. He waited and listened to the phone ring. He was certain it would go to voicemail. What seventy-year-olds were up at almost midnight on a Wednesday?

"Ben?" A groggy voice answered just before the final ring.

"We need to talk. It's about Veronica."

CHAPTER 7
ZEKE

Wednesday Night, October 22

Dzikamai Jackson strode from the parking lot down the shallow incline toward Peirce Mill, ducking under crime scene tape as he went. He stopped and stood still, surveying the scene, his eyes drawn to the vinyl sheets on the ground. Now that the scene was safe and the detectives had done their first go-through, it was time for him, the youngest crime scene technician in the department, to come in and do his part.

Dusk had come and gone, and now only the floodlights prevented complete darkness. This was a great aspect of living in this city. Here he was, only about four miles from the White House, and there was minimal light pollution.

The first reports of the incident had been called in just before one in the afternoon. The still-at-large shooter meant Dzikamai had to wait until the area was cleared, and the detectives had finished their initial investigation. So here he was, at Peirce Mill almost nine hours after the shooting took place, beginning his work. He carefully walked over the cool, dry grass. An outdoor crime scene was a nightmare. Trace evidence could be anywhere, and establishing a reasonable perimeter was a hopeless task.

The contamination, though. That was the true difficulty. Police officers and EMTs were often the worst offenders, through no fault of their own. Running through a scene trying to catch a perpetrator or attempting to treat an injured victim were necessary tasks but could destroy all sorts of evidence. He glanced at the small fenced-in area behind Peirce Mill. A historical marker told him that the stone mill was built by Isaac Peirce in the 1820s to grind corn, wheat, and rye. At least there were no animals on the grounds. That would have been a serious pain.

He knew he had to be meticulous. As well-respected as he was, he was still only twenty-four years old and an understudy in a case as big as this. The chief wasn't yet ready to give the crime scene to Dzikamai. He'd caught a break, though. His supervisor, Charles Wills, was allowing him to have a first go-through, so he wanted to make sure he got it right. Wills had told him it was a sign of the immense level of trust they had in him, and Dzikamai did not want to let him down.

The police had set up in the small gravel area between Peirce Mill and Peirce Barn. As he walked past the mill toward Rock Creek, still surging from the rain of the previous week, he could see again the four vinyl sheets that were spread over lumpy shapes, the white color in stark contrast to the green of the slick grass.

"Hey, Zeke," Detective Emilia Brown said as she approached him. "Five victims, four confirmed dead here, one in surgery. Looks like all four here were runners. From the shape of the bodies it appears one was shot first, and the other three were all shot while running away."

Even though the first syllable of his name was pronounced like a soft "j," Dzikamai allowed those who couldn't pronounce it to use the nickname "Zeke." Much easier for them than the name his Zimbabwean mother had given him. Even his American father couldn't always get it right.

Zeke looked down at the first body, lying just off the running path toward the bank of Rock Creek. He liked to form a snap opinion of the scene, but was always careful to not allow it to affect his forensic conclusions. A crime scene tech needed to look at every piece of evidence with a blank slate. Detective Brown was probably right, though. The other three, grouped together about ten yards farther down the trail, were all lying on their stomach, as if they had been gunned down amid attempted escapes.

"Any word on their identities?" he asked.

"Four dead. Two men and two women. A third male victim at the hospital. The women had their driver's licenses with them, one of the guys had a college ID card in his shoe, and the other had one of those Road ID things that says name and emergency contact. We're not releasing any names publicly yet."

He turned to face Detective Brown. She looked more like a punk rocker than a cop, with her spiked Mohawk haircut bleached blonde this week and piercings in her ears, nose, and upper lip. He liked working with her. She was the smartest person he'd ever met, but there was no one humbler. She was down to earth and, frankly, much more interesting than anyone else in the department.

"What about the fifth? The one still alive. Where was he found?" he asked.

"A bit farther south, still on the trail but down in the tunnel under Tilden Street," she replied. "What's your initial feeling?"

Zeke appreciated that the detective asked him as an equal, even though he was several rungs down the totem pole from her.

"First thought, I agree with your theory. Probably a single gunman, since it appears only one was shot before the others ran. He shoots the first victim from farther north on the trail, the others turn back down and run. He or she—for statistics' sake,

I'll say he—must have some level of proficiency with firearms, since taking down four people running away from you takes some doing. The fifth victim is still alive and manages to make it down the trail before falling."

He nodded in the direction of where the fifth victim had been found. "I feel pretty good on that last assessment, since I can see the droplets of blood going down the trail from here."

"I agree with almost all of that. Except ..." Detective Brown pointed at the three grouped bodies. "It's entirely possible the shooter just sprayed bullets in their direction and had a powerful enough gun to do the damage anyway. I got here after the bodies were already covered so I don't know what any of the wounds look like yet."

Detective Brown liked to joke that she was the true "enemy of certainty," an epithet she had told Zeke was originally given to an Austrian philosopher. She knew all sorts of things like that. Zeke had only worked with her a handful of times but had already learned more from her than he could have imagined. Don't let your own ideas get in the ways of the facts, she always told him. Hasty decisions made with imperfect information are how killers get away.

"Could be," Zeke responded as the detective walked up the incline back toward her car. "I'll let you know once I have more concrete findings."

As Detective Brown had alluded, it appeared the victims did not come in contact with their assailant, which made it unlikely there would be any trace evidence from the killer on the bodies. That assumption would not in any way change Zeke's methods, especially on a case with Detective Brown. Slow and careful precision was the only way to do his job.

He glanced at the rushing water, back to the old building, and then finally down at the four bodies in between. Time to go to work.

———

Satisfied he had completed his preliminaries and had covered the entire perimeter, Zeke walked back over to the first body. He pulled the sheet back to reveal a thin young man well over six feet tall. The man lay on his back on the trail, twenty yards north of Tilden Street. His open eyes stared up at Zeke, wide and frozen in a haunting gaze. Zeke studied the single bullet hole at the man's hairline.

He must have seen it coming.

He saw the shot and couldn't move fast enough. *That's a vision that will show up in my nightmares.*

The man, who looked like he was just a kid, was wearing a pair of tiny Nike running shorts and a runner's tank emblazoned with the emblem from a local running store. Definitely not just someone out for a casual jog.

"Guessing he was running forward when he was shot," Zeke said out loud despite there being no one within earshot. "Assuming he saw the shot, he was running toward the shooter. Why?"

Zeke considered that. Was it a combination of confidence and fear that said the best option was to charge the shooter? Or was he not aware the shot was about to come and was simply running normally? Or some other reason? That'd be for the detectives to think through further.

Detective Brown had given him access to photos of everything already collected in evidence bags. He swiped through the pictures until he got to one with cards taken from the first victim's small zipped pocket. He had a driver's license, credit card, and American University student ID, all showing that he was Mark Bandem, a twenty-year-old sophomore. He had a beaming smile in his student ID picture, the face of a young man at the beginning of a great adventure. Zeke glanced up at the man's face, confirming that this was indeed him, and that adventure had been violently cut short.

Zeke finished his examination and moved down the trail.

The next three victims were all lying on their stomachs,

head-to-foot in a row just at the north entrance to the tunnel. Blood coagulated in a combined pool beneath the bodies. All three were also students at American. Zeke sighed. A group out running together. Clothing and builds that suggested athletes, not just kids trying to stay in shape.

One head shot each.

Zeke furrowed his brow. He assumed the detectives had already noted this, the precision of the shooter. No chance this was just some dumb asshole with a gun. The odds that someone without training could take down three fleeing victims one by one without wasting a shot were astronomical.

"Detective!" he called over to Detective Brown, who was staring down at the creek from the parking lot, deep in thought.

"What's up, Zeke?"

"Do you know how many times the victim in surgery was shot?"

"Ah, shit. Did you not hear?"

"Hear what?"

"The fifth victim died just as they started surgery."

Zeke bowed his head.

"To answer your question, as far as I know it was a single shot, hit the base of the neck."

"Oh boy." Zeke shook his head in wonder.

"What?"

"The victims all have headshots. And look." Zeke pointed at several spots on the trail. "No extra shell casings, just the five."

Detective Brown nodded. "So, we've got five runners, presumably together—"

"They were," Zeke jumped in. "The four here are all from American University."

"Okay, I still need to confirm the fifth, but seems like a group all running together. Then something happens here and they're taken out one by one by our shooter, who is extremely capable with a firearm."

"I think you're going to have your hands full with this one, Detective."

"I agree. Would love a witness."

"Yeah, I was wondering about that. No one saw anything?"

"None that we know of. It's a busy trail, so I think there's a chance someone else saw what happened, but if they did, they're not coming forward yet."

"I'll have plenty of info for you and Wills," Zeke said. "But for now, I'm wondering what the first guy saw that led him to be shot in the forehead. It's not my job to speculate, but I'd guess this wasn't just some random shooter here. I think our first guy saw something."

"I'll think about it." Detective Brown pursed her lips. "I'll let you keep going. This is gonna take everything we got."

CHAPTER 8
BEN

Thursday Early Morning, October 23

G abriela and Ricardo Aguilar arrived at Ben's house just before two in the morning. Ricardo put down two small suitcases and exhaled deeply while Gabriela gave Ben a long hug. Ben welcomed them inside in a hushed voice. He hoped he sounded calm, but he knew it was unlikely.

Ben looked at the exhausted faces of his in-laws. He had only called them two hours ago and they'd thrown some clothes together and made the drive up from their home in Williamsburg in record time.

"I'd say you didn't have to come tonight, but I know there's no way you would have waited, and honestly, I'm relieved that you're here," Ben said. "I've never felt so helpless."

"We will find her. I just know it." Ricardo looked straight into Ben's eyes with a steely glint that made it clear he believed his own words.

"Tell us again, what is going on?" Gabriela asked. Sharp and to the point, as always.

"Okay. There are two different things here. First is that I got a text from Veronica saying to remember that she loves me."

Gabriela and Ricardo shared a look that Ben couldn't discern.

"Second, she didn't come home tonight, and there was a shooting along her running route."

"And there's a chance she was there around that time, you think?" Ricardo asked.

"Well, she goes on a run there during the middle of the day, and they said that the shooting happened early afternoon."

"But we have nothing concrete saying she was anywhere near?"

"No, you're right."

"We're assuming because it seems too coincidental other-wise, is that right?"

Ricardo really knew how to break down a theory with just a few questions. Ben was doing his best to keep up, but the more questions Ricardo asked, the more he wondered if he had jumped to a conclusion. *Was there a more reasonable explanation?*

"That is right."

"Why the text, then?" Gabriela asked.

He knew they didn't mean to sound like they were ganging up on him and his story, but boy, did the rapid questions make it feel like that. Although, he recognized he might just be projecting.

Ben had known Gabriela and Ricardo for over ten years now, and he still didn't know how they felt about him.

He'd met his future in-laws for the first time when they came up to DC to visit Veronica for a weekend, only a few months after they'd started dating. Veronica was as surprised as he was when her mother called on a Friday morning to tell her they were driving up from Williamsburg in the afternoon. Ben and Veronica both assumed they had heard of this new boyfriend and wanted to come check him out.

Sitting at dinner with them that night, Ben felt like a teenage boy trying to impress his crush's parents. It was a dynamic he had not known for a long time. Each comment he made elicited intense stares from both Gabriela and Ricardo, as if they were trying to see right into his mind and read his thoughts.

"That was exhausting," he had said to Veronica after her parents had gone to bed.

"Oh, don't mind them. They liked you. They're just always wary of any new person in my life," she had replied.

They were always friendly, but that early wariness had never subsided. He understood it was likely a product of raising an only child, but they seemed concerned at the idea of anyone getting that close to their daughter. Ben couldn't understand why they would be like that. Veronica could handle herself better than he could, that's for sure, and likely better than most.

She's probably still their baby girl. For that, could he really blame them? Would he be that different when Maria—and Nico —grew up?

He would have appreciated an ally, someone else he could talk to about the realisms of marrying into the Aguilar family. The rest of Veronica's family, though, were all still back in Mexico, and she had never shown any interest in visiting them. Something must have happened, he reasoned, that built walls between her and her extended family. She only ever talked about her grandparents, but they were gone before Ben entered her life.

Ben turned to face Gabriela. "That's the thing. I just don't know what that text could mean."

"You said on the phone before that her cell phone was off?" Gabriela asked.

"Yes. Which is again confusing."

Ricardo nodded. "Because if she were involved in the shooting and without her phone, it would continue ringing and not have been turned off. A phone that's off is either damaged or intentionally turned off."

"Exactly, and she always keeps it charged in her office, so it wouldn't have just run out of power."

"Look, Ben, Gabriela and I are, of course, concerned about our daughter. That's why we've come all this way in the middle of the night. But I'm not convinced she was involved in a shooting that she somehow had prior knowledge of. Nothing about that makes sense."

Ben looked down, with a slow and deliberate nod. Jeremy's earlier comments were swirling through his mind.

Imagine.

You end up catching your wife cheating on you, and just to make things even better, you bring up her parents for the big reveal. And somehow that ends up as the best-case scenario of all the possibilities? He was spiraling and knew it.

"Hey, Ben, I've got news." Jeremy came out from the living room and looked at Ricardo and Gabriela's shocked faces. "Oh, sorry, am I interrupting?"

"No, it's okay," Ben quickly said. "Ricardo, Gabriela, this is Jeremy Wiles."

Curt nods were the only response he got.

Jeremy continued, undeterred. "I've been watching and have made a few calls, but they have yet to contact all the victims' families." He turned to face Ben. "I can tell you this though—I just spoke directly with the chief of police, Andrew Branaman, and he guaranteed me that Veronica is not one of the victims."

"Oh, thank God." Ben exhaled, as Gabriela hugged Ricardo, letting out a ragged sob of relief.

————

"We need to go make it official and fill out a missing persons report." Ben sat with Veronica's parents in the living room after they had all given up their attempts at sleeping. Jeremy had gone home to get a few hours of sleep and check in with his wife. "I need to ask you two to watch Nico and Maria. I can't let them go to school today. I don't want them out there when we still don't know what's going on. Is that okay?" Ben looked aimlessly around the living room, scanning the bookshelves, hoping for something to take his mind off his fear for just a second. If either of his in-laws responded, he didn't hear it.

It was just before six in the morning and the kids would be getting up soon. The television was on, with a single reporter still at the scene. He announced that the fifth victim, who had been rushed to the hospital yesterday, was confirmed dead. The anchor reappeared and gave a quick recap.

"The shooter—or shooters—are still at large in an attack that left five runners dead on Rock Creek Parkway near Peirce Mill yesterday." A graphic popped up on the screen with five pictures. "The victims have been identified as Mark Bandem, Tyrone Jefferson, Mary Baer, Troy Peters, and Margaret Sund-ham. All five were members of the American University running club …"

Ben turned away as the anchor continued. That was an unexpected piece of news. But did it mean anything? "If those runners had been from Georgetown, not American, I'd feel like there might be some connection," he said, ostensibly to Gabriela and Ricardo, but really to himself. "It'd at least be something to go on."

"Does Veronica run with other Georgetown runners?" Ricardo asked.

"Not that I know of, no."

"Then you're just looking for a connection where there wouldn't have been one," Ricardo said with finality.

Ben sighed. "Do you actually believe that the shooting and her disappearance are just coincidental?"

"No, I do not," Ricardo conceded. "You told us that Veronica has a class at eight this morning, which means she would want to be in her office at least an hour before, right?"

"Yeah, she's always been that way, just like you and Gabriela are."

Both Gabriela and Ricardo had taught and researched at the

University of Guadalajara before uprooting for the opportunity to teach in the United States. Ben knew that decision, not taken lightly, was meant to help Veronica get into the best American college she could.

That move sure worked out for the Aguilars. Veronica breezed through her high school classes on the way to a full ride from the Massachusetts Institute of Technology. She moved up to Boston and aced not only her favorite math classes, but epidemiology, linguistics, history, and even ethnomusicology. Meanwhile, Gabriela now taught Latin-American history at the College of William & Mary, and Ricardo taught Spanish at Jamestown High School.

"So she'd be up right now getting ready for work. She wouldn't voluntarily skip a class. I think we can rule out something benign. Plus, wouldn't she be here for the kids getting up?" Ricardo asked, knowing the answer.

"Definitely."

All of Ben's infidelity worries had gone away when he woke up after a fitful couple of hours and found his wife still missing. That she would not be here to see off the kids before school was unheard of.

What could have happened, then? Not off in some hotel room, not a victim in the shooting, and not here at home where she belonged. So where could she be? He had no answers.

He headed upstairs and poked his head into Nico and Maria's room.

"Psst." The kids rolled and stared through bleary eyes. Ben didn't believe in giving them an alarm of their own yet. For as long as he could—or as they would let him—he and Veronica enjoyed being the ones to wake them up each morning.

Ben tiptoed around and stood in front of their bunk beds, Maria on the bottom and Nico on the top, both looking at him from underneath Bluey duvets. They looked so much like their mother, with none of Ben's fair skin, blue eyes, or freckles. Ben didn't mind. Why shouldn't he want his children to look like the love of his life?

"Nico. Maria. Time to wake up."

"Where's Mama?" Maria asked. "Why isn't she in here with you?"

"I need to tell you something." Ben took a deep breath. "Your mother had to go away for a while."

"Why?" Nico asked, brushing his hair out of his eyes and blinking.

"It's hard to explain, Neek, but it will all be okay."

Nico nodded, but Ben caught the sadness in his eyes. He could see his response had the opposite effect as intended. "Look, it's going to be tricky without her here for a bit, so I have a surprise for you two. You don't get to see the surprise until you come downstairs, though, so get up and come down for breakfast."

Ben blew them a kiss and closed the door behind him. He hoped that the idea of a surprise would be their takeaway from that brief conversation, and they'd come bursting out of the room any second. If it took several minutes, he'd know he needed to go back in and have a second talk.

He was walking down the stairs when he heard the doorknob move, and within seconds, two blurs had whizzed past him down into the kitchen.

"Abuela! Abuelo!" they squealed with delight.

After extracting themselves from extended embraces, Nico and Maria both turned back toward Ben. "You didn't tell us they were coming," Maria said, hands on her hips.

Ben crouched down and smiled. She had some sass—both twins did. They definitely got that from their mother. "I know, my sweet. That's the surprise for you. They're both going to stay here for a while."

Ben shot a relieved smile at Gabriela. She nodded back at him.

Ricardo grabbed Maria's hands. "There's another treat for you too."

"What is it, Abuelo?"

"You and your brother don't have to go to school today,"

Ben watched her eyes light up. Despite his fear, seeing it made his heart soar, if only temporarily.

Ricardo continued, "We figured since we came all this way, we'd like to spend the day with you and your brother."

Maria and Nico could barely contain their excitement. They both began jabbering loudly as they moved into the dining room with Ricardo to eat their cereal.

Ben sat down next to Gabriela in the kitchen. "I'm going to go ahead and go over to the Alexandria Police station and fill out a missing persons report. Jeremy said he'd meet me, and we're going to drive up to Peirce Mill and see things for ourselves." Ben paused to look at his mother-in-law, seeing her eyebrows raised, showing her disapproval. He knew his in-laws were not keen on Jeremy's involvement and wanted to keep everything within the family. "I know, but he has a profile that might help me get more information that I might not get if it's just me."

Gabriela sighed. "It's not that we don't appreciate his help and his profile, and we know he's your best friend." She paused, glancing over at her husband entertaining the kids in the dining room with funny faces while he ate. "The thing is, V never fully trusted him. She told us that everything about him after the shooting last year felt insincere. Like he was playing on his hero status."

This surprised Ben. Sure, he had known that there were plenty of skeptics about Jeremy. There were plenty of think-pieces in the *Washington Post* and *New York Times* wondering about his true motivations.

"Was he actually in it for the betterment of the country? Or was he just looking to cement a legacy?" the *New York Times* reporter had speculated.

But Veronica? He had no idea she had similar thoughts. They had chatted about Jeremy's presidential campaign often, but he hadn't known she had any stronger feelings than he did.

"She told you this?" he asked.

"We haven't had long discussions or anything like that. She has just mentioned it a couple times. I also think she didn't want to admit it, but she was jealous of him on your behalf. She's sure you're going to be president one day," Gabriela added.

"It definitely has been wild to watch my best friend go from early career Secret Service agent to celebrity and maybe the next president in just a year."

Gabriela nodded as she turned and studied the framed photo of the whole family, mounted on the wall behind the couch. Veronica and Ben had a photoshoot when Nico and Maria were six months old and loved this photo of the four of them at the edge of the Tidal Basin by the Franklin Delano Roosevelt Memorial.

"I just want her to come home," she said, her voice barely above a whisper, subconsciously rubbing her left pinky, the same finger her daughter lost decades ago.

CHAPTER 9
ZEKE

Thursday Morning, October 23

T he vinyl sheets were gone, and the bodies had been transported to the medical examiner down on E Street. Not much else had changed since Zeke had gone home for a couple hours of sleep.

He looked down the trail. Dawn was just beginning to illuminate the scene, and Zeke took it all in for a second time with rested eyes. He always returned after his original evidence collection, not least because it was true what they said: the guilty did tend to come back to the scene of the crime. Most important, though, was that now he could look at the scene again, not for minutiae, but on a macro scale.

Zeke walked down to the edge of Rock Creek. What was a raging river at the time of the shooting had slowed back to a meandering stream, and even more of the bank was visible than when Zeke had gone home. He let his eyes wander, moving from the bank and surveying the entire area.

The trail ran past Peirce Mill, between the building and Rock Creek. A small wooden fence separated the trail from the embankment, just north of Tilden Street, and a line of trees flanked the creek. The Peirce Mill Dam spanned the creek just upstream of the Tilden Street bridge. Beach Drive NW ran above a steep bank on the opposite side of the water.

Zeke walked down to the edge of the water. Without the surges of the previous day, he could see an object wedged against the roots of the trees. He carefully pulled on his gloves, reached in, and pulled a runner's bottle out of the water. There was no telling whether it was related to the crime, but it didn't look like it had been in the water for days. It was a handheld water bottle, designed with a pocket to hold keys or a phone, but this pocket had been torn off. *Might as well bag it.* Anything could be evidence.

Two men stood up above him on Tilden Street, just beyond the crime scene tape, watching Zeke from a distance. He saw them looking and gave a cursory nod before turning back around. Whether reporters or simply curious bystanders, he had no interest in listening to questions about the shooting. He hadn't worked many yet, but every crime scene so far had people pushing through the tape, trying to glean whatever information they could.

If you thought people gawked at car accidents, just wait until you work a murder scene. He shook his head. Curiosity was one thing, but actively trying to see dead bodies? He would never understand that.

Zeke pulled on wading boots and stepped out into the water, following it downstream, picking up anything out of place, anything that could end up the missing piece of the puzzle.

Once he was satisfied that he had found all possible new evidence, he stepped out of the water and back onto the trail. The two men had disappeared, likely disappointed in the lack of gruesome details to tell their friends.

"Should have known you'd beat me back here." A voice came from behind Peirce Mill as Detective Brown emerged, her Mohawk not nearly as sharp as it had been hours before.

Zeke winked at her. "You know you can't beat me back to a crime scene."

"Oh, don't you get all high and mighty on me," she said. "When did you leave?"

"I was done at around three thirty this morning and got back here just after six."

"Yeah, thought so. I didn't get back home until five, and here we are. Back again before seven."

"What were you doing after I left?"

"Detective work, Zeke," she gave him a slap on the shoulder. "I know you think you're the entire department, but it turns out there are a few others who work here too."

"Ohhh." Zeke feigned being deep in thought, his left hand stroking his chin. "Yeah, I think I might have heard something about that. Sounds unnecessary to me, anyway—I got this under control."

"Do you now? Okay then, hotshot, tell me something I don't know."

"Well, the high water earlier this morning might have concealed some valuable evidence that I've now collected. I wanted to come back out here and do another look before Wills comes out for a follow-up in a few hours."

"Good for you, Zeke." Detective Brown cocked her head with a smile. "But you'll have to do better than that. Why do you think I'm back here so soon if not for that exact reason?"

"All right, how about this? The location of the casings suggests that the shot that killed him was taken by the southeast door of Peirce Mill. I'm thinking that the building is of more importance than the trail." He hesitated before continuing. "Just a thought, but I wonder if something illicit happened inside there and then our shooter ran into eyewitnesses after."

"Okay, I'll grant you that's an interesting theory, boy wonder."

"There's one big problem it causes, though."

"Yeah?"

"If this was a crime that turned into a murder, then the perpetrator was willing to kill to hide whatever was happening. There's a decent chance our shooter isn't done."

CHAPTER 10
THE GIRL

I first killed a man when I was twelve years old. It should have been difficult, but in a way, it was the easiest thing I had ever done. A small squeeze, and in an instant, a life ended. An evil life, a life intent on ending mine, but still a human life. Should I have felt something other than pride? Some sort of remorse?

Maybe I truly was my father's daughter.

Growing up the way I did, I knew my way around guns from an early age.

"A gun is just an extension of your arm," Dad would say. "Point and pull. The rest will take care of itself."

I assumed at the time that there was probably more to it, but he was right. The rest was inside your head.

"Look, it's not like I want to teach you gun safety already," he had confided in me when I was only ten. "It's simply a fact of our life that you need to know how to protect yourself. Remember when you saw me have to use one?" I shuddered at the thought of seeing him shoot that man over what seemed to be nothing.

He saw the look on my face and said, "I know, but I had to do it to protect our family. He was stealing from us, and it could've become dangerous for you. I had to be proactive."

We had a small grove of trees just inside the back gate, and us kids who lived in the compound practiced shooting at cans and other small *objects that we'd set up on fallen logs or low branches. My first time shooting a gun, the recoil knocked me right over. My brother laughed and my face burned. But I persevered. I stayed outside for hours, shooting right through the dinnertime calls of my parents, long after the rest of the compound had retired inside. I would not leave until I hit the empty Coca-Cola can wedged in the cohune palm tree.*

That was a good memory.

My father wasn't much for gun safety, was he? He talked a good game, but what other father would let their twelve-year-old child play around with several guns and an unlimited amount of bullets? Sure, I was technically supervised by the unspeaking, unsmiling sentry named George who kept a distance and reported back on my activities, but it wasn't like he was actually there to stop me if I tried anything.

I never liked George. Not the sort of thing you're supposed to say about someone who's dead, but it's true. He was surly and his penchant for grimacing did not impress young me.

That good memory of shooting at Coke cans? I lied a little bit. That was actually a lot of good memories wrapped into one. Night after night of shooting until dark. The "ping" as the bullet hit the Coke can. The thrill of running back inside to tell Dad I'd hit every one.

Then the bad memory.

The evening when my nightly target practice became much less theoretical. When a man rappelled down the wall into the wooded area at the back of the compound, unseen. When a shot rang out and George crumpled, his blood staining the green grass beneath the trees.

The man stepped out into the small clearing and looked directly at me. I still don't know exactly what his expression meant but I could tell it wasn't good news for me. I glanced at what was left of George and an instinct I didn't know I had took over.

Him or me.

He made the mistake of holding his gun down by his side. He didn't see that I had a gun near me. Not the last time that underestimating me cost a man his life.

I like to tell myself that I closed my eyes as I bent down, grabbed the pistol off the ground and fired. Like there was some skill inherent deep inside me that took over.

That's not exactly how it happened, though. The less glamorous, but truer, version is that he got distracted by a noise at the top of one of the palm trees. He looked for a split second, and I swung my arm down and grabbed the gun. I fired the entire clip at him.

I flew backward from the recoil, so it was only after I'd scrambled back to my feet that I saw the damage I had done. It turns out Dad was right. If your stance isn't set, the recoil knocks you down.

I still remember my first thought as I slowly walked over and looked down at the dead body, blood gushing out from a single hole in its forehead.

It doesn't matter how many times you miss—you only have to hit the Coke can once.

CHAPTER 11
FRANCISCO

Thursday Evening, October 23

Francisco could not believe it. His target, the reason he had spent those nights freezing on rooftops, was gone. Nowhere to be found. And now he had no idea how to find her.

Okay, stop.

Think.

Where could she have gone? Home, presumably. But of course, that was the first place he checked. Now here he was, hours later, still wandering the streets of Old Town Alexandria.

As he turned onto North Fairfax Street and passed the Alexandria Visitor Center, he realized that this problem might have further reaching issues. A delay he could handle, but if he legitimately could not find her anymore, well, his boss was not one to take disappointment lightly. Francisco knew this well, since his boss often turned to him to handle such disappointment.

The most recent disappointment ended up in several plastic bags at the bottom of Lake Ilopango. He had been a local butcher who decided he was no longer keen on laundering the organization's money. Now that butcher's apprentice was in charge and eager to provide his services. Ruthless persuasion, Francisco's boss called it.

Francisco had twice before taken out members of his own crew for disappointing the boss. But now, this disappointment would likely lead to his own death if he didn't salvage the situation. He knew his boss would do it in person, too. Luckily, he was still in El Salvador and none the wiser. Better to keep it that way for as long as possible.

He continued walking, passing Market Square, the location of the oldest continuously running farmer's market in the country. Francisco had read that George Washington himself had once sold produce here.

Knowledge is power. He'd never travel anywhere without knowing the place's history.

As the sky darkened, Francisco decided it was time to stop wallowing and take some steps. Not just to find her, but for his own safety as well. He was going to be looking over his shoulder for a while now.

Time to step out of the shadows. Shadows were where people got killed and no one ever noticed. Now he needed to become more public. Publicity could be his safety net.

But what kind of publicity? Public to whom?

Ben. The husband. That was the obvious answer.

He had to get close to Ben. Who would know more about where his wife had gone?

He thought for a few minutes as he wandered, before a smile grew across his face. He knew just how he would approach it, and felt much more content. A few events would need to happen first, but now he had the beginnings of a new plan. This was good. Maybe there would be no delay after all.

He stopped and gazed past the gates at the Carlyle House. The stately stone mansion had been the home of John Carlyle, one of the founders of Alexandria. Carlyle's first wife was Sarah Fairfax, and Francisco made a mental note to check later if it was a coincidence or not that he was standing on Fairfax Street.

Knowledge is power.

"It's fantastic, isn't it?" A soft voice from behind made him turn his head. "Built in 1753 and still looks spectacular." A young woman stopped just behind him and shook her head in wonder.

"Yes, it is nice." He stuttered. "I—I didn't know the exact date."

Her eyes sparkled in the twilight, and she gave him a smile that just about knocked him off his feet. "I'm Miranda. I think we ran into each other, literally, the other night, over on Royal Street?"

He concentrated, making sure he did not say anything that made it clear he knew she was the babysitter of the Walsh children, and had seen her from the rooftop and intentionally ran into her afterward. "You're right, yes. Sorry, I think I was in a hurry because of the rain. I'm Reynaldo, I just recently moved here."

Never give a stranger your real name. Your name should be guarded under lock and key, only to be let out when you deem it safe to do so.

"Nice to meet you, Reynaldo. I live over on Oronoco Street. What brought you to Old Town?"

"I'm a graduate student at George Mason," Francisco lied easily. He could lie in any scenario and not blink an eye. It wasn't some random skill, either. He stole a polygraph machine years ago and practiced on it. The trick, as easy as it was to say, was to believe the lie. If you believed your own lie, how could any person or machine tell you otherwise?

"I'm from El Salvador and have been trying to get into a graduate program here in America for several years now," he continued.

"Oh, that's wonderful, and your English is great! What are you studying?"

"Thank you! I have studied English for ten years. My program is criminology. The criminal mind is fascinating to me, so I want to do something related." Maybe now wasn't the best time to tell her why he spent so much time considering the morals of those who do evil deeds. Or at whose command he started learning English so many years ago.

"Wow. I wouldn't want to spend any more time thinking about criminals than I have to."

"It's definitely not for everyone." Francisco gave his best benign smile. "You knew the date this place was built. Do you mind if I ask you a question about it?"

"Yeah, go for it."

"So, this Carlyle was married to a member of the Fairfax family. Was this road named Fairfax when he built the house, and was that why he built it here?"

"Wow, that's a good question. You must have done your research before coming here!" Miranda flashed another dazzling smile and continued, "I'll preface by saying I don't know the second part for sure, but the street was called Fairfax before the Carlyle House was here. The street that the gardens back up to, Lee Street, was at that time Water Street. The water level came all the way up to just below it, and I believe he used the back entrance by the water for his merchant business, to keep it separate from the social gatherings and events that would happen toward the front of the house."

Francisco stared for a second too long.

"Sorry, didn't mean to overwhelm you with that," Miranda said, trying to hide a grimace.

"No, don't apologize. You know so much. I was just impressed."

"Well, I love history. I figured since I live in such a historical place, I would be remiss to not learn as much as I can. But you! Knowing about John Carlyle and Sarah Fairfax. I bet that most Alexandria residents don't know their story."

"I tried to learn some before I got here, so that it would feel more familiar to me."

"It must be quite a culture shock being here. Are you on your own?"

"Yes, just me. I left my sister and all my friends back home."

"That must be hard. I know about being alone."

Francisco could see that last sentence slipped out before she had a chance to stop herself. He stayed silent and let her keep talking.

"Hey, look, if you need anyone to help out with it all, I'm over on Oronoco and Washington. It was nice to meet you." She gave him a final smile and headed down the street.

"Hold on," he turned quickly, his eyebrows raised. "Oronoco and Washington? As in Robert E. Lee's home?"

She looked back, surprise on her face. "You know it?"

"Yes, I told you I studied before I came here. It's across from the Lee-Fendall House. That's my favorite historic house in this area."

"Yes, I do live in Lee's boyhood home."

"That's incredible. I'd love a tour of it sometime. Wait. I meant …" He fumbled over his words.

Best way to put a person at ease was to act a little unsure of yourself.

Miranda responded with an easy smile. "Don't worry, I know what you mean. I'd be happy to make that happen."

CHAPTER 12
MIRANDA

Thursday Evening, October 23

Miranda was annoyed at herself. It wasn't that she tried to hide her wealth, but she was enjoying a perfectly normal conversation with a guy who did not know her background, nor did he already look at her in a certain way because of the events leading to her wealth.

It was a matter of time anyway, she thought, especially since she did tell him to come by if he needed anything. Why did she blurt that out?

Probably that jawline.

In most interactions she was the one being ogled, but he had a suave confidence to go with that runner's physique. How could she pass that combo up?

She thought she had recognized him as she was walking toward him but thought better of it until she realized he was staring at the Carlyle House. Maybe he was a history buff too? She figured it wouldn't hurt to strike up a little conversation. It was probably fine anyway, but for a minute there, she had been able to forget about her past, and it felt nice.

Not that she wanted to get rid of all the memories. There were plenty of good, but the recent bad ones sometimes felt like an albatross around her neck. She suddenly wondered if Reynaldo had also read "The Rime of the Ancient Mariner" and enjoyed it as much as she did. *I might actually like this guy*, she thought with a sad smile. Wouldn't that be something? After years of being pressured to find a guy by overbearing but well-meaning parents, she'd met someone now that they were gone.

Mom and Dad.

And Tracy.

All gone just like that.

That was a memory burned in; it would never go away. The four of them in the family Camaro, out together headed to Crystal City. They had just enjoyed a nice dinner together in Old Town, and were heading north on Potomac Avenue, having a good time and reminiscing about similar outings when all four were much younger. Tracy, her sister who had been three years older than her, insisted the convertible top be lowered, and the two had been sitting in the back seat waving their hands in the wind.

They had just passed Potomac Yard Park when a dark Escalade rolled by on their left. It hovered just in front, and then inexplicably flicked its turn signal and went to merge into their lane. The driver must have thought he'd cleared them, since he didn't hesitate at all. Her mother jerked the wheel to try to avoid the SUV but only succeeded in getting pushed past the bike path and down a steep embankment into the small pond that lay at the bottom.

The screams as the car accelerated down the bank would never leave her.

The car hit the water and she had no more memories after that. She was later told that she was unconscious for just over two days. When she woke up, she had three broken ribs, a concussion, and a giant vertical laceration down the left side of her face. But none of that could possibly compare to the pain she felt when her doctor, as kindly as possible, told her she was the only one who made it out of the pond.

Her parents and sister were gone, just like that. All that was left was the rest of her life to carry the weight.

Her parents' status brought the story of their deaths to the front page of *The Washington Post*. Her father, Ulrich Belle, had bought the Washington basketball team ten years prior. After numerous seasons mired in mediocrity before his arrival, the team and its fanbase were as disparate as ever. He had set about fixing the entire culture. On day one he promised a new regime, a focus on fundamentals, and a team to feel good cheering for.

Fast forward a decade, and he had lifted the Larry O'Brien Championship Trophy three times. He turned the franchise into the toast of the town. The political journalists had liked to joke that he was the only unifying force left in the District.

For the worst possible reason, she became a household name overnight. The die-hards already knew who Ulrich's two daughters were, but now everyone knew the name of the one who had survived. Even though it had been a year since the accident, she still got the look from just about everyone she met. That look of such pity that made her want to run screaming.

People fundamentally don't know how to react to someone else's tragedy. There were plenty who tried to latch on to her tragedy, make it about themselves and how sad it made them. More tried their best to continue to make it clear they would never forget, as if it somehow helped her being reminded over and over what happened. All she wanted was for people to be respectful, and to ask her what she wanted or needed rather than assuming. Why did most of the world have such a problem doing that?

She looked ahead and saw she was about to pass her second pretty face of the night. Ben Walsh was walking toward her, looking like he was on the verge of a breakdown.

"Ben!" She called out, yet no response came. "Ben," she said again, only yards from him now.

He raised his head, eyes wide. "I'm sorry, I didn't see you."

Up close, Ben looked like someone whose will to live had

just been plucked away. She knew that look well, having seen it in the mirror for months after the accident. There was something badly wrong. This man, whom she'd only ever seen immaculately put together, was dressed in a Georgetown hoodie and Under Armour sweatpants tonight. The bags under his eyes could give her largest suitcases a run for their money.

"What's going on? You don't look good at all." Miranda stopped next to him. "Talking about whatever it is always helps. Trust me on that one." She never again took for granted the ability to talk things out.

"I guess I'm just wandering aimlessly out here anyway." He looked around, as if only now realizing where he was. "I just needed to get out of the house for a second."

"What's going on?" Miranda asked again.

"Did you hear about the shooting in the District yesterday?"

It was a sure sign of the gun issues that plagued the country that she had to ask, but she needed more details. "Which one?"

"Up in Rock Creek Park—five runners were killed."

"Okay, yeah, I did hear about that. They haven't found who did it yet?"

"So." He took a deep breath. "I don't know what happened, but my wife is missing. And she normally runs on that route on her lunch break every day."

"Holy shit. Oh my God." Miranda paused for a second. "Wait, but she's not one of the victims?"

"No, and there's no proof she was for sure there or anything. But how coincidental would that be, that there was a shooting in the same place she might have been and now she's missing?"

"So did she just not come home?"

Ben sighed and shook his head. "It's more than just that. She sent me a weird text yesterday morning saying she loves me and to remember that. I have no idea what to make of it."

"Okay Ben, look, your wife is one of the most incredible people I have ever met. I refuse to believe anything could or would happen to her. There must be some explanation."

Something about her trust that Veronica was all right seemed to give Ben a visible lift. His hunched shoulders straightened slightly.

"What makes you so sure?" he asked.

She paused, trying to come up with the words.

"I'd like to think I'm a great example of the fallacy of thinking bad things only happen to bad people, but there's just something about her." Miranda had always marveled at Veronica's strength, and conviction, and that made her believe nothing could happen to Veronica. Even what she did with her spare time was impressive. She volunteered teaching math to the incarcerated. She even went out of her way to counsel and meet with the most hated man in America, Jacob Jordan, because she believed anyone can get better. "A woman who'll look the man who tried to assassinate the president in the eye and not flinch is someone who can get through anything."

"I've always thought that was one of the best examples of why I fell in love with her," Ben said as he nodded along. "She has this ability to care deeply and is the most empathetic person I've ever known. She's so sure that there's something going on with Jacob, some... thing not explained, because she can't reconcile the Jake she knew from her class with this murderer."

"I swear I recognize him from something," Miranda said. She was fascinated with his story. What caused him to attempt to assassinate the president? She read all the profiles of him—his family life, all of it. She let out a small chuckle. "Sorry, I didn't mean to get us off topic there."

"I just don't know what to do." Ben looked up at the cloudy sky and watched a plane enter its final descent into Reagan National Airport. "In the books and movies, people in my position jump into action and all of a sudden become MMA fighters or something. Liam Neeson would have figured it all out by now and killed a dozen people in the process." He gave a sad laugh.

"I think I might be the only person you know who can

empathize with that sentiment," Miranda conceded. "It's been a year and I don't know who killed my family. All I want in life anymore is to get a chance to look them in the eye and ask why they didn't look in their blind spot. In real life you don't get to avenge wrongs just by sheer force of will."

"I know logically that you're right, but I still can't get it out of my head that there's something I should be able to do."

"Of course you can't, and I don't think you should have to. It's rational to want to fix everything, but just make sure not to hold yourself to some weird Jason Bourne standard, okay?"

"If only," he sighed. "Can I ask you for a favor though? Can you help Veronica's parents with watching the kids if need be? I'm not planning to run off or anything, but I just don't know."

"Absolutely, just let me know. Also, if I were you, I'd go to campus and talk with her colleagues. Just to get an idea of what her morning was like. Maybe you'll find some clue there."

CHAPTER 13
BEN

Thursday Evening, October 23

Ben got home to find Veronica's parents engaged in a feisty game of battleship with Nico and Maria. His in-laws were doing a valiant job of not showing their concern in front of the kids. It was hard telling them that Mom had to go away for a bit, and the kids had several questions, but having their grandparents coming to stay had satisfied them, at least for the time being. Ben was relieved they weren't a few years older or else this would be much trickier. He hurried them along to bed before sitting down with Gabriela and Ricardo.

"Sorry, that was a longer walk than I meant it to be. I ran into the kids' babysitter and we chatted a bit."

Gabriela looked up and her eyes flashed. "What would your babysitter have to say that's so important right now?"

Ben realized he needed to tread lightly. Even years later, he still felt like he was in an ongoing audition.

"Do you remember last year, when the owner of the Washington basketball team and his wife and daughter died in that car accident?"

"I think so."

"She's the one who survived, the youngest daughter. She moved here to Old Town after it happened. I didn't realize I needed it, but it was nice to talk to someone who knows about worry and tragedy." He held his hands up before either of them could jump in. "I know, and I agree, nothing is certain, but there is a real chance something has happened."

"What did she say, then?" Ricardo asked.

"She suggested what I'd been thinking this afternoon, that I need to retrace V's steps and go to campus and try to figure out what she did before she left."

Ricardo raised his eyebrows but did not comment further.

Ben grabbed his phone off the end table and checked his email. He had a couple responses from her colleagues, but all he'd learned was that neither of them had interacted with her at all that morning. He had not even bothered to look at his work phone since the morning. Congresswoman Moore had made it clear to take as much time as he needed. His deputy would cover for him.

"Have you two been to the Georgetown campus since V started teaching here?"

Both Gabriela and Ricardo paused and looked at each other. "I don't think we have. I've heard it's a spectacular place," Gabriela replied.

"If you'd like I can call Miranda and ask her to watch the kids tomorrow morning so you can come with me. I know it's not the best circumstance, but you're probably itching to do something, too."

"That's kind of you," Ricardo responded. "But we want to minimize the upheaval for Nico and Maria, so I think it's best if we stay with them.

"I always knew she'd end up at a place like that," Gabriela said. "The way she understood numbers and patterns just made our minds boggle."

"I've been trying to pick up things through the last few

years and have gotten very little. Veronica and I joke about how my profession is all about communicating with laypeople and hers is militarily against it," Ben said.

"I remember the day she came downstairs in the morning and gathered us in the kitchen to explain that if you have a room of twenty-three or more people in it, there's a greater than fifty percent chance that two of them share the same birthday." Ricardo glanced at Gabriela. "She must have been sixteen?"

Gabriela nodded. "She gave us the full proof, too. Now we're both well-educated people, but she was throwing around factorials and combinatorics, and I had no idea what she was talking about. I made her explain it slowly about ten times before I understood."

"That was when we realized she was destined to teach math. That she could get us, two people who never had any aptitude for it, to understand this paradox meant she could teach anyone anything," Ricardo added.

Ben couldn't help but smile. "I have a similar story. I wasn't necessarily a slouch in math, but I didn't get far past intro calc in college. She sat me down and explained a posteriori probabilities and Bayes' Theorem, and in about half an hour, I understood it." He gave a self-deprecating shrug. "Well, at least I think I did. Although now she's gotten comfortable talking about things like Galois Theory, and I can't even come close. I think she thinks I'm getting it, but I barely can understand the words she's saying."

"When we moved here just after her fifteenth birthday, she had to jump right into high school despite not knowing much English at all. I think that math must have always come naturally, but it was her life jacket those first few months. She struggled with the language, the culture, everything really, but she found solace in math. It was the same everywhere. As long as she could just about understand what the question was asking, she could answer it."

Gabriela walked over to Ben and pulled him close. *Must have aced tonight's audition*, he thought.

"She's out there. She knows how much we care, and she'll come back. I know it."

CHAPTER 14
THE GIRL

When I was thirteen years old, I watched my brother die in front of me. There's a sentence that took me a long time to fully come to terms with.

Kelvin had been the one I always wanted to emulate. He was just over five years older than me, that golden age gap close enough to make his achievements seem attainable but far enough away to look up to without any competition.

He was the one my father could always rely on. Especially after Mom passed on. Turns out, no number of armed guards can keep brain cancer at bay.

I was the favorite, but if there was something that needed doing right, Kelvin was the go-to. And that included the rest of the organization.

After the heroic derailing of the attempt on my life, I was part of the organization proper, too. Dad used me for odd jobs, little undertakings just to get my feet wet. It helped that I had my growth spurt early. I was fully grown by my thirteenth birthday, and puberty had been kind to me. I could have passed for twenty.

I guess that's why the three of us were all hunched together in the Jeep at half past three in the morning. My father and Kelvin each carried shotguns, with handguns tucked away under their belts.

I was there simply to be the lookout. I wasn't the one Dad was grooming to take over the family business.

Yet.

The two of them pulled black ski masks over their faces and crept out of the car toward the house that lay quiet at the end of the dark street. I stayed behind, sweeping my eyes around the residential area. I looked right and watched a mother holding her baby looking out a bedroom window. I stared until I saw her put the child down and turn the light out.

I had heard enough of their conversations in the buildup to know that this was the house of one of my father's rivals. He didn't have many anymore, but this was the latest pretender trying to take the throne. They had found this out after months of painstaking effort, finally getting a lieutenant to flip on his boss and give up the address.

It didn't even take that much effort in the end.

In the end, we didn't have to apply that much pressure.

Only three toes.

I watched from the back of the Jeep, ever alert and aware, as they crept up to the front gate, then past the immaculate lawn and up to the porch. That lawn should have been a clue. Normal people don't insist on that type of perfection. People who do don't get snuck up on.

I realized I was holding my breath. I was still new to the life even though I had subconsciously known for many years what it was. The night was still, and I let the silence envelop me as I watched them tiptoe to the front door.

The man we were after had not only stolen from my father but had killed two of his couriers three months before. In the following days, Kelvin had convinced Dad that it was not the time for a proportional response. We would bide our time, collect our intel, and make our move. Cut off the head. I was not supposed to know all this, but I was still just as good at sneaking around and eavesdropping as I had been as a child.

The two of them entered the house, making quick work of the lock on the front door. That was when the alarm bells should have started ringing.

If this really was the house of the head of the second biggest drug-running operation in the city, why was security so lax? I don't know if it gave them any pause, and I never spoke with my father about that night again. Maybe they truly believed they were catching this rival off guard. I've never known my father to make a mistake like that, though.

I waited.

And waited.

And waited.

And waited.

I could feel the blood pumping through my veins. I was sure anyone inside the house could hear my thumping heart.

Several times I came close to getting out of the Jeep. I wonder if I'd be dead right now if I had.

I wonder if Kelvin would be alive.

Finally, two shadowy figures emerged from the house. I squinted as hard as I could to see who they were. As they scurried off the porch and into the yard, I recognized my father and Kelvin, trying to stay low.

"Get in the front and start the car!" My father hissed, trying to make his voice loud and quiet at the same time. I bolted into action.

"What's going on?"

"It's a trap. There's no one inside!" My father and brother crept out of the yard and onto the sidewalk.

"I don't understand," I replied. "If it's a trap, then what—"

I heard the shot before I could finish speaking. I heard the squelch as it hit its target. I watched my brother, five feet away from the Jeep, twist and crumple, a marionette with the strings suddenly cut. He landed face down on the sidewalk, the back of his head replaced by a gaping red hole. I'm thankful I never saw what his face must have looked like.

"Get down!" my father yelled.

I ducked under the steering wheel as three more shots echoed out in the erstwhile quiet night. Glass shattered above me and I pulled my knees closer to my chest, trying to make myself as small as possible. I couldn't tell if my father had been hit, so I chanced a glance up.

"Stay down!"

I ducked again, doubling the grip on my knees.

I don't know how long I waited there, but I expected death at any moment. I heard distant shots, and then nothing but quiet.

I eventually allowed myself to peek out. My brother lay in a puddle of blood too large for my brain to comprehend.

I threw up out the front window.

I glanced out again, and threw up for the second time.

But where was my father?

I stepped out of the car. I'm still not sure from where I got the bravery.

Was it even bravery?

I tried to figure out where the shots had come from. Kelvin and Dad had come out the yard and turned to their right to make the last few steps to the car. He was hit from behind, so it must have been from near the house with the mother and child.

I jerked when I saw the light come back on. The same upstairs room I'd seen earlier. Yet there were no women or children there now. Only a hulking figure, covered in blood. He looked straight at me, whirled around and disappeared from sight.

The figure came out the front door seconds later and walked toward me, every step deliberate. His pace told me all I needed to know. The danger was over.

My father had his shotgun in one hand and a machete in the other. I still don't know where he found it, or from whom he took it. Anger was etched all over his face, but I could also see a deep sadness he was doing his best to suppress. He looked me up and down when he got to the car.

"Are you all right?" he asked.

"Yes, I'm okay. What happened?"

"They're dead."

"Who?"

"All of them."

CHAPTER 15
BEN

en drove down Reservoir Road, flanking Georgetown University to the north, and turned just beyond the giant Medstar Georgetown University Hospital. He headed down the small road toward the department of mathematics and statistics.

Friday morning. Almost forty-eight hours since Veronica's cryptic text.

As he walked into St. Mary's Hall, skirting by the School of Nursing and Health Services on the first floor, he thought to himself just how young college students looked nowadays. It was thirteen years since he'd graduated, and with a bit of quick math he realized that it'd be thirteen more years until his kids were ready to go to college.

I'm already walking around here looking at it as a parent rather than a student, he thought. Students and faculty bustled around, hurrying to and from classes, and he stood still for a second and thought about how little Veronica's disappearance seemed to have affected anything. He knew that there would be some scrambling to see who could cover her classes, and that students would miss her while she was gone, but the rest of the students, university, and even world just kept turning. It was immensely sad, and yet, somehow, just a little bit reassuring.

Ben climbed up to the third floor and approached the office of the department administrator, an exceedingly likable lady in her seventies. With the amount of math she had picked up over the years, Ben thought she could probably teach all the department's classes on her own by now.

"How can I help you?" she asked without moving her eyes from the crossword puzzle she was working on.

"Good morning, Denise. We've met a couple times, I'm Veronica Walsh's husband."

"Oh, good morning!" Denise looked up and gave Ben a friendly smile. "I heard you had called and that Dr. Walsh is going to be out for a few days. What brings you here?"

"I'm going to go into her office and grab a couple things. I wanted to let you know first so you know there isn't some stranger rummaging around. I don't know how many of her colleagues would recognize me."

"Smart thinking. Do you have a key to get in?"

"I do."

"Well, go right ahead, then. Let me know if you need anything."

Ben thanked her and headed to Veronica's office. He wasn't a regular in Georgetown's math department, but he knew his way around. He pulled out the spare key that she'd made for him years ago and entered her office. The space was immaculate. He always marveled at how she managed to keep her office looking like it was straight out of a catalog when her colleagues' offices were often cluttered, disorganized messes.

Ben picked up the framed picture next to her closed laptop computer. The faces of his family beamed up at him. They had taken this selfie on a trip to the Bahamas last summer. He loved it and had gotten it framed twice as soon as they got home. The other sat on his desk in the Rayburn House Office Building. Nico and Maria's smiles shone brighter than he had ever seen, and Veronica looked stunning. Most important though, her face was one of utter contentment and peace, a visage not often seen with kids in tow, no matter how lovely they are. Whoever said vacation is just parenting in a different location captured it perfectly, but this trip was the exception that proved the rule.

Ben thought back to the day the doctor told them that they would be having twins. Veronica did not believe it. Even after seeing the ultrasound for herself, she was still convinced there must be some mistake. He never got a clear answer out of her as to why she was so adamant she wasn't having twins. Not that either of them could now imagine life without both Nico and Maria.

Flash forward seven months. Veronica's water broke and he rushed her to the Inova Alexandria Hospital. Ben had pulled up at the front door, and a nurse with a wheelchair had come running out, when Veronica saw a poor, sick woman struggling to walk after being dropped off by a taxi.

"Ben! You have to go help her." She pulled her hand away, not allowing him to help her out of the car. Beads of sweat dotted her forehead.

"Are you serious? I have to get you inside the hospital!"

He would never forget that look. Her eyes bore straight through him.

She spoke slowly and enunciated every word. "Ben. I am fine. This is what is supposed to happen. There's a woman over there who might not get the help I'm about to get. So, what you're going to do is leave me with this nice nurse here and go make sure that woman gets in and is helped."

Always thinking of others. She was selfless to a fault, combined with the strongest will he had ever known.

"Ben?"

He turned around to see a tall and slender man standing in the threshold, dressed in a purple gingham button-down and slim chinos that made him look even more the beanpole than he already was.

"Hi, Dan. Good to see you."

Dan Flint was a professor emeritus who had been at George-town for over forty years. He had recently turned seventy-five but looked no older than fifty. Possessing a keen wit and a tendency for sarcasm, Dan was always Ben's favorite person to mingle with at Veronica's departmental events.

"Where's Veronica?" Now was not the time for sarcasm, and Dan got straight to the point. "She's gone for a bit unex-pectedly?"

"Hold on, come on inside." Ben ushered him into the office and shut the door behind the pair. "Look. I want to keep these circumstances as quiet as possible around here. Veronica wouldn't want any unnecessary upheaval. That's why I called the chair and said that Veronica would be away for a bit."

Dan's eyes grew wide with concern.

"You're a good friend to both of us, and her absence will be more conspicuous to you than most. The thing is that V didn't come home on Wednesday. I last heard from her late that morn-ing, and then that shooting happened by Rock Creek where she runs at lunch each day."

"Holy Mary." Dan put his hand over his mouth.

"I've been racking my brain for what other reason she would have to not come home other than something to do with the shooting. I don't even know if she was there, and, even so, what would have happened. I'm here just to try to find out whatever I can about what she did Wednesday morning to piece things together."

"Let me see. I finished teaching my complex analysis class just before eleven that morning. As I walked by her office, I went to peek in but she was on her cell phone. I didn't see her again. She had nothing scheduled that afternoon, so I assumed she had found some quiet alcove to think about research."

"She was talking to someone?"

"Yes, she was sitting at her desk looking at her computer while talking."

"That must have been right at the end of her office hour, which means it's possible no one else saw her before she left."

"I could have stopped and waited to talk to her. I didn't need to go back to my office," Dan said, the distress evident in his voice.

"You couldn't have known." Ben opened Veronica's computer. He entered a string of digits and the lock screen disappeared. Her password was endearingly nerdy and sweet: 144 1597 233. The twelfth, seventeenth, and thirteenth Fibonacci numbers in order, representing the date of their wedding. She seemed to think it was a normal thing to know what those numbers were. Ben, on the other hand, had taken more time than he'd like to admit to memorize them in case he ever needed access.

The front page of *The Washington Post* reloaded as he clicked on her internet browser. She had no other windows open.

"I wonder if she saw something on her computer that prompted this all. She's got the *Post* front page up."

Ben scrolled down the page. The Democratic presidential primary was in full swing, with all the candidates trailing former Secret Service agent Jeremy Wiles in the polls. His combination of expansive progressive ideas and his heroic recent past had national pundits considering him formidable in the upcoming general election.

None of this was news to Ben.

Further headlines informed Ben of various other political and national intrigues. But these weren't the headlines Veronica had looked at Wednesday. Ben wanted to see those.

"You can probably look up what was on there two days ago," Dan said, as if he knew what Ben was thinking. "But if I were you, I'd first find out who she was talking to."

"You're right. I can pull up our phone plan app and see who she was on the phone with last. I can't believe I didn't think about that earlier. Wait." Ben paused. "She was on her cell phone, not her office phone?"

"Yes, definitely a cell phone."

Ben's mind spun. He couldn't imagine any call she could have made that would lead to the text she sent. They joked about it, but they were that couple who could talk about anything. Ben didn't like to say they had no secrets between them—because really, how can you know that for sure?—but he knew he could always tell her what was on his mind. Since he knew her parents hadn't heard from her, he couldn't come up with anyone else who she would have felt comfortable talking to about whatever it was that was going on.

What even is going on? Ben thought. He didn't have the faintest idea how to connect the dots between a strange text and a mass shooting that she just might have been near. Who could even say there were dots connecting the two in the first place?

Ben pulled up the page, clicked on Veronica's phone number, and scrolled through her phone calls. "Looks like she received a call from some number I don't know at 10:50 on Wednesday, and then the last call she made was at 11:04. The number … wait." Ben blinked and read it again. He shook his head, refocused, and read it a third time. "No way. How could he not …?"

He looked up at Dan, his contorted face laying bare the betrayal he felt. "I'm sorry, I have to go."

He slammed the laptop shut and marched out the door.

CHAPTER 16
ZEKE

Friday Midday, October 24

"Now it's our turn to figure out which of all your forensics is a clue and which is just crap." Detective Brown winked at Zeke.

"That's why they pay you guys the big bucks, Brown."

Brown and Zeke stood in the hallway and watched as co-workers filed out of the meeting room that they had all occupied together. Chief Branaman was the last to leave.

"Brown. Jackson." He gave them each a small nod and continued walking down the hall as the two of them fell in step behind him.

"Chief," Zeke said.

"What do we have so far? There was a lot of talk in there about forward steps, but I want to hear the most up-to-date state of play."

"We've got five dead runners, all from American University, out running together. Feels like there must be witnesses out there but we've blasted out that we're looking and no credible responses so far."

"Okay. I met with Wills, but I want to hear from you too, Jackson. Talk me through what you saw."

"Four bodies at the scene, one gunshot wound each, all four shots were either head or neck. No evidence of any missed shots."

Chief Branaman stopped. "No evidence of missed shots?" he repeated.

"Nope. No casings other than the five shots we observed on victims, and it appears our shooter was firing in the direction of the bridge, so we scoured and found no bullets lodged anywhere on its face."

"So, unless our perp got incredibly lucky, we're looking at a pro here."

"Seems that way."

"I want updates as soon as humanly possible. There's a lot of attention on this right now. I practically had to turn my phone off because of how many times Jeremy Wiles has called."

"*The* Jeremy Wiles?" Zeke cocked his head.

"Yep. He called to find out if a friend of his was a victim. Pestered so much that I finally just got the name and confirmed for him she wasn't one of the five. Now he's just been calling for updates. The guy doesn't take no for an answer." He puffed out his cheeks and walked off in a huff. "Campaigns," he muttered.

"Well, this is officially the highest-profile case I've ever worked on," Zeke said. "That dude is gonna be president."

"Secretly hoping this is your big break, aren't you?" Detective Brown cracked a sly smile.

"You know the country doesn't have a position of chief crime scene technician? I'm just saying that's a spot that I could fill."

"Maybe you and Jeremy Wiles could make a good team, what with you two having the biggest egos in a city full of them."

"I'll take that as a compliment."

"As I knew you would."

They walked in silence until Zeke asked, "What do you

think of this task force the chief has set up? The mayor seemed pretty riled up in that meeting."

"I think he and the mayor have to do something, if only for optics. I don't think there's anything here yet that Fahey and I can't handle, but I understand the need to look like it's all hands on deck. Murdered college students, especially white ones, get national attention no matter where you are."

"That makes sense. Where is your partner, anyway?"

"He had to run, so I'm catching up with him in a bit." She sighed. "My cynical mind thinks there's something else to it also. I'm thinking Chief probably wants the public perception to be that we're all working on this, not that it's being led by a young-looking female detective with spiky hair."

"That makes sense too. Unfair, but I could see the chief thinking that." Zeke paused to take a sip from the water fountain. "Do we know anything about the victims yet besides the obvious?"

"Only the basics so far, but we'll definitely dig deep to see if one of them in particular was the intended target. Troy Peters was big in his acapella group, Mary Baer was vice president of her sorority, Margaret Sundham had been a stellar youth runner, but burned out and was only rediscovering her love of running now, in her senior year. Each of them has stories like that. I made the calls to all the parents, and it was excruciating."

"That must be the worst part."

"It really is. And none of the five live close enough for me to have at least done it in person. The families are all here now, though."

"We need to find this guy, and fast."

"You're not wrong about that."

"Speaking of, I have some preliminary results from that water bottle."

"Oh, yeah? Go on."

"We were able to extract DNA from it. It's running right now. We might know very soon who it belongs to."

CHAPTER 17
BEN

Friday Midday, October 24

"Hey, what's up Ben? Any news?" Jeremy's voice came through the phone far too calm, far too friendly, and Ben's emotions spilled over.

"What the fuck were you doing not telling me?" He gripped the steering wheel tightly as he turned out of the university parking lot, nearly careening into two students on vespas.

Ben heard Jeremy scrambling to pull his campaign office door shut.

"Hold on, what?"

"V called you! The morning she went missing, she called you and you said nothing!" Ben hissed before taking a quick breath to keep the tirade going. "You—"

"Wait. Stop. Slow down." Jeremy cut him off. "Let me speak."

"Tell me why!"

"That's what I'm trying to do! Look. You're riled up and I get that, but there's a benign explanation. Give me a chance."

Ben wanted to keep screaming at Jeremy for his betrayal, but his need to hear Jeremy's reasoning won out. "It better be a fucking good reason." He took a deep breath. He needed to calm down and focus on the road. He would be no good to Veronica if he ended up in a ditch.

"She did call me, but only because she wanted to ask about my schedule and whether I'd be around for your birthday. She said she was planning something and hoped I'd be there."

"My birthday isn't for another six weeks."

"I know, and I told her that I couldn't be sure because of the campaign schedule. Apparently, whatever she's planning is a thing that needs to be thought about well in advance. You know I want to be there for any celebration of yours. We also chatted about art and discussed planning another visit to the National Gallery. They've got a great new exhibit on Bernini there."

That last line rang true to Ben. Jeremy had been obsessed with art history ever since he'd learned of the Isabella Stewart Gardner heist as a kid. He and Veronica had bonded over their shared love when Ben and Veronica started dating. "That still doesn't explain why you didn't tell me."

"I didn't tell you at first because Veronica is planning a surprise for you, and I wasn't going to be the one to give it away. I didn't tell you after she went missing because I thought —and maybe hoped—that it was just some misunderstanding and she'd be back quickly. It was nothing consequential, so I just decided to stay silent. Then once it was clear something was actually wrong, it didn't feel right to tell you because I'd refrained from telling you before."

Despite himself, Ben could feel his resolve softening. He wanted to stay mad. But most importantly, he just wanted someone to blame. Someone to blame meant an opportunity to find out what was going on. As angry as he was with Jeremy, he thought he had found a clue, a tiny piece of hope, and that was now gone. He allowed himself the anger because he thought it meant moving forward, that there was some lead he could follow. He was back to nothing.

"I just really wanted you to know what had happened," he

said, resigned. "I convinced myself that you knew something because I wanted to believe that I was closer to finding her."

"Look, I want to get her back just as much as you do, and I'll do whatever I can to make that happen. But you've gotta understand there's no way I was involved in whatever happened."

Ben remained silent. He had a thousand thoughts flying through his head. How could he have thought his best friend was in on his wife's disappearance? What kind of crazy conspiracy did he imagine was going on?

No, it made no sense. Jeremy was ambitious, maybe to a fault, but the same could probably be said about Ben. Jeremy had skipped a lot of steps most people were supposed to take when running for president, but could Ben really blame him? He stopped Jacob Jordan's assassination attempt on the president. That was literally his job description. Was it really fair that Ben couldn't shake the feelings of jealousy? Those feelings that Jeremy was somehow cheating the system and getting away with it by using his celebrity to fuel his presidential run?

It had been one thing watching his friend get to throw out a first pitch at Fenway Park, the childhood dream of so many kids who grew up in Boston. He'd even been thrilled for Jeremy when he casually dropped that he'd met Natalia Rochev backstage at the Grammys and they'd hit it off. He didn't begrudge his friend marrying the queen of pop herself, and his best man speech killed that night. But why did Jeremy have to decide he wanted the presidency? Politics was Ben's world. Jeremy could have any world he wanted, why did he have to wade into Ben's?

Ben didn't want to think about it, but he was pretty sure the jealousy must be why he was so quick to assume Jeremy knew something and had kept it from him. Maybe he really did want to bring Jeremy down a peg or two, and hoped this would be how.

You're supposed to be logical and always in control. As much as he hoped it were true so he could find an answer, Ben could not find any logic in Jeremy being part of it.

"Talk me through what you've done and found out," Jeremy said.

"I went over to Georgetown to see if I could get a sense of what she did in the hours before she texted me. I figured maybe I'd find some hint about where she went."

"Yeah, that makes sense."

"There was nothing obvious in her office, but I talked to Dr. Flint. You remember him from their holiday party last year?"

"Dapper and charming old guy, yeah."

"He saw V in her office on the phone shortly before she must have left. I checked it out and saw two phone calls right around that time. Yours was the most recent."

"Was she supposed to be out the rest of the day?"

"She didn't have any teaching or office hours, so I assume she was going to be doing some research, which I guess she could do from anywhere."

As he sat at a four-way stop, waiting for a young man and his dachshund to cross the road, Ben considered his next question. Going from accusing Jeremy to asking for his help in a matter of minutes left him feeling uneasy. *Swallow your pride*, he thought. *Most important is finding V.*

"Look, I'm driving back home from Georgetown right now, do you think you could look something up quickly for me?"

"Dude, just like that?"

"I know, I know. I can only say that I'm desperate to find her and was willing to believe anything."

"All right, fire away."

"The other phone call was a number that I don't know. Can you look it up for me?"

"Yeah, no problem. What is it?"

Ben pulled over into a back street of Georgetown, near Dumbarton Oaks. He looked at his phone and read out the number.

"Great, I'll call you back."

Ben put the phone down and pulled back out, heading toward Rock Creek Parkway to take him south, back to Alexandria. He had barely any time alone since Veronica hadn't come home, and as he sat in the driver's seat, he realized his concealed loneliness was threatening to burst out. It took only forty-eight hours for him to accuse his best friend of … what? Kidnapping and maybe murder?

Get a grip, Ben. What would Veronica be doing if you were missing? He had to smile at that thought. She'd probably have been able to persuade the National Guard to put her in temporary control. He would have been found within half an hour.

The sound of his ringtone brought Ben out of his thoughts. He glanced down at his cup holder, saw Jeremy's name come up, and quickly grabbed it.

"Yes?"

"Hey, man. I got the number. Probably good you asked me, actually. I was able to pull a couple strings."

"Go on."

"It's a collect call number for a prison. I gave a friend a call and found out it's Red Onion State Prison. A supermax way down in the far corner of Virginia."

"Jacob. She must have been called by Jacob Jordan." Thoughts swirled through his mind. Could Jacob have said or done something? Could he be behind the shooting, despite being in prison? What did he know? For all Ben knew, Jacob was still barely talking to anyone. He never spoke to anyone after he got arrested, and only said what he had to at the trial.

Or maybe this was simply the scheduled time that Veronica had set up to talk to him. Ben didn't know much but he knew that you can't just call someone in prison, they have to call you. She was always so guarded about it, so he didn't have much to go on.

"Why would he do that?" Jeremy seemed to be having the same thoughts.

"Well, you know V talks to him once every few weeks? She was the reason he first spoke after the trial was over—he asked if he could call her."

"I had no idea. I knew hers had been his favorite class in college, but not that they had such a relationship."

"Oh yeah, absolutely, from early on that semester she would come home and talk about this mathematical wunderkind she had in one of her courses. She said the sky was the limit with him. He was proper and polite and aced everything she put in front of him."

Ben thought back to when Veronica learned what Jacob had done. He had graduated from Georgetown a few years before, and Ben hadn't heard his name since. He found out later that Jacob had been a graduate student in the University of Michigan's prestigious Applied & Interdisciplinary Mathematics program.

Ben had been at work on a Saturday, getting all the pieces in place for Congresswoman Moore's *Thank You* tour after being reelected. The shooting caused Congress to go into lockdown so he didn't get home until late that night. When he arrived he found Veronica sitting on their couch, hunched over, holding onto a pillow tightly.

The more she followed the trial the more confused she became.

"I get that you might not fully know a person, but the out of character part of this is that his plan just seems so dumb," she had said. "How could someone so rational do something so irrational?"

Ben hadn't had, and still didn't have, an answer.

"She just can't wrap her head around this smart, polite kid being the one who shot a congressman and attempted to assassinate the president," he explained to Jeremy. "And the biggest thing is the irrationality of it. He never struck her as irrational."

"Wasn't the Unabomber a great mathematician? I still remember that line from the CNN "Crimes of the Century" episode on him. Something like: 'He was a brilliant mathematician … who hated society.' My best guess is this guy had something similar inside."

"She's never wanted to discuss what she and he talked about. She often seemed frustrated when she'd tell me he had called her," Ben said. "Like she knew there was something buried down there but that she could never actually get in."

"What do you want to do? Remember, she called me after talking to him, so I can't imagine whatever was discussed was that important. She didn't mention it to me at all."

"I have to call him. Or figure out how to get him to call me. I have to see if he knows something. It's strange, actually, I was just talking to someone about him yesterday."

"Really?"

"Yeah, I ran into Miranda Belle when I went for a walk yesterday. She said she's always looked up to V and was so impressed that she was willing to try to see the good in a murderer like Jacob Jordan. She was fascinated by the case and said she's read everything about him."

"I wouldn't have pegged her as the type to be interested."

"She said there was something so familiar about him, like she knew him from somewhere. I know she's not much older than him so I wonder if she could've overlapped with him at Georgetown at all. He certainly would have remembered her."

"No doubt. Everyone who has ever met her remembers the occasion." Jeremy paused. "I hope she's doing okay."

CHAPTER 18
MIRANDA

Friday Evening, October 24

Miranda floated around the estate as if she were walking on air. Tidying up here. Putting away a few dishes there. The buzz and excitement of a budding new relationship made the most mundane tasks seem joyful.

Reynaldo had called. He asked her out, she said yes, and he would pick her up tonight at eight.

She hummed happily to the tunes running through her head as she picked up around the foyer, just in case things went extremely well and she let him in after. Not that this house needed any help. If anything, she worried he wouldn't even notice her after being blinded by the interior.

It had been a long time, even before the accident, since she had something like this to look forward to. She paused for a second and thought about how Tracy would always help her get ready for dates when she was younger.

Grief was a tricky thing. Sure, it decreased over time, but that decrease was anything but linear. It spiked when least expected, and that pain could last five minutes, seventy-two hours, or a week at a time.

She had heard grief described as a ball bouncing around a

box, with a pain button on one side of the box. The ball got smaller over time, and so the chance of hitting the button decreased, but when it hit the button, the pain was just as strong. That was the best presentation of grief she'd ever heard, and it stuck with her.

The ball hit the button dead-on and forced her to take a seat in her dressing room. She stared at her clothes and all of a sudden wondered what it was all for. She knew she had to go on and continue living for her family members who couldn't, but the truth was she was just sad and lonely.

Who did she have to tell if things went well? Or, with her dating luck, who could she reliably bitch to if he turned out to be a dud?

Now's not the time, she thought. She picked herself up.

"Look at yourself." Miranda spoke into her golden arched mirror. "Look at me. I'm funny, I'm honest, I'm engaging, I'm kind. I deserve to get back out there and live my life. Mom and Dad and Tracy would want me to do this. They would be upset if they knew I've been backing out of social engagements for months." She took a deep breath and started looking through her many closets.

An hour and a half later, Miranda was fully dressed and had finished putting her face on. She wore a black two-piece satin dress inspired by a Taylor Swift look from a Grammys red carpet and complemented it with a white lace shrug.

She gave herself an up-and-down look in the mirror and smiled at what she saw. She had no idea where they were headed. All she knew about their destination was that Reynaldo said it was fancy, and she certainly looked the part.

Miranda was reading in her library, a room she had converted just off the main entryway, when the knock came on her front door. She hesitated, not wanting to appear too eager, and then crossed the foyer and opened the door.

"Hi, Reynaldo." She held back the full-watt smile, the one that she had been told could stop trains in their tracks, but figured the smile she gave was still plenty powerful enough to show her excitement about the upcoming night.

Reynaldo greeted her with a quick hug, and she ushered him into the entryway. He wore a light blue tee shirt under a navy slim fit suit that made him look even taller than he already was. His pants stopped just above his ankles and he wore loafers with no visible socks.

He has this vibe, Miranda thought, *like he is in complete control of himself. He's a man who knows exactly who he is.*

Reynaldo gaped as he looked around. "This house is incredible! And you. You look amazing."

"Thank you, that's very kind." Miranda shrugged his compliment off. *Be demure*, she could hear her mother's voice saying inside her head.

He noticed her glance away. "If it helps, I once lived in an even bigger house."

Miranda swiveled to face him squarely, surprise and bewilderment etched across her face. "Wait, what?"

Reynaldo flashed a mischievous smile. "Another place, another time. Come on, let's head to dinner. Plenty of time there to tell tales of misspent youth." He glanced outside. "I hope you don't mind, I figured it'd be best to take an Uber. I, for sure, am planning on having a drink."

"Not at all, but I would like to know where we're going, and I haven't gotten that out of you yet!"

"Good point. I got us a reservation at a nice place in DC on 7th Street. I've been told it's incredible, and I've never had fancy American food so I'm curious!"

"Lead the way." Miranda opened her front door and followed Reynaldo outside, enjoying a feeling of hope she had not experienced in a long time.

CHAPTER 19
JEREMY

Friday Night, October 24

"Jeremy Wiles." Jeremy picked up his phone after glancing at the unknown caller message. He leaned back in his chair and looked out over his campaign headquarters, full of staffers despite it being almost 9 p.m.

"Mr. Wiles. It's a pleasure to get to talk to you one on one," a man with a thick accent replied. "I have news for you."

"Who is this?"

"This is Robin Verheijen."

"No way." Jeremy perked up. "You got my message?"

"That I did. And if my sources are correct, I have information you would very much like to hear. I assume you know of my reputation from that previous encounter of ours?"

"I know you're the man who can find anything that's lost. I know you work on the boundary of both our, and international, laws. I know you have a particular affinity for lost paintings from Dutch artists. I know you're as respected as you are wanted. I know you previously attempted to call me and were rebuffed, for which I apologize sincerely. Does that sum it up?"

"That's quite nice. Take out that final sentence and I might put that on my next business card."

"What do you have for me?"

"Let me tell you a story."

Jeremy held his phone away from his head as he let out an exasperated sigh. He had been warned that Robin was the type to talk someone's ear off before getting to the actual point.

"Go on."

"It started well before this, but we'll start our story in the early hours of March 18th, 1990."

"Robin, all due respect, but I know the story of the Gardner Museum heist."

"Two thieves, posing as policemen, entered the venerable Boston museum under the auspices of checking on a disturbance." Robin continued as if Jeremy hadn't even spoken. "They handcuffed the two guards, threatened their families, and left them tied up in the basement. What happened next, you ask? Did they methodically steal the most valuable art in the museum? No, I tell you! Titian's *Rape of Europa?* Untouched! Raphael, Botticelli, even Michelangelo himself? Ignored!

"But what room was looted? What room could that be? Why, the room containing only those works of art from the legends of my country. Yes! The Dutch Room! Three Rembrandts, a Vermeer. Even a Govert Flinck was taken!"

"Robin, please, I know about all thirteen works of art stolen, including the five Dutch pieces," Jeremy said, rubbing his forehead.

"Then you'll know of course that one of the early suspects was none other than Whitey Bulger himself, and, by proxy, the Irish Republican Army? And, though that turned up nothing, the police took a long, hard look at the Boston Mafia?"

"Yes, Robin." Jeremy was starting to wonder if this was all worth it. "I do, in fact, know that. I would not have reached out to you if I had not known."

"So tell me then, where do you think the lost art is?"

"That's the whole point of you, isn't it?"

"Yes, yes. You, a man with considerable reach, still would

have no chance of doing what I do. That is the point I am making."

"So, what do you have for me, then?"

"I'm guessing you, too, believe that Bobby Donati was the mastermind behind the heist? That he did it to use the art to negotiate the release of Vincent Ferrara, as he was caught up in the middle of the Patriarca family civil war and needed Ferrara on the outside to protect him?"

"You already know this. I laid this out in my first message to you."

"Well, my friend, you are in luck."

"Tell me."

"As it turns out, Bobby D was the true mastermind. And he did bury much of the art, as he told Ferrara in prison. Now, the location of the buried art remains a mystery, but a particularly uppity low-level mobster who was in on the secret did manage to sneak back and sequester one work away. That is where I come in."

Jeremy realized he was holding his breath, hanging on every word. The Gardner heist had been an obsession of his since he'd first visited the museum as a child and looked upon the empty frames, still hanging in their original positions. After his abrupt rise to fame and fortune, he realized he was finally in a position to attempt a lifelong goal he'd never believed possible: find the lost art. He maintained a deeply held belief that the art was still out there somewhere, and there was at least one person still alive who knew where it was.

That was why, after meeting with local police and FBI agents, and seemingly exhausting all possibilities, he had stumbled upon Robin Verheijen. A showman and storyteller, he was known as the expert on lost Dutch art. Jeremy figured if anyone had an idea as to the whereabouts of the Dutch pieces from the Gardner it would be him.

So here he was, listening to a man suspected of several art

heists and forgeries, just because he might give him the info Jeremy had been craving for decades.

"I tracked down the son of this mobster who shall remain nameless, and, well, let's just say we talked."

"What did you find out?"

"Look out at the front door of your campaign office, Mr. Wiles."

"How do you know I'm in my office?"

"Oh, Mr. Wiles. Don't insult me." Robin laughed.

Jeremy stood up and peered past his staff. He saw a man dressed in a United States Postal Service uniform place a rectangular box up against the exterior of the door.

Jeremy's lower lip dropped. He stood, mouth agape, as the man turned around and disappeared back into the crowd.

"I take it you see my gift? Excuse me, not a gift. A service. Assuming you will send the money you promised, this is where we part company. You've seen my reach, so I know you will pay. Goodbye, Jeremy Wiles."

Jeremy strode out to the front door. He grabbed the box and held it up. It looked a bit bigger than the average diploma frame. He averted his gaze so as to not lock eyes with anyone as he casually walked back to his office.

This is an issue with having glass walls, he thought. Privacy is easily achievable with the blinds, but it's conspicuous. He pulled all the blinds down anyway. Some things were too important.

He opened the box and slid out a canvas inside a protective casing.

"Oh, my God."

CHAPTER 20
ZEKE

Friday Night, October 24

Zeke entered the internal briefing room. Everyone working on the Rock Creek shooting had been hurriedly summoned, and as he glanced around the room, he saw not only the chief of police, but also Mayor Angela Wood in attendance.

This must be something big, he thought. While a mass shooting was undoubtedly a high priority in its own right, he did not think that the mayor would be in attendance unless she had been briefed ahead of time about a new development. Especially not at almost ten at night.

Detective Brown stood up at the front of the room and cleared her throat. "We have the DNA results from the water bottle found at the scene." Every time she spoke, Zeke marveled at her gravitas. She had them all hanging on her every word. The chief had made a mistake when he didn't make her the outward focal point of the investigation.

"As you all know, we do not believe this was a premeditated crime. As such, it is likely that our killer did not have time to clean up the scene, especially since it happened in broad daylight on a relatively busy trail."

Zeke nodded along. He was the one who had told Detective Brown that theory and, after he laid it out for her, she fully supported it.

"As you also know, we recovered this water bottle from the scene, wedged between the bank of the creek and a root. It is unclear how it pertains to the case, but as it is the only object that did not get swept away by the water during the storms, we believed it could give us a clue as to someone who was there around the time of the incident.

"I brought you all here because the DNA has come back, and it's a doozy."

The detective stopped to take a swig of water as the anticipation built around her. Zeke knew that they had finished their analysis, but the result came back while he was at dinner, and his boss took it straight to Detective Brown. He was as much in the dark as the rest of the room.

"There is no DNA match."

Confused whispers spread row to row. Zeke glanced to the back of the room and noticed the mayor nodding along. *Good enough for me*, he thought. If the mayor already knew this and is still here, there must be something coming.

"But," Detective Brown continued. "We can tell the DNA is genetically similar to someone whom we do have on file. This makes it likely that our person of interest is closely related to said individual."

"You're killing them all, just spit it out, Jesus Christ!" Her partner, Detective Martin Fahey, roared. That was exactly what Zeke had been thinking.

She threw her partner a mischievous wink, and then turned back to face the crowd. "The DNA we found appears to be from a relative of Yancey Portillo."

The name meant nothing to Zeke, but he heard a voice behind him groan. "Oh, fuck me. You're kidding. Portillo?" He looked around and saw shocked and scared faces throughout the room. *Who is this guy?* He stared at the ashen face of a veteran detective who looked like he'd seen a ghost.

Mayor Wood stood up. "Ladies and gentlemen, we know that he was seen entering the country a few days ago. Now we have this. I think we have to believe this is connected, and I want you all to know everything there is to know about Yancey Portillo as soon as humanly possible. This might be connected to his international drug ring now, which would mean their violence has come to the district. We need to find him and whomever else might be here immediately."

She walked toward the exit. "I wish you well. Good luck."

Zeke nudged Detective Fahey as they left the meeting. Martin Fahey was a behemoth of a man. The former body-builder stood at six feet seven and weighed close to three hundred pounds, all of which he claimed was muscle. Up close, Zeke always found it hard to disagree.

"So, what's the story with Yancey Portillo? That was quite a reaction from everyone in there."

Fahey's handlebar mustache twitched. The thirty-nine-year-old fixed a deadly serious gaze on Zeke.

"He's the only bad guy I've ever heard of who legitimately scares me. I mean, look at me. I can take care of myself, right, but he's a whole different level, man."

"Why would he be here?"

"Word is he's looking to expand his empire into America. His base of operations is in El Salvador and he's got no competition. The last time there was any, he took them all down in a single night. Some Keyser Söze shit."

"You're kidding. Why haven't I heard about him?"

"Probably because he and his organization have never gone after civilians. Well, at least in a way that can be proven, or would be noticeable here. But this changes things. Think of the scariest gang or cartel you can imagine. He could squash them like an irritating mosquito."

"Wow." Zeke hadn't anticipated this. "That's terrifying."

"It is. You watched *The Wire*?"

"Of course."

"Imagine Omar and Marlo wrapped into one body. Ruthless, cunning, smart, you name it. Lucky for us the man does have a code." He paused. "Or, at least, he used to. Who knows anymore?"

"You know quite a bit about him."

"Yeah, I do. Honestly, it's been a bit of a hobby for me, keeping up with him. He's outside our jurisdiction but the tales are the stuff of legend, so I like to keep up. Makes me sleep better at night if I at least know what he's up to, rather than letting my mind wander. I'll tell you one story. When he was younger and just starting out, he got a sit-down with the head of a big smuggling organization in San Salvador. We know this because right after that meeting, the man walked into the police station and turned himself in and disbanded his gang. He didn't ever tell what Yancey said, but this nineteen-year-old kid destroyed that gang with just a few words. There's a kicker too: a week later, the same guys were doing the same smuggling, but under Portillo's command. To this day, no one knows what he said. He built an empire from there. Any crime in El Salvador goes through him. Now they've picked him up on a security camera at Miami International Airport about ten days ago. The story was in the *Post* this week."

"Does he have relatives that we know of?"

"That's the tricky thing. The simple answer is we don't know. He came from a big family, several brothers and sisters, and we believe he might have many children of his own too. The two kids we know about are dead. But his inner circle is practically impenetrable, so it's hard to know for certain."

Detective Fahey puffed out his cheeks. He gave a little shake of his head as he let his gaze drift above Zeke's frame.

"This is a whole new ball game if Portillo has anything to do with this. You, Brown, me, all the rest who are on this case. We need to watch our backs. You've never seen anything like what you might see now."

CHAPTER 21
MIRANDA

Friday Night, October 24

Reynaldo pulled out her chair and let Miranda seat herself before he took his own seat at a small square table.

"Chivalry. One point for you." Miranda smiled as they opened their menus.

The restaurant was small but not cramped, with a cozy atmosphere. The brick walls were painted white, with white frames holding minimalist art set against the bricks. They ordered drinks and entrees and settled in.

Reynaldo turned his palms upward. "So, what makes Miranda Belle tick?"

"Wow, that's quite a question." Miranda thought for a second. "Normally the first questions are 'Where are you from?' and things like that."

Reynaldo smiled. "I don't like to talk about small things. I want to talk about big ideas, aspirations, feelings."

"Well, let me turn it back to you first, then." Miranda laughed. "You tell me and then I'll reciprocate."

"I can't argue with that. For me, it is providing for my family back home. I have lots of relatives back in El Salvador and I want to be successful so I can help them as much as possible."

"That's a lovely goal. Can you tell me about them?"

Reynaldo let out a deep sigh. "Actually … I haven't told you the full story of why I am here. I'm not just a graduate student."

Miranda felt the air thicken around them. "What do you mean?" she asked as she leaned back, confusion and worry creeping in.

"I guess we'll just jump right in. I wasn't intending on bringing this up so quickly, but I feel like I can trust you."

"You can."

"Okay. So there's a man—no, he's more than just a man—back in San Salvador, where I'm from. He's cunning and incredibly smart. *Increíblemente*. His name is Yancey Portillo. Do you know this name?"

"No, I don't think so." She paused and tilted her head. "Wait. Wasn't he in the paper recently? Some drug lord?"

Reynaldo gave a quiet chuckle. "To say he is some drug lord is to say Lionel Messi is some soccer player. The thing is, I'm actually—"

"Good evening! Apologies for intruding." A server appeared with their meals. "I have the baked potato chowder for the lady, and the tripe pappardelle here for the gentleman. Bon appétit!"

Miranda gave Reynaldo a conciliatory grimace after the waiter was gone. "Sorry, that was really awkward timing. What were you saying?"

"I was trying to tell you that I'm actually a refugee. I had to flee El Salvador for my own safety."

"Oh, my goodness! What happened?"

"The man I was telling you about, Yancey Portillo. He … well … he killed my parents. And my brothers. I'm only alive because they sent me away." He took a deep breath. "I was the first to get away. The rest were supposed to come as soon as they could, but they weren't able to find a way fast enough. Your government doesn't move quickly, even in these cases."

"I'm so sorry, Reynaldo. That's just awful."

"I now care deeply about how the rest of my family—my cousins and aunts and uncles are doing. I worry every day that I will hear bad news."

He straightened up in his chair and shook his head with a soft chuckle. "I'm sorry, I told myself I wouldn't bring this up. This is a date, it's supposed to be fun! You're just very easy to talk to, and I haven't met anyone yet in America who I can talk to about my family."

"No. This is actually really nice to hear." Miranda looked Reynaldo directly in the eyes before quickly averting her gaze. "Wait. I'm sorry, I don't mean that it's nice what happened. I just have a similar story." She squeezed her eyes shut and grimaced.

"Seriously?"

Miranda looked back up and continued. "My parents and sister were killed last year. A car accident. I was the only one who survived. The thing is," she continued. "Since then, I haven't been able to connect with anyone. It's like I have this albatross around my neck, this guilt at being the one who survived." *There I go again with the albatross analogy.* She stifled a groan and continued. "No one knows how to talk to me anymore and I don't know what to say either. So, you're definitely not scaring me off, or making me feel uncomfortable by mentioning your parents. If anything, I feel like I'm talking to someone who really knows what it's like."

She could feel herself starting to ramble. "You know how when you go on a trip, and you have all these experiences and then can't wait to tell your friends or family once you get home? And then they're never as excited about it as you want them to be? Because how can they be? They're not the ones who were part of the shared experience. They can hear about it, but they'll never feel the same feelings. This is like the negative version of that to me. Everyone has hardship, and sometimes comparing tragic tales is a waste of time. It can feel like no one actually really, truly, can empathize. So, I just pretend things are more okay than they are."

She looked at Reynaldo with a grimace that turned into a glimmer of a smile. "Now it's my turn to apologize. Didn't mean to just unload that all on you there. Clearly, I should be talking to someone about all of this."

Reynaldo gave her a gentle smile. "Maybe we both should be. But for now, talking to each other seems to be going well."

He raised his wine glass and gently clinked it against hers. "A toast. To kinship and kindred spirits!"

They both ate in silence for a couple minutes until Reynaldo asked, "So, you are friends with that couple who live on Royal Street? Where we almost ran into each other the other night."

"Yes. Yes, I am. Ben and Veronica. They're wonderful. I don't know if they know it, but they're the best friends I have here in town."

"That's great! Tell me more about them."

Miranda thought it was slightly odd he was interested, but figured he must not know many people here yet. And, hey, she did first see him outside their house, even if he didn't seem to remember bumping into her.

"Okay, well, Ben is from Boston and is the chief of staff to Congresswoman Chamique Moore. You might have heard of her—she's become a big deal pretty quickly."

"I haven't, but the only reason I even know who the US president is right now is because of that assassination attempt last year. I'm not very knowledgeable on American politics." Reynaldo did know one or two Salvadoran politicians who owed him and his boss many favors, but he didn't bring that up.

"Well, I wouldn't bet against her running for president in the future. She's headed straight to the top. Anyway, he's something of a big deal too as her number two. Meanwhile, I believe Veronica grew up in Mexico and then came here with her parents sometimes in her teens. She's a math professor at

Georgetown and is probably the smartest person I've ever met. She's also been incredibly kind to me ... they both have."

"I think I saw one of the children in the window as I went past."

Wow, he is thorough, she thought. She tucked that thought away for later. *Thorough can be good but can get creepy quickly.* "Yeah, probably. They're twins, five years old. They're sweet kids. A funny mix of their parents' disparate looks!"

"I went through Mexico on my way here to the United States. Do you know where in Mexico she is from?"

"I don't know, she doesn't ever really talk about it. I think she once mentioned southern Mexico. Like close to whichever country is just south of it? Sorry I'm not great with geography," she added.

"Interesting," he said, with an inscrutable look that she tried to decipher and failed. "Anyway, enough about them, let us get back to you."

———

As they were preparing to leave, Reynaldo suggested they walk to the metro and take it back to Old Town. "Mount Vernon Square metro stop is just by here. Would you like to take it back? I'm new to it, so it's still exciting to me."

Miranda glanced outside and shrugged. "Why not? It's a pretty night for a little walk."

The two of them sat, side by side, in the almost empty metro car, as it whizzed through the darkness under the nation's capital. After several minutes, the car emerged onto a bridge across the Potomac River.

"What a city," Reynaldo said breathily, finally taking his eyes off Miranda to look out at the monuments that made up DC's distinct skyline.

They disembarked minutes later at Braddock Road station, the northernmost of the two metro stops in Old Town. The pair walked down Oronoco Street, and Reynaldo slipped his arm inside hers. She smiled and let it stay. They stopped in front of her house.

They both held the embrace a few seconds longer than anticipated. Reynaldo beamed at her.

"This was fantastic, and I enjoyed spending time with you this evening. I just want to quickly say that I'm very traditional, though, so I think the night should end here, as much as I'd love to get an invite inside." He spoke breathlessly, as if not getting the words out immediately would mean they didn't come at all.

"You'll never know if you were about to get an invite or not." She gave him a mischievous smile. "I'll give you an idea, though." She leaned up and gave him a kiss on the cheek.

"Until next time," she whispered in his ear and promptly turned and went inside.

Once she closed the door, Miranda snuck over and peeked out the window and watched Reynaldo walk farther down Oronoco Street and out of sight. She walked into the kitchen and poured herself a glass of her favorite chianti—from the Montepulciano region of Italy, of course. As she walked out to the terrace, she tried to remember the last time she'd had such a good first date.

She heard a rustle in the trees on the edge of the property. She put her glass down and peered out to see which of the squirrels that practically lived with her was making the fuss this time.

As she walked farther out into the yard, she turned around slowly, savoring the night and the promise of nights to come.

Miranda sighed. This was contentment. She could not remember the last time she'd felt like this. Happy.

The thump felt like a hammer hitting her spine.

She barely had time to comprehend it before the second came, and then there was nothing.

CHAPTER 22
JEREMY

Saturday Morning, October 25th

"Top o' the mornin' to you, boss!"

Jeremy watched as Ernest walked into the office, his paisley tie loose and his socks mismatched. He was eager, but a morning person he was not. Jeremy knew the to-go cup in his hand was at least his third.

"Ernest, you grew up in New Mexico," Jeremy chided.

"Sure, but you Bostonians talk like that all the time, I hear," Ernest grinned as he put his briefcase down at his desk with a loud thud.

Jeremy stifled a yawn and glanced at his watch. Six-thirty in the morning. Another early morning after another late night. And it was worse when he was out on the campaign trail. At least his current schedule allowed him to spend a bit more time at home this week.

When you're married to a pop star who is rarely home, you work hard to be home when she is.

Natalia had been far more receptive to his plan to go for the presidency than he'd anticipated. Date after date, and then night after night, he put off telling her. He even wondered if maybe he could be happy with what he had. A nationwide hero, soon-to-be married to the most recognizable pop star in the world. More important, married to a genuinely kind and thoughtful woman. What kind of person would look at that life and think it wasn't enough?

But Jeremy knew. He wasn't cut out to be the trailing spouse, to use a term he learned from a diplomat friend. He needed to be the protagonist.

That's the thing about being a former gifted kid. Not just that, but a charming and classically attractive one. You spend your childhood being told how special you are. You ace your tests, your good looks are always noted, and adults fall over themselves gushing about what a good conversationalist you are.

But there are lots of kids who get told that. All but a few end up working at decent paying no-name jobs, just like their peers they were told they were better than.

Jeremy hadn't wanted to join the Secret Service. He didn't admit this to anyone, even Ben, because that would be an admission of defeat. He needed to look like everything was going exactly as he had planned.

Not that he'd been passed up for job offers at places he wanted to work. *Especially* the position working for Congress-woman Moore that went to Ben instead. He never told Ben he'd applied for the same vacancy. Sure, Ben was the one with the policy and government degrees, but Jeremy was so competitive he wanted to know if he could get offered a job above his best friend.

It took Jeremy far too long at Harvard to realize that Bill Parcells was right. *You are what your record says you are.* It didn't matter if he was the best at everything if he only ever coasted. He enjoyed college exactly as he was led to believe he should. He put in enough work to look decent and had plenty of extra-curricular fun. But for the first time in his life, he didn't stand out.

But look at me now, he thought. The most recognizable face in just about every room he entered.

He wished his parents were still alive to see this. They had tried to hide it, but they'd been so disappointed by his college stagnation. Then again, their untimely deaths—a stroke and an aggressive brain tumor, respectively—had provided a spark, telling him he had to become something more than what he was. With no siblings, he was the only one left to carry on the Wiles legacy.

"What do you have for me, Ernest? In early on a Saturday, that's what I like to see."

Ernest beamed back at him. That's all it took. Throw a little bone here and there, show you appreciate the people helping make your dream a reality.

"Figured we could chat schedule before the day starts in earnest." He raised his eyebrow, making sure Jeremy caught the pun.

Jeremy chose to ignore it. Got to keep your people humble, too. "What are we looking at?"

"As you know, you have a packed schedule today. Local non-profits, a few heads of organizations, just straight back-to-back shaking hands and wooing important people all day long. A dinner with the senior Senator from Ohio tonight, and then you're done at around eight."

Jeremy nodded along as he spoke. He was happy to be spending some time at home, but it did mean campaign meetings with the worst types of people. Being out in the country, holding rallies and kissing babies, that was where he felt good. People would show up looking for hope, and he could see in their eyes they often left believing they'd found it.

But here in DC, no one offered a thing without a promise of something in return. So, while Natalia was also home for a little while, he'd asked his staff to set up as many meetings as possible with anyone who was anyone. This week wasn't about securing votes, but endorsements. It was right around the time that some of the highest ranking Congressional Democrats would begin their endorsements, and even getting a couple of them on his side would provide a massive boost.

"When do I meet with Congresswoman Moore?" he asked.

"I...," Ernest's voice faltered. "I'm sorry. We couldn't get you on her schedule this week."

Jeremy looked down and put his hand to his forehead. When he looked back up, he said, "I'm sorry, what do you mean you couldn't?"

Ernest looked down at his notebook and flipped a page. "They said they were happy to hear from us, and would find a time in the future, but that the Congresswoman was, I quote, 'busy working on important policy', so we're out of luck this time."

"When did we reach out to them?"

Ernest cocked his head. "Several weeks ago, I'd have to check the exact date," he said, after a couple seconds had passed.

"No, that's fine. Give me some time in here, and then let's rally the troops and start the day." Jeremy looked past Ernest into the empty space behind. "Well, once they actually arrive."

After Ernest left, Jeremy grabbed his phone, before thinking twice and putting it back down. Nothing in Congresswoman Moore's schedule happens—or doesn't, in this case—without Ben's approval. So, why didn't Ben let him meet with her?

Jeremy assumed he already knew the answer. Ben wasn't great at hiding his feelings—hell, he'd just accused him of kidnapping under twenty-four hours ago—so Jeremy could see the jealousy. Jeremy knew better than to take it personally, he'd do the same thing in Ben's shoes.

He wished Ben could have looked past it and agreed to join his team. He was headed to the top. How else was Ben going to get there? If everything went as planned, this was a fast track to the White House. Surely a little competitive streak wouldn't stop Ben from jumping at that opportunity.

Or so Jeremy had thought.

Ben was on edge right now, Jeremy understood that. If Natalia were missing, there's no telling what he would do. Any other time he'd have gone through with the call and asked Ben what was up.

He glanced again at the time, wishing it wasn't moving like molasses. Just one day to get through before he could get off the grid tonight, if only for a few hours.

He couldn't wait.

CHAPTER 23
BEN

Saturday Morning, October 25

Ben sat in his study, the digits punched into his phone, not sure what was stopping him from pressing the call button. Nico and Maria were with Veronica's parents, enjoying Saturday morning cartoons in the living room. How his heart ached for them. He and Veronica were supposed to be superheroes to them at this age. No matter what the situation, their parents were there to fix it. He could see it in their eyes, just how much they had grown up in these past four days.

Kids always understood more than anyone thinks. He tried to convince them that their mother was just away for a few days, but they could tell something was wrong. Even if they didn't know exactly, they understood the anxiety and fear, despite how well he and his in-laws tried to hide it.

He had no idea how to call a prison, so he spent some time searching online and found out that there was no real way to call an inmate. An inmate could call someone, but inmates could not be called, and guards and prison staff were not likely to pass on a message.

So here he sat, with the prison number in his phone, debating whether it was worth it or just a lost cause. *Gotta check the box,* he thought. *Worst case scenario is there's no lead or I can't even talk to him, and then I just move on.*

What the hell. Just do it. He pushed the call button.

"Red Onion State Prison," a cheerful young voice answered. Ben was taken aback. He had expected a grunt, or at most a grumpy monotone answer. The woman on the other end was anything but.

"Hi …" Ben trailed off as he tried to get his act together.

"Yes?" The voice chilled.

"I'm sorry. My name is Ben Walsh and I have a request that I'm pretty sure you're going to say no to." He paused and took a breath. "My name is Ben Walsh, and I need your help. My wife is missing, and I think one of your inmates may know something about it. I need to speak to Jacob Jordan. Can you please let me talk to him?"

"That's not possible, sir. Inmates cannot receive calls and I am not at liberty to relay messages."

"Wait. You might know. He calls a woman every week or so, right?"

"I can check that, hold on."

Ben waited, wondering what checking meant. *Did she have that info on a computer in front of her? Or did she have to go talk to someone?* There was so little he knew about prisons. He felt guilty for not knowing more, realizing how lucky he was to have never had a reason to.

Veronica knew a lot more than he did. She had a passion for criminal justice that surpassed even the majority of his co-workers. She went to the local prison every few weeks to help tutor math. And of course, she had her scheduled calls with Jacob Jordan, the most notorious criminal in the country. The man who tried to assassinate the president and then remained silent from arrest, to arraignment, to his trial and sentencing. Not a single word.

"You know what really bugs me every time I go, though?" Veronica had asked Ben a few months before.

"What?"

"The way we all treat inmates. Or even former inmates."

"How do you mean?"

"Isn't the point of a jail sentence supposed to be rehabilitation? For all but the very worst offenders? So why do we as a society still judge people even after they've finished their sentence? The point is that they've completed it. They're allowed back into society. So why is it a stigma forever? And don't even get me started on the fact that released felons are still not allowed to vote in most of the country. Every week I look at these young men and think about how life will never be easy for them again whether they get released or not. A Black man in the district gets caught with a tiny bag of drugs and it ruins his life. He goes to jail, normally for years, and then when he gets out, he can't get hired anywhere for the rest of his life, while a White hedge fund owner gets caught with the exact same thing and no one even cares. It's just not right."

"You know you're talking to a policy person, right?" Ben had smiled. "I absolutely agree with you. You really should get involved, do some sort of advocacy. You already make a great difference in these people's lives, but I bet you could do so much more with your voice."

Veronica had pursed her lips, weighing it in her mind. "I think you're right, but I don't want to have a loud voice. I just want to do what I do best. You're the one who can make a difference."

Ben hadn't believed her, and he still thought that she should get involved somehow. Well, once she came back home safe and sound.

The operator returned. "You're right. He has a single call each week. This is a favor. Normally we do not give out that info."

"That's my wife! Veronica Walsh. She's the one who is missing!"

"I'm very sorry to hear that, sir."

"I know you guys don't like giving prisoners messages, but he called her right before she disappeared. I need to know if she said something, if he knows anything. Can you please, in this instance, just tell him she's missing and let him decide if he wants to call me?"

The no longer cheerful voice gave a deep sigh. "Give me a callback number and let me see. No promises." She listened as Ben relayed his cell number, and promptly hung up the phone.

Ben slumped back into his chair. He looked around the study, with its shelves alternating between math texts and historical tomes. He couldn't wrap his head around any of this.

Veronica had texted him on Wednesday, saying she loved him and to remember that. That was right after she'd gotten a call from Jacob Jordan and she had called Jeremy. Jeremy said it was just to discuss upcoming birthday plans for him, which made sense to him since she was tremendous at planning extravagant experiences each year. But then what caused her to send that text?

And did the shooting in Rock Creek Park have anything to do with it? She went running there during the day, yes, but how could she have been at all part of that? It was too coincidental. But if it was connected, then she knew about a shooting before it happened. What did that mean? Most of all, what about it could have made her disappear?

Ben's head swam. But as he sat there, he realized a clue he had overlooked in her office. He had been looking for anything that could provide evidence. He hadn't looked for what was not there.

Her running backpack. He scrambled upstairs and into their bedroom. He pulled open her closet and flipped through her clothes as quickly as he could.

No backpack.

She must have taken her running backpack with her. Which meant she did go on a run.

But how would that work? *She sends a cryptic note and then goes on a run like everything is normal?* Each thought just led to more questions.

Ben felt like his brain was on a spin cycle as his thoughts tumbled around. Was it even a cryptic note? Was she maybe just saying she loved him with no extra context? But wouldn't that be even more coincidental?

"Ben?" His mother-in-law's voice rang out from the living room.

"Yes, I'm upstairs."

"We were going to get some takeout for brunch. Want to help us pick out a place?"

He nodded and attempted a smile. As he followed her down into the living room, he made sure his phone volume was set on high, just in case.

———

Ben laughed as they sat at the dining room table an hour later. He watched Nico and Maria argue over who got the last piece of the giant biscuit. Crumbs from hastily eaten breakfast sandwiches were strewn around the table. Even his laughter felt hollow, though. What kind of husband was he to allow himself to be happy for even a moment when his wife was missing?

The *West Wing* theme rang out from Ben's pocket, and he begged off into his study before answering. A robotic voice asked him if he was willing to accept a call from Red Onion.

Yes, of course.

Ben held the phone against his ear, his heart thumping.

"Dr. Walsh is missing," a high-pitched nasal voice came through the speaker.

"Jacob? Is this Jacob Jordan?" Ben realized he had never heard Jacob's voice until now.

"Dr. Walsh is missing," the odd voice repeated. "Dr. Walsh is missing."

Ben took a deep breath. "Listen, Jacob. I know she talks to

you often. You called her on Wednesday, and then she disappeared soon after. Can you tell me what you talked about?"

"Dr. Walsh is missing."

"Yes, but I'm here. I'm her husband. Can you talk to me?"

"Dr. Walsh is missing. The proof didn't fit in the margin."

"What do you mean by that? What proof?"

"The proof didn't fit in the margin. Dr. Walsh is missing. The proof didn't fit in the margin." Jacob's nasal voice took on a songlike quality as he repeated the same phrases over and over.

Ben sighed, exasperated. "Jacob. This is very important. What did you talk to my wife about?"

A long silence hung in the air until Jacob spoke again. "Dr. Walsh," he spoke deliberately, his voice still in a far higher pitch than sounded natural, "is missing. The proof. Didn't fit. In the margin."

"Are you trying to give me some clue? I don't understand."

"Dr. Walsh is missing. Goodbye." The phone clicked off.

Ben slumped into the chair behind his desk, dumbfounded. He knew that Jacob hadn't spoken during the entire trial, but he assumed it was a tactic. Better to say nothing when your guilt is basically indisputable. But this? Did he actually have a mental impairment? Something that had grown progressively worse? Surely Veronica would have mentioned this.

He could feel his pulse slowly returning to a normal rate. He had been so sure that this would be the breakthrough, the missing piece of the puzzle.

Though Ben was by no means mathematically inclined, he had managed to learn plenty just by proximity to Veronica over the years. After taking a quiet moment to think, Ben realized that he recognized the phrase Jacob had said.

The proof didn't fit in the margin.

It referenced a famous seventeenth-century French mathematician named Pierre de Fermat. Fermat annotated his copy of Diophantine's *Arithmetica* and, in particular, wrote in one margin what would become known as Fermat's Last Theorem:

that there is no integer solution to the equation if n is greater than two. What brought such notoriety was his additional comment. He wrote, in Latin: "I have discovered a truly marvelous proof of this, which the margin is too narrow to contain."

The theorem was noteworthy for its brevity and clarity. Anyone who ever studied geometry in school learned the version where n is two: the algebraic form of what is likely the most well-known mathematical theorem in existence, the Pythagorean theorem. The proof of the Pythagorean theorem, when explained well, can be accessible to even the most math-phobic. The idea that there was no solution for any power greater than two was astonishing.

Fermat's remark was only published after his death, and attempts to prove his conjecture helped to birth the mathematical field of algebraic number theory. That was Veronica's field of expertise, but what could Jacob have meant? Ben didn't know what he was supposed to glean from that quote. He also didn't know if Jacob was *compos mentis* enough to have been attempting a cryptic clue anyway.

Ben typed out a quick email to Dr. Flint, asking if Fermat's Last Theorem had any relevance to Veronica's current work. He tossed his phone down onto the couch once he was done, with much more force than he meant to. Two phone calls that could have explained things, and nothing at all to show for either. Maybe he'd rushed too quickly toward them as potential clues. Or maybe he just didn't ask the right questions.

His frustration level rose again. This time, though, he was angry at himself. Why couldn't he be better at this? He had conquered every challenge he faced so far in his life, so why was attempting to be an amateur detective so much harder than anything he'd ever done? He retrieved his phone from under the couch cushion, made sure it was on high, and left the study, slamming the door behind him.

Nico rushed to greet him as Ben reentered the family room.

Ben couldn't help but smile as he picked up his son and swung him through the air. People kept telling him to enjoy these moments, as they'd get fewer and farther between as they grew up. It felt to him like something adults spoke into existence. If you posit that it's just destiny that eventually your kids will despise you, it is much easier to accept when it happens. He had disagreed with his parents growing up—who hadn't?—but he'd never hated them and couldn't understand how it happened to others.

The hatred came once he was well into adulthood. But that was down to their own actions.

He looked at his in-laws, each of whom were watching him expectantly. He shrugged and gave a resigned shake of his head. "I don't think he's fully with it. He just kept repeating a phrase to do with a famous mathematician. I don't even know if he could tell who I was."

"What mathematician?" Gabriela asked.

"Fermat. I know about him, through V, but I don't understand what it could possibly have to do with anything. I could look it up, but I'm pretty sure that she taught a bit about him in one of the classes Jacob took from her, so maybe it's just some sort of name recognition going on in his brain." He grimaced. "I guessed that there was something up with him, but I don't think I realized how bad it was. I'd be surprised if his lawyer isn't trying to move him to a mental institution."

"But you said that V has been talking to him pretty often? I don't understand," Gabriela said.

"I don't either. I can't imagine he had much to say. I wonder if she was trying to coax the old him back out or something." He paused for a second, thinking. "Unless he was just playing some trick on me? I just don't know."

———

Ben spent the entire day with Nico and Maria. Gabriela and Ricardo had insisted on it. The police are in charge of looking for Veronica, they had said. It's your job to make sure these kids know they still have a father present.

They laughed. They played. Ben allowed himself to be distracted for the first time since Veronica's disappearance. It was a nice feeling.

Now the kids were asleep. The grandparents were asleep. But there was no way Ben could sleep. He had given up on the idea of sleep hours ago. So, here he was, just after midnight, sitting in his study. If the phone calls didn't have anything to do with her disappearance, then maybe it was something she saw on her computer.

In truth, he'd been waiting all day for everyone else to go to sleep so he could get back to searching for clues.

The Washington Post's front page was the last thing she had looked at before closing her computer. He wondered what she had seen, and if it even had anything to do with this.

Surely there's a way to find out? He had a thought just as his phone rang, an unknown number. He scrambled to pick it up off the nearby couch.

"Hello?"

A deep robotic voice spoke. "Stop looking for your wife. She's not coming back."

"Who … who is this?" Ben's voice trembled. "Do you have Veronica? Where is my wife?"

"Stop investigating," the chilling voice continued.

"Or what?" Ben found a courage he didn't know he had. He'd watched enough crime shows to know that if someone was calling, then he was close to hitting a nerve. But what nerve?

"There will be more consequences." The lack of decipherable tone made the sentence all the more ominous.

"What do you mean more?"

"More people will die if you do not stop."

"I'll never stop looking for my wife."

"Forget about her. Or else you'll soon have to forget about Maria. Or Nicolas."

"If you fucking come near—"

"Ah, now you're getting it."

Ben stopped. "What do you want?"

"You heard. Stop searching."

"And what? If I stop, you'll just bring her back?"

"Go to the first boundary stone. You'll find one of your consequences there. Maybe it's her."

CHAPTER 24
JEREMY

Sunday Early Morning, October 26

Jeremy heard his wife Natalia tiptoe down the stairs. It was into the early hours of the morning and he had not yet gone to bed. She'd be coming around the corner any second to check whether he had fallen asleep in his chair once again. It had become an almost nightly ritual, whether here at home, or in whatever state, in whatever county, he ended the day. Running a successful campaign did not provide much opportunity for quality sleep.

At least here in their Georgetown home he had his comfy chair, worn down from years of use, soft in all the right spots.

She crept into the living room before stopping and straightening. "Oh! You're awake. I was sure I'd find you passed out down here," she said with a sly grin.

Jeremy grinned back. "I still keep you on your toes, don't I? Still full of surprises?"

"Ha! As if." She laughed. "I don't think you could surprise anyone to save your life. You're not the type. Good thing I married you for other reasons."

"And what would those reasons be?" Jeremy raised an eyebrow and winked.

She responded with an exaggerated up-down look. "I mean, you're not much to look at, so I guess it must be your mind?" She shrugged.

"Ouch. Good thing you aren't interested in giving a stump speech for me." He mimicked her voice, a combination of her California valley girl upbringing and her Russian roots. "My husband: he's not great, but I guess you could do worse, so you might as well vote for him."

"As if I'm not cornering the thirsty frat boys' vote for you."

That was certainly true, he thought. Having an international superstar as his wife, and an absolute knockout at that, did capture the attention of many who might otherwise not be predisposed to politics.

She was selling herself short, though. She was one of the few unifying forces left in the country. Just wholesome enough that parents could go along with their kids' obsession, and just provocative enough that those not interested in her music stayed for other reasons. And there were few who did not like her music. She'd burst onto the scene from complete obscurity with a debut album and hit song that eventually won her the coveted Grammy sweep: album, record, and song of the year, along with best new artist.

Critics liked to say she must have been created in a pop lab somewhere deep underground. She had the range of Ariana Grande, the girl-next-door vibe of Taylor Swift, and the sheer vocal power of Christina Aguilera.

Now, a decade on from her introduction to the world at age seventeen, she was still the undisputed queen of pop. Her fifth studio album had just been released, and she was in the process of planning an extensive world tour that was originally scheduled to start just before Christmas. With the campaign ramping up, they had discussed that maybe it would wait until after the general election. She liked to joke with Jeremy that being first lady wouldn't mean any more security than she already employed.

Jeremy smiled widely. "Well, we are building a broad and expansive coalition," he said, spreading his arms wide.

"So, what are you doing still awake?"

"I guess I didn't realize how late it was." He glanced over at his computer and stared for a second. "I got an email with some really exciting news a few hours ago and I've sort of been basking a bit, I guess." Jeremy looked back, straight into Natalia's eyes, his own aglow. "I know you don't pay too much attention to politics, but I assume you know who Bart Marsden is?"

She nodded noncommittally. He could tell that there was at least a fifty-fifty chance she did not know, so he pressed ahead.

"He's the current Chief Justice of the Supreme Court. He's been on the court for forty-seven years now and rumors have been swirling for what seems like a decade now about whether he would retire. I've tended to assume, instead, that he will outlive us all.

"I just got an email from him. We've been in contact before, but now he says that he isn't planning on retiring anytime soon, unless I win the general. He said he'll only step down if I'm the one picking his replacement."

By now his eyes were ablaze. "Can you imagine that, Nat? Me! I could be the one who chooses the next Chief Justice! Do you know how few presidents have had that opportunity?"

She chuckled and shook her head. "Babe, you must know the answer to that is no."

"Okay, fine, it was more rhetorical," he smiled at her. "But think: just like that, I could be an era-defining president before I even really get started."

"Don't you still have a primary to win?"

"You really know how to keep me grounded, don't you?"

"Just saying. I imagine an endorsement from the Chief Justice would go a long way to wrapping that up?"

"Yes, but here's the thing." He leaned in and lowered his voice. "He told me to delete the message as soon as I'd read it, and that it absolutely could not be public. He said if word got out that he had decided this, he would then claim it was fake and show 'proof' that I made it up."

"How cryptic. Why would he tell you that then?" She scrunched her face together. "What does he gain from telling you?"

"I have absolutely no idea. Probably because it's almost two in the morning, and I don't think my mind is at its sharpest now."

"Did you sneak out and go see a movie tonight? I know you have ways to get past your Secret Service guys."

Jeremy laughed. "I did, in full incognito mode—it was great. I still don't know why you won't join me in this tradition."

"Seeing a movie at a random Regal theater in Potomac Yard every Saturday night isn't my thing, babe, you know that."

"It's not just that now, though," Jeremy replied. "Now there's an extra thrill of being there unnoticed by the rest of the moviegoers. It adds a whole new level to the fun that wasn't part of it when I started this four years ago. Thank God they decided not to tear it down when the city was building that new metro station."

Natalia turned her back and started walking toward the stairs. "Well, this is all fascinating, but feel free to come and join me upstairs," she cooed as she pulled her pajama shirt up and over her head.

"On my way!" Jeremy scrambled up and started after her.

The jarring tone of his phone stopped him in his tracks. He looked down and saw Ben's face staring back up at him. He looked back up to see Natalia waiting patiently, making no attempt to hide that she was topless. If ever there was someone who would take pride in showing off their body, it was her.

Jeremy groaned. "I have to answer," he said more to himself than Natalia. "Ben wouldn't call in the middle of the night unless it was an emergency."

He picked up the phone. "Ben?"

Jeremy heard hyperventilating on the other end. After a second, Ben started speaking quickly and frantically.

"Ben! Slow down I can't tell what you're saying." Jeremy strained to try to discern any words, but was able to pick out just two:

"She's dead."

CHAPTER 25
BEN

Sunday Early Morning, October 26

Ben knew Jones Point well. During the year in which he lived down near Mount Vernon, he would ride his bike on the trail up the Potomac River and to Jones Point Park. Located on Hunting Creek marsh, it had been inhabited for over 9,000 years. Archaeological finds suggested hunter-gatherers had been in the area as early as the Paleo-Indian period.

By the time Europeans first came over to North America there were several American Indian settlements in the area. As with most of American history, that didn't last long. Settlers felled all the trees in what was once a wooded area, and by the late 1600s they had been replaced by rows and rows of tobacco. Enslaved peoples and tenant farmers worked the land. The area was likely named after Charles Jones, one such tenant farmer, but so little was known about him it was impossible to know for sure.

If it weren't for Jones Point, Alexandria might never have become what it did. An inspection station for the tobacco grown at Jones Point was built on what was now Oronoco Street and was the origin of the newly growing port town.

Ben wasn't sure why all this knowledge had come to the forefront of his mind. Probably because he was doing his best to block out all the other thoughts in his head. The thoughts that, if he allowed them to, would render him catatonic. He turned around as he heard the car approach.

"Talk to me. What's going on?" Jeremy asked as he stepped out of his car. They stood in the Jones Point Park lot, almost directly below the Woodrow Wilson Bridge on the south end of Old Town Alexandria. "Is it V?"

"Follow me," Ben replied, his voice giving away nothing. He turned away and walked quickly.

Jeremy accompanied Ben as he turned off the Mount Vernon Trail and onto the dirt path that led through the trees to the old Jones Point Lighthouse.

"Ben, you've got to talk to me. Where are we going?"

"I—I got a call. To come out here to find something. I don't know who it was, they didn't say much, they just told me to come here." They passed to the south side of the lighthouse, walking up onto its river-facing porch. Ben stopped and looked down. He pulled out his phone.

"They told me to stop looking for V." Ben's voice was barely above a whisper. "Then they said to come here, to the boundary stone." Ben pointed down at the stone set below the glass on the edge of the porch.

When Washington, DC, had been originally mapped out, they erected stones along the entire boundary as markers. DC was originally shaped as a diamond, with Jones Point as the southernmost tip. The boundary stone at Jones Point was the first one placed, in 1791, making it the district's oldest artifact. Washington, DC, returned its land west of the Potomac River to Virginia in 1847, partly due to abolitionists not wanting the District to be associated with the slave trade in Alexandria, but the stone remained.

"Ben ..." Jeremy started cautiously. "What do you see? What's there?"

Ben's breathing quickened. "I can't look again, you look … just shine your flashlight over the side of the porch." He turned away and threw up.

Jeremy peered over the porch railing. There was a man-made buildup of logs keeping the water from lapping up against the wall of the porch.

He couldn't see anything at first, even though the ground was only a few feet below him. But when he strained his eyes, he saw a shape that did not belong. He turned his phone's flashlight on and pointed it toward the shape.

The light found her feet first. As he turned his wrist, the rest of the grisly scene became clear.

It wasn't Veronica, though.

The woman whose body was dumped in the logs and branches was Miranda Belle.

———

Jeremy and Ben stood together thirty minutes later in the clearing near the lighthouse, watching the police converge. Jeremy had suggested going back and waiting at their cars for the police, but Ben did not want to leave Miranda alone.

Why her?

Ben racked his brain. What did she have to do with V's disappearance?

Miranda had moved nearby after the death of her family, and she had been his and V's go-to babysitter for months now, but how could the voice have known that? Was the house under surveillance?

A dark thought began to form in the back of his mind. Miranda had asked him about Veronica the other night. She wanted to talk to him about her. Could she have actually played some part in this? Was she killed not because of what she knew, but because of a falling out between kidnappers?

How could that be, though? The woman whose entire family

was killed, ending up as part of some conspiracy? She did seem a little clingy about Veronica, but surely that was just because of her tragic circumstances.

He wanted to voice this thought but knew Jeremy would tell him it was crazy. He didn't want to be judged, he wanted to believe there was some reason, other than proximity to him, that this innocent young woman, who had suffered so much already, had been killed. He also, as with Jeremy before, wanted to have someone to blame.

Ben realized the other reason he was trying to rationalize this senseless death. To keep the fear at bay. Mass shootings happened so often that he, like so many other Americans, knew how to process the emotions in the aftermath. This, though, was different. Someone killed a friend of his and sent a pointed message to him to come find her. The initial shock had worn off, and he was petrified. He looked down at his hands and for the first time noticed just how much they were shaking.

"You know that you and I are going to be their first suspects, right?" Jeremy shot Ben a concerned look. "And I hate to say it, but you more than me. You called me, and with my history they may not look at me twice for this. But you ..." he trailed off.

"I got a call though," Ben replied weakly. "Someone told me to come here."

"People can do all sorts of fake things now. They won't necessarily believe that wasn't your doing. More important is whether you have an alibi for the last several hours." Jeremy tilted his head slightly toward Ben, inviting him to respond.

"I mean, I've been home all night. But V's parents and the kids were all in bed by about ten, so no, I guess I don't really have one."

"I got you. I'll make sure you're covered," Jeremy said.

"Thanks, but you don't have to do that. I'm feeling guilty enough as it is."

"I know. Honestly, I don't think I've been a good enough

friend recently. I was really pissed when you all but accused me of having something to do with her disappearance, or at least having covered up some important detail. But I thought about it for a while and realized you'd only have thought that if I had given you any reason to. So, I just want to say I'm sorry for that."

Ben turned and looked out over the river. He could see Fort Washington across the way in Maryland and knew George Washington's Mount Vernon was just around the riverbend on the Virginia side. He always loved water. Nothing brought more inner serenity than standing on a beach, or riverbank, and looking out over the water, listening to the waves lap up against the land. He would stand still and appreciate the dichotomy between the stillness of the surface and the invisible activity just below.

His eyes filled with tears as he remembered meeting Miranda for the first time. She had been seated on a bench in Alexandria's Waterfront Park, her feet dangling over the water. The sun had just set on a beautiful, unseasonably warm February day, and he and Veronica were enjoying a stroll after a splendid meal at their favorite Italian restaurant, on the corner of King and Union streets. Veronica noticed her first and pointed Ben in her direction. He saw a young woman, sitting alone and sobbing into her hands, as people walked by without even breaking stride.

"We have to go talk to her," Veronica had said. Ben agreed, although he often wondered if he would not have had she not pulled her hands away from her face, showing herself to be devastatingly beautiful. He liked to consider himself an enlightened man, but it worried him that he was much more willing to help once he saw how she looked.

They slowly approached her.

"I'll speak first," Veronica whispered to Ben. Ben hung back slightly as Veronica crouched down next to the weeping woman.

"I'm sorry, I don't mean to intrude, but can I help you with anything?" she asked tenderly.

The woman looked up at her with puffy eyes. "My gosh, I'm sorry. I didn't mean to make a scene." She quickly began to wipe her eyes, a futile attempt to hide the evidence.

Veronica has such kind eyes, Ben remembered thinking. All anyone had to do was look at her once and they felt like they could completely trust her. Those eyes were laser-focused on this woman.

"It's okay. No one should ever apologize for showing emotion," she said with a gentle smile. "I'm Veronica, and this handsome man lurking behind me is my husband, Ben."

"Nice to meet you. My name's Miranda." She paused to grab a hairband and pull her hair into a ponytail. "I'm sorry again, I've just had a really hard time recently." She grimaced and looked down, as if voicing that had made the tears almost come back up.

"Oh, my goodness," Veronica's face fell. "I thought I recognized you."

"That was a pretty big picture of me in the paper wasn't it?" Miranda forced a small chuckle that lacked any semblance of warmth or happiness. "Right next to the quotation saying I wanted privacy."

Veronica turned to face Ben. She whispered, "Do you remember the story in the *Post* a bit ago? The baseball team owners who were killed in a car crash along with their daughter, leaving only the other daughter alive." She gave a furtive nod over her shoulder. "She's the other daughter."

She turned back toward Miranda. "Can we help with anything?" she repeated. "Actually, we were going to go get some ice cream. Would you want to join us?" Veronica gave Ben a little shrug.

"You know, I'd actually really like that," Miranda said. "I've been so lonely but haven't had the energy to do anything social at all."

As they walked up King Street, discussing which of the many ice cream options they should choose, Miranda gave Veronica a sad smile and squeezed her arm. "Thank you."

Ben was brought back to the present by the sound of more sirens closing in. Jeremy turned to him.

"Come on," he said. "Let's go back to the parking lot and meet the detectives. This must be them."

Ben looked once more back at the portico, shivered, took a deep breath, and walked forward into the trees.

CHAPTER 26
BEN

Sunday Early Morning, October 26

"Are you two the ones who found the body?" Detectives Emilia Brown and Martin Fahey introduced themselves and wasted no time.

"Yes," Jeremy answered.

"No," Ben gave Jeremy a stern look. "I did, and I called Jeremy to come out here."

Detective Fahey looked straight at Ben, taking in his disheveled appearance. "And you just happened to be wandering around out here in the middle of the fucking night?"

"We can discuss all the details later," Detective Brown jumped in. "Please, can you lead us to the body?"

They walked in silence. Ben led the way, following the same route he had done with Jeremy less than an hour before.

As they approached the lighthouse, Ben stopped. "Up ahead, just beyond the porch. I don't want to go any farther."

The two detectives looked at each other and Detective Fahey nodded. "You go ahead and check in with the first responders," he said to his partner. "I'll stay here with these two."

"He wants to make sure we don't leave while they're not

looking," Jeremy whispered to Ben. "He definitely does not trust us."

The lumbering detective glanced over. "Does the stage whisper work better when you're actually on a stage? Yes, of course I don't trust you. You just brought us out to see a body that no sane person could have possibly found accidentally."

"Look ..." Ben started.

"Fahey! You gotta come over here." Detective Brown waved her partner over. He acknowledged her before turning back to Ben and Jeremy.

"Stay put," he growled.

Despite Jeremy saying they should follow the detective, Ben did just that. He watched as more law enforcement officials descended upon the scene. The crime scene tape went up, not that it was needed to keep anyone out at four in the morning. Critical conversations happened in hushed tones, as if the dead would be offended if they used their regular voices.

Ben felt numb. Fear, sadness, and exhaustion all collided, leaving him unable to fully comprehend the night's events. All he knew was that someone wanted him to come here and find Miranda. *But what did it have to do with Veronica? Why did the voice make him think V was here?*

After almost an hour, Detective Brown eventually came back over to Ben and Jeremy. She gave them both a conciliatory smile. "I know this is hard, but I appreciate you both waiting here. Now, Mr. Wiles, I'm a bit of a political junkie ... don't you have a busy schedule coming up today?"

"I have a town hall tonight and a few other events, yes," Jeremy said.

She nodded along. "Okay, let me just ask you quickly, then. Tell me about tonight and your whereabouts."

Jeremy quickly recapped, skipping the details of what Ben's call pulled him away from. She thanked him and said he was free to go. With an understanding nod from Ben, Jeremy turned to leave.

"If they give you any trouble, just give me a call," he whispered as he walked past Ben.

Detective Brown looked Ben up and down. She took a deep breath. "Now, I take it you've got a bit more of a story, yes?"

"It starts with my wife," he said. "I don't know how or why, but somehow her disappearance is connected to this."

As soon as he started talking, it all came tumbling out. He told Detective Brown about the cryptic text, his wife's disappearance, his hunch it had something to do with the shooting in Rock Creek Park, and now the phone call he got telling him to come to the boundary stone. The detective stood and listened, jotting down notes, her expression unchanging.

"Okay," she said when he was finally finished. "Let's start with the obvious, then. It seems reasonable to assume that the call you received came from the killer. Someone who wanted you to find her body, but to make you think you were coming to find your wife. To what end would they do that? Why make you think that?"

"I was thinking about that a little while I was waiting," Ben replied. "I don't get it, though. It definitely made me come out here and look for myself first. That's all I can think of. I came out here and found her first, then called Jeremy and you guys."

"You think that the point was to get us out to find the body, but the caller didn't want to call directly?"

"No, now that you say it out loud, that sounds ridiculous. They threatened my family if I didn't stop looking for V, and then said to come out here. They used a specific word. Consequences, I think. That I should come out here to see one of the consequences of me looking for her."

"Where is your family now?"

"Back at home. I woke up my father-in-law and told him I had to go out, and then called him to say what I found." He thought as he spoke. "Wait. I guess I left that out. I called him, then Jeremy, then the police."

"Why didn't you call us immediately?"

"I really don't know. I wasn't thinking straight. I knew I had to tell my in-laws that it wasn't Veronica, and then I think I just needed a friend here."

Detective Brown nodded, her eyes showing a sympathy Ben was not expecting.

"Hold on," Ben started as he saw a figure walk by in the periphery. "That crime scene guy." He pointed to the investigator taking photos of the body. "Did he work at the shooting scene by Peirce Mill?"

Detective Brown turned around and followed his gaze. She saw Zeke surveying the scene, mentally going through the checklist in his mind. "Yes, he was at the Peirce Mill scene. Why?"

"Is it okay if I ask him a question?"

"Sure, but let me come and be there while you do."

They walked over to the edge of the crime scene tape.

"Zeke!" Detective Brown called. He looked up and gave her a big toothy smile. "Hey Detective, what's up?"

"This is Ben Walsh. He was the one who found the body. He says he's got a question for you." Zeke's smile disappeared and he gave Detective Brown an incredulous look, before facing Ben.

"Shoot."

Ben studied Zeke. He had not realized before just how young this man was. He must have been barely out of school. How did he end up the one crime scene tech for such a high-profile shooting?

"Okay, so this might be a weird question," he started, feeling out Zeke's receptivity. "You were working at the shooting scene. I saw you there."

"I'm sorry, when?" Zeke interrupted. "When were you there?"

Ben shot a nervous glance at Detective Brown.

"You're telling us that you've now been at two recent

murder scenes," she said. "Get to your point, because that doesn't sound great for you."

"I saw you on Thursday morning. I went out to Peirce Mill because I heard about the shooting and knew that my wife often ran on that trail. You were picking up something from the riverbed, I couldn't tell exactly what it was because I was too far away. Can you tell me, was it a water bottle?"

Zeke looked to Detective Brown for instruction. She responded with a single nod.

"It was."

"Was it a CamelBak handheld one?"

Zeke perked up at the new info. His eyes got wide and he again looked for Detective Brown's permission before responding. "That's exactly it. You know whose it is?"

Ben hesitated, sensing the heightened tension.

"I do," he said. "It's my wife's. She carries it with her while she runs. This means she really was there, doesn't it? She must have seen something." He paused, considering the consequences.

Detective Brown and an astonished Zeke stared at each other, both understanding the implications.

"What? What is it?" Ben asked, his head swiveling between the two of them.

"Look, Ben. We're going to need to ask you some more questions. Will you come back to the station with us?" Detective Brown's firm voice made it clear it was not really a request.

CHAPTER 27
JEREMY

Sunday Morning, October 26

Jeremy slept for just over an hour and was already back at it. Campaigning was going to be the death of him. He looked in the mirror and could not shake the feeling that he already looked a decade older. He looked at his hairline and was convinced it had receded in the last few months.

Agreeing to go on the *Today Show* seemed like a good idea at the time, but after the early morning he had, he was worried he would fall asleep in the middle of the interview.

If his video setup had been with his old comfy chair, he knew he actually would have struggled to stay awake, so he was glad to be seated in his study, in front of a bookshelf with strategically placed intellectual books.

"Joining us this morning, we'd like to welcome Democratic presidential candidate and current front-runner, Jeremy Wiles!" The host, Bethann Johnson, introduced him with a beaming smile. "Good morning, Mr. Wiles. It's good to have you with us."

Jeremy smiled, a practiced, politician's smile. "Thank you for having me. It's an honor to be asked to be a part of your show."

"You're the big story here, we're happy to have you."

Jeremy nodded his head in a quiet assent, with another polite smile. Bethann Johnson had only been the anchor of the morning show for a couple months now, but she had earned a reputation over her years of work in the media as a smart and tough, but fair, interviewer.

"So tell me," her co-anchor Dante Bromley asked. "What have you found to be the hardest part about campaigning?"

"Getting makeup applied for interviews like these." Self-deprecating humor always hit the target during a campaign. The two hosts laughed on cue.

"How does it feel being the front-runner, and potentially going up against your old boss in the general election?" Bethann asked.

"I have to disagree—I don't think anyone can claim to be ahead right now, before any votes have been cast."

"But surely your lead in the polls is a big deal right now?" Dante followed up.

"I agree that polling is important, yes, but I think it should only be used internally. People see these polls and then decide their favorite candidate can or cannot win, and that changes how they eventually vote. I'd rather polls were private, so that no voter feels that pressure. To that end, no, I don't want to put any stock in what the polls are saying."

"That's an interesting consideration," Bethann said. "Now, we know a campaign is very busy, so what's coming up next for you?"

Although it had been a rushed decision between himself and Natalia, Jeremy thought it was the best thing to do. He cleared his throat and prepared to shock DC.

"Apologies, but may I switch gears and talk about something personal?" Jeremy asked.

"Of course, go right ahead."

Jeremy gave his best intense stare into his camera and spoke. "Some of you who are watching this might have seen the news about the shooting in Rock Creek Park in Washington, DC, on Wednesday. My prayers go out to the victims, but I also want to mention something else that happened that same day."

The hosts shared a look, mirroring each other's arched eyebrows. He knew he should have asked them ahead of time and given them the opportunity to prepare for this, but he pressed ahead regardless.

"Most of you might not know who she is, but Veronica Walsh went missing in Washington right around the time of that shooting. She is a math professor at Georgetown and the wife of Ben Walsh, who is chief of staff to Congresswoman Chamique Moore and my best friend."

Bethann and Dante were silent, doing their best not to appear shocked.

"Someone knows something about where she is, so I'm asking all of you to be on the lookout. We'll put up a picture of her." He looked into the camera, hoping Bethann would understand the intent in his eyes.

She did.

"All right, we need to go to a break, but we'll be right back with more information on Veronica Walsh. This is the Today Show."

Before either of them could say anything, Jeremy spoke. "I know, I'm sorry I just sprang this on you, but things are happening really fast and I needed to do something. Natalia and I talked about it this morning and decided on this."

He could see and hear the commotion he had caused. Someone in the background was shouting about a graphics editor, and why did she have to be in the bathroom. Staffers ran in and out of the screens, dropping documents in front of the hosts.

Dante spoke in a hushed voice. "We can run with this, if that's what you want. Do you have more to say if we give you the floor when we come back?"

Jeremy nodded.

Bethann said, "I'll start and say a few words, and then we'll pivot back to you and just take it away. They'll give you a sign when it's time to go to our next break."

A producer called out, "Thirty seconds!" and a graphic popped up on the screens showing Veronica's Georgetown faculty picture and her name.

"Quick, what number should we put up for tips?" A showrunner poked his head on-screen so Jeremy could see him.

"Let's use my second phone," Jeremy responded and gave him the digits.

The countdown started and Jeremy watched as the staffers disappeared and the hosts turned toward the main camera.

Bethann took a deep breath.

"And we're back, still here with presidential candidate Jeremy Wiles. He had some breaking news for us, and we now have on-screen a picture of the missing Dr. Veronica Walsh, along with a number to call if you have any information. Now, we'll also post this information on all our social media channels, but Jeremy tells us there's even more to this story."

Jeremy took a deep breath. It probably looked a bit performative, he thought, but in essence that was what he was doing. He needed to make a show to get people to pay attention. That's what it was all about in this business.

"Late last night a young woman was killed in Alexandria, Virginia. The police are looking into it, so I can't give out details or anything like that, but there seems to be some connection. Ben Walsh was called by the likely killer." The last sentence slipped out before he could stop himself. He knew he'd be getting an angry call from the police for giving away that information.

"Wow, so we might be dealing with some sort of serial killer?" Dante asked.

"Could Ben Walsh tell the voice of the person who called him?" Bethann followed.

Jeremy shrugged, "I don't know, Dante, but I do know the

answer to Bethann's question. The caller used one of those voice modulators." He figured now that the info on the call was out he might as well lean in.

He continued, "I was with Ben at the crime scene only a few hours ago. I almost wasn't able to join you this morning, but I thought it would be important to use my platform. The most important thing right now is finding Veronica Walsh." He nodded to Bethann, queueing up her next line.

"We also want to show you this tweet that was just put out, from our friend Natalia Rochev, the queen of pop, and Jeremy's wife." The on-screen graphic switched to a tweet that read:

Please help us find @Veronica_Walsh_Math, missing in Washington, DC. We have set up a $25,000 reward for any information that leads to her being found safe. Thank you!! xoxo

"Jeremy and Natalia are graciously offering a reward to help people come forward if they have seen Veronica Walsh," Bethann said. She turned to Jeremy. "Now one final question, does this change how you are planning to campaign?"

Jeremy's expression was somber. "Obviously the primaries will go on, and I hope this is all resolved very quickly, but yes, this is going to necessitate an immediate change. I'm suspending my campaign operations until Veronica is found. I will use my platform to continue to spread this message until it is no longer needed."

Bethann Johnson turned back to the main camera one more time. "There you have it. Jeremy Wiles, current front-runner for the Democratic nomination, is suspending his campaign effective immediately, until missing Washington, DC, woman Veronica Walsh has been found. Jeremy, thank you very much for your time. We wish you, and Ben, all the best in your search for Veronica."

CHAPTER 28
BEN

Sunday Morning, October 26

"Take a seat right in here, and we'll be with you shortly," Detective Brown directed Ben as she gestured toward a room with a plaque outside that read *Interrogation Room B*. Ben wondered who must be in room A, since it seemed like the entire station was abuzz about Miranda's death. It was a few minutes before nine in the morning, and the detectives were just about ready to continue the conversation from the crime scene.

Ben wiped the sleep from his eyes. They had allowed him to rest at the station for a couple hours, but somehow, he felt even more tired now. He had not wanted to wake his in-laws, but he needed to tell someone, so he called Ricardo. Turned out, Ricardo had been sitting awake in the living room waiting for Ben to return. Ben told Ricardo a few more details about the phone call and finding Miranda's body. He hadn't wanted to say too much more to him before figuring out what the police wanted, so he assured Ricardo it was just customary follow-up procedure to be asked to stay and answer more questions. Ricardo strongly suggested that Ben call a lawyer, but he had brushed his father-in-law off, promising that he would call one if questions turned adversarial.

Detectives Brown and Fahey sat across from him. They were adamant this was not an interrogation, that this was simply the best place to ask questions, but it did not feel that way to Ben. He felt small and insignificant as they stood and looked down at him from the opposite side of the table.

"We need to ask you some questions about your wife." Detective Fahey spoke first. "And this is some messed-up shit, so you better be truthful with us." He glared at Ben.

"Where is your wife originally from?" Detective Brown asked.

Ben looked up with surprise. He stared at her, his brow furrowed. "What does that have to do with anything?" he asked.

"Look here, we're the ones asking the questions." Detective Fahey slammed his fist on the table and made the entire room shake. He turned to his partner. "You promised he'd cooperate."

Detective Brown looked at Ben and simply said, "Please answer the question."

"She's from Guadalajara, Mexico. She and her parents moved to the US when she was sixteen, I believe."

Detective Brown nodded as he spoke, although barely listening. Distracted by something in her own mind, Ben assumed. "And how much of her childhood do you know?"

Ben opened his mouth, then closed it. Hadn't he just a few days ago been upset when yet again Veronica had shut down conversation about her upbringing?

"She said she grew up poor and didn't like to talk about it," he finally managed to say. He regained a bit more confidence. "What does this have to do with anything?"

Detective Brown ignored his question. She shook her head, as if trying to wrap her mind around a tricky new piece of info. "Is she fully Mexican?"

"What do you mean?"

"We've seen pictures of her and her parents. I have to say, the facial features just don't seem to match up."

"So what?" Ben realized as he said it just how little he knew of so many important moments from his wife's childhood. He felt an immense sorrow come over him. His wife was missing, and now these questions made him wonder just how much there was he didn't know. His world felt like a Jenga tower toward the end of a game, wobbly and precarious, ready to fall apart whatever the next move.

"Please." Ben hoped his voice didn't sound as desperate as he knew it was. "What is this about?"

Detective Brown looked at her partner. They gave each other a small nod. She turned and opened the interrogation room door. Zeke walked in, carrying a water bottle in gloved hands. Ben raised his eyebrows.

"Good morning, Mr. Walsh," Zeke spoke with an off-putting formality. "Can you tell me for sure if this bottle does belong to your wife?"

Ben studied the bottle. "Can you show me the bottom of it?"

As Zeke shifted his hand so that Ben could see the bottom of the bottle, Ben looked at the two detectives. Each of them shared the same quizzical look.

"Veronica always likes to draw a pi symbol on her stuff. She jokes that someone else might have the same initials as her, but it's unlikely anyone else would put a mathematical symbol instead."

He squinted at the bottle and continued, "Normally she does it very small so that it's not conspicuous. It should be … yes! Right there near the center. You can see a pi symbol. That's definitely hers." Ben took in a long, deep breath. Fear and hope both bubbled up to the surface in equal amounts, overwhelming him. This proved that she was there, but what did it actually tell?

Detective Brown grabbed the bottle and turned it upside

down. He was right: there was a tiny, single-centimeter-tall symbol, written in blue sharpie. She exhaled a deep sigh.

"Ben." She looked him dead in the eyes, her own eyes imparting the seriousness of her ensuing question. "Does your wife have any connection to El Salvador?"

"No," he responded without hesitation. "Why are you asking me so many questions about her past? We now know she was at the creek that day, and now we can find her."

Ben's mood pivoted from gloom back to hope. He had a lead. Veronica must have been near the shooting, seen something, and ran. *She must have seen who did it*, he thought. But why not immediately go to the police? Could she not go to the police? Was she too scared? And where was she in the meantime? Questions swam around in his head, and each spawned several more.

"Let me explain the situation." Detective Fahey's voice broke the spell. "This water bottle was found at the crime scene. It contains DNA from a close relative of Yancey Portillo, one of the most dangerous drug lords in the world." He saw Ben's eyebrows arch. "I mean it, this guy will make your scariest nightmare seem like a children's story. And we have word that he's in the country."

Detective Brown seamlessly continued. "We're investigating what went down over by Peirce Mill and now, because of what you told us at the Miranda Belle scene, we've come to find that this bottle belongs to your wife. She is missing and you assume that she was near the crime scene. This bottle confirms it."

She stood up and leaned back against the one-sided mirror. "Now, you understand why we're asking questions about her past."

Ben sat in stunned silence. He unwittingly fiddled with his wedding ring until he looked down and realized what he was doing. He put his hands back in his lap.

Zeke spoke up. "The kicker here, Mr. Walsh, is that the DNA is clearly female. I confirmed that again before you arrived here. So, what are the odds that the female DNA on your wife's water bottle, that just so happens to be from a relative of a hall-of-fame-level bad guy, is not your wife's DNA?"

Ben felt his chest constrict. For a second, he thought he was having a heart attack. His face turned hot and red, and his breathing became shallow. Veronica, his endearingly nerdy and sweet wife, might somehow be related to some crime boss. How could this be possible? He knew her parents. This had to be a mistake. Cops always look for the simplest answer. There must be some other explanation. Something a bit more complicated. But who else could have used her water bottle? It was always with her or in her running bag.

Seeing Ben's red face, Detective Brown spoke. "Ben, we need to know as much as we can about Veronica. Are her parents nearby?"

"Yes, they've been staying with me since she went missing," he said in a voice barely above a whisper. His breathing was heavy and ragged.

Detective Brown nodded. "Okay, I'm going to need you to call them and bring them down here. We need to talk to them as soon as possible. I'll let you make the call."

"They're probably awake already, but someone needs to watch the kids." His heart sank as he realized the obvious choice was in a body bag, likely at the coroner's office only a few blocks away. He had not had time to process her death yet. Even though he wasn't very close to Miranda, he still felt an overwhelming sadness. She was just starting to begin her life again after all she had been through.

Detective Fahey shrugged and walked to the door. Detective Brown gave an understanding nod and said, "If the kids are awake, they can bring them here. We'll find a spot for them, don't worry."

"One more thing." Detective Fahey turned back. "Your wife isn't missing a finger, is she?"

Ben felt the blood drain out of his face. "How could you know that?"

The massive detective simply grimaced, nodded to himself slowly, and walked off without another word.

Ben numbly picked up his phone and dialed his mother-in-law to ask her to come and answer questions about the woman he'd thought he knew better than anyone.

CHAPTER 29
THE GIRL

I was fourteen when my life changed irreparably.

By then, I was the undisputed number two in my father's organization. Sure, I was not part of the official hierarchy, but those were titles only. They meant nothing when it came to who my father relied on to get the job done. Everyone knew it too, and no one complained, though there was some initial grumbling when Kelvin died and I first began taking his place.

That ended, one year before, when I showed up at the compound holding the severed finger of our greatest rival, Maynor Mejia.

He was the latest of the young bucks trying to muscle in on my father's business. He and his twin brother, Osmin, had created a bit of a name for themselves. We realized that we needed to cut them down, make a preemptive strike before they could amass more power and become a real threat. So, while my father and his "best" men debated and argued for hours as to how to get past Maynor's security, I went out and did the deed myself.

It took me under half an hour to infiltrate his outer ring of security and sneak up into his room where he was taking a bath. Soft rhythmic music was playing. His head was tilted back, his eyes closed as he enjoyed the serenity.

He never even opened his eyes.

I realized I needed some proof of what I'd done. My father would *hear about it, but others would likely claim it was their victory. So, I took my knife back out of my pocket and sliced off his pinky finger.*

I have to admit, I do have a flair for the dramatic.

I sashayed right into my father's office and dropped that finger on top of his roundtable, giving it just enough force that the finger bounced a couple times before coming to rest. Everyone stared at it and then one by one turned their gaze on me.

"What is this?" Orlando, my father's deputy, asked.

I shrugged.

He turned and glared at my father.

"What did you do?" my father asked me, his voice soft, yet utterly menacing.

I flashed a playful smile and spread my arms wide. "I solved your problem. You and your boys weren't getting anywhere, so I did it."

Orlando sputtered, "Wait, that's Maynor's finger?"

"Well, you couldn't expect me to fit the whole body on my bike." I winked at him and shrugged once again. That raised a chuckle from a few of the lower ranking men in the room.

"Where?" My father's booming voice silenced the room.

"I left him where I found him, in his bathtub. There's a lot more than just water in there now, though," I responded, as calmly as if I were just telling him I'd finished taking out the trash.

His expression never changed, but I saw the glint in my father's eye. "Gentlemen, I thank you for your time. Your proposals and ideas are appreciated, but it appears you've all been outdone by my daughter." He turned to Orlando. "Set up another meeting soon to deal with the fallout."

They knew not to question me anymore.

I was his ace in the hole. No one outside the organization knew. And who would guess it was a thirteen-year-old girl? For just about a year, I was his assassin. I stuck with the severed finger idea too. Something of a calling card.

Like I said, I'm a bit of a show-woman.

My notoriety grew. Well, not my own, but the notoriety of the mysterious assassin working for my father. I absolutely loved it. I had a singular purpose.

That is, I loved it until just a couple weeks after my fourteenth birthday.

After taking down a particularly vicious nobody, I was a little too casual in my getaway. I was seen swinging a pinky around as I sauntered up to the front entrance of our compound.

Again, a show-woman to a fault.

I learned later that word spread quickly through the underworld. It turned out all our competitors—and I use that word lightly—were so keen on figuring out who the mysterious assassin was that they had been sharing information for months.

It's good to have your work recognized.

One of them eventually got to me. I was out on my bike, headed on a not-at-all murderous outing to the grocery store. All of a sudden, my front wheel stopped, and I went flying over the handlebars. I was dragged into a white van by two men and had a burlap sack thrown over my head.

My first thought? Excitement. This should be fun.

I was not scared. Not in the slightest. I get it, that is what anyone would say after the fact, but it was the truth. I knew that my father would save me, or, failing that, I'd do it myself. My confidence even threw off my captors a little bit. I watched the skinny one continue to glance nervously at the fat one.

I was the assassin. I was an integral member of the greatest crime and drug organization the country had ever seen.

Or so I thought.

I heard the ransom call. I think they allowed me to hear it because they knew what was coming. These dumbasses told my father that if he did not relinquish his reign of San Salvador, then they would kill me slowly, with the only evidence left being my own severed pinky finger.

I knew my father was a ruthless businessman, and I knew that his reputation was built upon the fear factor he had cultivated for years. But I did not realize just how far he was willing to go to hold onto that status.

He laughed.

He laughed and laughed and laughed.

My own father listened to the kidnappers, thought for half a second, and then laughed at them. I heard his voice turn deadly serious. "Kill her. Or don't kill her. It doesn't matter to me, and it won't matter to you."

The two kidnappers, such nobodies I still don't know what cartel or otherwise they belonged to, looked at each other with confused expressions as he continued.

"You have messed with my organization, so what you are right now are living corpses. You are dead men who just happen to not be dead yet. Do what you must, but know this: your time is running out."

I sat there in shock. My father had just told my kidnappers that I was expendable. He cared more about his reputation than his own daughter.

"He's bluffing," Fat said. "She's too important."

"Agreed," Skinny responded. "We need to make it clear we're willing to do this." He picked up the garden shears from an admittedly impressive spread of torture equipment and walked over to me. I could smell his rancid breath as he leaned in close. "How about we give her a taste of her own medicine?"

"Whoa, wait, wait, wait." I started gasping. This was happening far too quickly. "I can help you."

Skinny showed all his yellow teeth as he flashed me an evil grin. "I don't need help from some dumb kid, no matter how many people you've killed." He looked over at Fat and jerked his head toward me.

Fat came over and grabbed my hand and splayed out my fingers. I struggled but was no match.

Skinny grabbed my pinky, swung the shears closer, and chopped down hard.

I passed out. I don't know what happened next.

When I woke up the room was empty. It was just light enough for me to see. No Skinny, no Fat, no torture tools. I was still handcuffed around the pole in the middle of the room. My hand was throbbing, but I couldn't bring myself to look at it. I could feel that there was something wrapped over where my finger had been. I retched. I would've thrown up but there was nothing left.

I have to get out of here, *I thought.*

And there's no rescue party coming.

Those two thoughts allowed me to push through the pain. The handcuffs were no problem. All of us had been taught early on how to get out of handcuffs. It was simple, in truth, if you were willing to handle a bit of discomfort. Dislocate a thumb, pop the hand out. Easy.

I grimaced and squeezed my eyes shut as I dislocated my left thumb and then squeezed my hand out of the cuffs. I realized that my father had never told us how to get the other cuff off, barring dislocating both thumbs. I assume the idea was then you could pick the lock? I wanted to have one fully functioning hand so I let the cuffs dangle from my right wrist.

Now, the door. I crept slowly over to it and felt around in the dark. It had a single lock on it. I was almost offended. Five minutes later and I was half a mile away, no problem. I never even saw Skinny and Fat. What a botched attempt that entire kidnapping was.

It was at that moment, ducked behind a shrub in case the kidnappers were close, that I made the most important decision of my life.

I didn't go home.

I ran in the other direction. I ran until I couldn't anymore.

I took a break.

Then I kept running.

CHAPTER 30
BEN

Sunday Morning, October 26

Ben got up and greeted his in-laws with a quick hug each, and they sat down together in the station's conference room. To make Gabriela and Ricardo more comfortable, the detectives had decided an interrogation room was not where they wanted to be having this discussion.

"What is this about, Ben?" Gabriela asked. "On the phone you said our Veronica hasn't been found, but that we needed to get down here as quickly as possible? And we're just supposed to leave Nico and Maria with those officers out there?"

"Yes, I'm sorry I couldn't tell you more. Honestly, I don't know more. But the detectives have some questions for you."

"Why do they want to talk to us?" Ricardo started to stand back up. "They can't think we had something to do with it?"

"No, no that's not it," Ben said. "It's just, they need more info on her childhood. Apparently, there might be some connection. I can't really wrap my head around it."

Ricardo lowered himself back into his seat. Gabriela and Ricardo looked at each other, fear and understanding written all over both of their faces.

"What? What is it?" Ben asked.

The door opened and Detective Brown walked in. "Good morning to you both, and I thank you for coming down here with such short notice." She sat down across from the three of them and opened up her considerable notebook. Gabriela looked up at Detective Brown's extravagant hair with a startled expression. The detective caught her gaze and smiled. "Yes, I get that a lot. I'm a little different from your typical cop."

She code-switched back to detective mode, leaned back in her chair, crossed her arms, and sighed.

"I need to know about your daughter's upbringing," she said. She filled them in on the events of the early morning and brought them up to speed on the DNA and water bottle.

"I have one question. I imagine it might lead to more, but this right now is my only question: why is your daughter's DNA a familial match to a notorious drug lord?"

Gabriela bowed her head. Ricardo stroked her back and gave Detective Brown a defeated look.

"This was never supposed to be our story to tell," he said with a shake of his head. "We hoped we would never have to." He turned to face Ben. "I'm sorry, Ben. You should have known all this a long time ago."

Ricardo turned back toward the detective. "We'll start at the beginning, I guess."

"Sorry, hold on. Just one second." Detective Brown said. "Detective Fahey is our Portillo expert. He's supposed to be in here too. Fahey, come on!" she called out the door.

Detective Fahey lumbered in and sat down with a thud. "Mea culpa. Needed some quick sustenance." He held up a hand to show unmistakable white donut powder on the tips of each finger.

"Okay, please continue," Detective Brown said.

"Do you know the story of Yancey Portillo's assassin?" Ricardo asked.

Detective Fahey smiled and nodded. "I knew it," he said as

he leaned back, hands clasped behind his head. "I fucking knew it. Holy shit."

Catching Ben's bewildered expression, Ricardo continued. "Yancey Portillo, an infamous drug lord, crime boss, or whatever term you prefer, is the scariest man in El Salvador. For a short while, though, there was one person who was scarier. After Yancey's son Kelvin was killed in a botched attempt to take out some rival, word spread of a new fear from the Yancey organization."

He took a breath to compose himself. "Yancey had a new anonymous henchman. No one outside his organization knew who it was, but everyone feared them. The rumor was that most on the inside didn't even know who it was. This *asesino* killed under Yancey's orders and always left the same calling card: a severed pinky from the victim's left hand."

Ben gasped and shuddered.

"No one ever found the actual missing fingers, but you could be sure if a body turned up with only nine fingers, it was the work of this mystery *asesino*. It took about a year, but someone finally figured out who the *asesino*—or *asesina*—was. Yancey's fourteen-year-old daughter, Alessandra, was seen carrying a severed finger back into his compound."

"She's legendary in those circles," Detective Fahey jumped in. "People still talk about her in hushed tones."

Ricardo nodded. "She was kidnapped by rivals a few weeks later. While she was held, she had her own left pinky cut off as retribution. Yancey wasn't interested in negotiating, so she had to escape on her own."

He looked at Ben, with a kindness in his eyes Ben had rarely seen. "This is where we come into the story. This extraordinary fourteen-year-old didn't go home after she escaped. She said there was nothing left for her if her own family wouldn't protect her. So she ran away. She stole a motorbike and crossed the border into Guatemala. She lay low for a couple of days before continuing on into Mexico. She made it all the way to

Guadalajara. And that is where we found her. On the streets of our home city. We took her in—she became ours. We went to the courthouse, told them she was an orphan with no documentation and that we were adopting her. That day Veronica Aguilar was born. We knew that she was likely safer in the United States, so we moved to this country soon after."

Ben put his head in his hands, his eyes bulging in shock.

"For the last however many years, the most mysterious and legendary assassin Latin America has ever seen has been right under my nose?" Detective Fahey could barely contain himself. "This is unbelievable. I thought she must be dead. Everyone thought she was dead!"

Ben could practically see smoke coming out of his ears.

"Alessandra Portillo has been missing and presumed dead for over twenty years." Detective Fahey continued. "The conventional wisdom was that those jokers who kidnapped her had killed her. Not that they fared any better. Their bodies were actually found, though, with stuff done to them I absolutely am not willing to say out loud."

Ben sat silent. He couldn't believe what he was hearing, couldn't make it make sense. None of it made sense. Gabriela reached out and took one of his hands in hers. "I'm sorry, Ben," she said in a quiet voice. "Our Veronica loves you very much and made us promise to never mention her past."

Ben tried to speak but his voice felt hollow, like someone else's words were coming out of his own mouth. "I want to say this can't be, there must be some giant mistake, that it doesn't make any sense, because it doesn't at all in my brain. But … somehow, I know it's true. Not wanting to talk about her past, the ways she'd steer conversations away from her childhood, even…" He stopped, his eyes wide. "Even that time I dropped our carving knife, and she caught it behind her back without even looking. She just kept saying she got lucky, but I always thought it was nuts that she even thought to try it." He paused again. "Wait, no, no, no. It can't be. She's so against violence! She won't even kill bugs!"

Detective Brown looked at Ben with a determined expression. "Ben, you do realize what this means? She was likely at the scene where five people were murdered. Your wife is our lead suspect now."

CHAPTER 31
BEN

Sunday Morning, October 26

"Umm, Ben. Look."

Ricardo's words brought Ben back from his stupor. He looked out the back seat window—he couldn't claim the passenger seat over his mother-in-law—and was never more appreciative of its tint.

"Shit." He gulped, looking at a line of reporters stretched down the block, their trucks and vans haphazardly blocking neighboring driveways.

"How could they know?" Gabriela said, her voice hoarse and barely detectable.

Ben sighed. "The same way they always know. Because every institution in this country leaks like a sieve!"

"What should I do?" Ricardo asked.

"They left my spot open—how kind of them—so just go ahead and pull in. You two go inside immediately. I'll handle it."

Ricardo slowly pulled up to the curb in front of the townhouse. There was no use hiding. Reporters had seen the car and were already scrambling over.

Ben took a deep breath and pushed his door open. A dozen

or so reporters crowded around him as he shielded his face with his forearm.

"What do you have to say about your wife? Did you know she was a monster? How could you marry someone like that?"

Ben recognized a few of the shouting reporters from Capitol Hill. *Of course this would turn into a political story as well.* He shoved past them as best he could. A well-timed shove sent a cameraman back a step, crushing the dahlias Veronica had recently planted. But it gave him a hole to burst through, and he finally moved past the horde.

"But don't you want to tell us your side?"

He heard the question as he reached the front stoop.

His side. What did that even mean? It was always *their* side. Ben and Veronica, the DC power couple, as they liked to call themselves behind closed doors.

He should say something, shouldn't he? He understood spin as well as anyone in this town. If you don't control the narrative, someone else will fill that void.

Ben turned around and cleared his throat.

He looked out at the reporters and the words all died in his throat. He couldn't do this. This couldn't be happening to him.

Let someone else control the narrative for now. It couldn't get any worse, could it?

CHAPTER 32
FRANCISCO

Sunday Midday, October 26

F rancisco sat alone in his study, contemplating his next move. Friday night had been thoroughly enjoyable, but he had work to do. Everything else was a distraction now.

Especially after Jeremy Wiles went around to all the Sunday morning shows, making impromptu appearances discussing the disappearance of Veronica Walsh. Now the entire country knew her face and would be looking out for her.

His phone lit up, and he glanced down and saw the name flashing back up at him.

Mierda.

He picked up the phone, his hand trembling slightly.

"Update me." The voice on the other end was full of conviction.

Francisco took a deep breath. "Things have not gone to plan so far, sir."

"This is not news." Yancey Portillo had a deep and commanding voice. As far as anyone knew, he sounded like this from the day he was born. "For decades, I thought my daughter was dead. We held a ceremony for her. You were there, just a child. Then, when we found out she's been alive this whole time, it became your job to find her. She is now missing, and Americans are dead. American police are involved. Tell me why I shouldn't come get rid of you right now."

Francisco summoned up all the courage he had. "Because I'm the best you have, and you'd be hurting yourself if you got rid of me."

Yancey chuckled. "I have always enjoyed that you're not scared to speak your mind to me," he conceded. "But you're not the best I ever had. The Alessandra I knew would take you apart, piece by piece. Is that what happened? You underestimated her?"

Francisco sighed. "What do you suggest now? I hear you're also in the United States."

"I am. I was here on standby, but now consider that I am here to clean up any messes. And I see a large mess right in front of me. It is clear that my daughter has retained her formidable skill set. Therefore, we must change tack. Do you have anything to go on right now?"

There was a quiet pause. "No," Francisco admitted after a few uncomfortable beats.

"Okay. Then what you need to do is follow the husband. He is searching desperately and there's a chance she might eventually reach out to him."

"I was planning tha—" Francisco began to respond but Yancey cut him off.

"But following won't be good enough to get ahead of this. Your best move is to befriend him. Convince him you can help and then you'll be there ready to act when the time comes."

"What will you do?"

No answer. Francisco looked at his phone. Yancey was gone. He would have liked to know his boss' plans. Now he would have to keep one eye over his shoulder at all times, just in case.

He didn't even get the chance to tell Yancey that befriending Ben was already his own plan.

He turned on the television and perked up. The police were holding a press conference. A mammoth of a man was standing behind a podium. Francisco turned the sound up and listened.

"We have a suspect in Wednesday's shooting by Peirce Mill. We are asking for assistance from the public in the apprehension of Veronica Walsh, also known as Alessandra Portillo. If you see her, do not approach, but call the police immediately. She is considered armed and dangerous. We are circulating her picture with all present news agencies and on our social media channels."

Well, guess that's not a secret anymore, Francisco thought. Interesting that the police believed she was the shooter. He tucked that tidbit of info away, just in case he could use it later.

The giant detective continued on. "Veronica Walsh is a mathematics professor at the University of Georgetown, but we have recently learned she is also Alessandra Portillo, the long-missing daughter of Salvadoran drug kingpin Yancey Portillo. She disappeared over twenty years ago from San Salvador, but before her disappearance, despite her youth, she was Mr. Portillo's assassin of choice. We have learned she fled to Mexico, changed her name, and made her way to the United States where she settled down.

"We do not have any motive yet, so we are treating her as a continued public threat. We will provide any updates as and when we are able to do so, but for the time being, please be careful. And again, if you see her, alert authorities immediately. Do not engage. Thank you."

Francisco watched on as the detective answered a string of questions from the media members present. Now her husband must know. Convincing him to trust Francisco just got easier. He had been wondering how to go about doing so if the husband were not aware of his wife's past. Now he had a plan.

He thought back to the memorial service they had thrown for Alessandra. He could still place himself in the moment. Standing there next to his father, Miguel, trying to hide the tears streaming down his face. She had been three years older than him, and he looked up to her like a sister.

The life of a child in the inner workings of organized crime was not easy. Life lessons were harsh and were doled out swiftly, often at ages far younger than appropriate. The few of them whose fathers, and sometimes mothers, worked together grew up alongside each other. The hierarchy meant that Alex, as they all knew her, and her brother were on a pedestal above the other children, but that had not stopped them as kids from all playing together when they could.

Alex had been the one who taught him important life skills, like how to tie his own shoes and how to palm a knife without cutting himself. He could still remember exactly where he was when he heard Alex had been kidnapped. He and a few of his friends were playing soccer in the street outside Yancey's compound when their entire world turned upside down. The gates opened and car after car streamed past, as if escorting a head of state.

Francisco had been standing and watching, wondering what was going on, when the last car stopped in front of him. His father opened the door, and he scrambled in.

"What is happening?" he asked, noticing the frightened look on his father's face.

"Someone took Alex."

Francisco could feel his pulse pounding inside his head. This wasn't possible. She was the best of all of them, not only the fiercest and scariest, but the most loyal, most kind as well. Why would someone take her? He, of course, had no idea that she was the one collecting victims' fingers on her father's behalf.

That had come as a shock when he asked his father. How could it be her? Hadn't they all just been talking together the day before, trying to determine who the assassin must be? He had become convinced it was his own father and many of the other kids agreed. Even Alex had agreed it was most likely his father!

There had been worry, and everyone sprang into action, but there had not been a full panic. They assumed that she'd come back unharmed soon, either through Yancey's doing or her own. It was only when Yancey, Miguel, and a couple others stormed the building in which she had been held captive and did not find her that they really began to panic. When Yancey brought everyone together and told them that the kidnappers were dead, but there was still no sign of Alex, a full inquest began.

Two days later, Miguel sat down at the foot of his bed and looked at Francisco with heavy eyes.

"Son, we think Alex is gone for good. We have to prepare for life without her now." Francisco's eyes brimmed with tears as he listened. "We have to be strong now, like she was."

As Francisco grew up, there were various rumors of sightings over the years. No body was ever found, so there was an unspoken feeling that maybe she was still out there somewhere.

The rumors gradually changed and grew more sinister in nature. Maybe it was true she was still out there, but now as an opposing force? No other theories of what happened to her held up as well as the theory that she ran away and turned against her own. Just like that, she was again the crime world's bogeyman, the tale to tell kids at night to make sure they behaved. Only this time, the stories were told inside her father's organization.

Don't forget to put your dishes away, or else Alessandra will come scoop you up in the middle of the night.

Then, just a few months ago, Yancey came to Francisco, now a firmly established lieutenant, and entrusted him with whispers he kept hearing in the United States. A woman with a mysterious background was working at an American university. And what's more, the whispers mentioned she was missing her left pinky finger. Yancey did not want to bring the cavalry, especially in a foreign country, so asked Francisco to go and find out if this truly was Alessandra Portillo. Francisco had under-stood it was not actually a question.

Now here he was, on what felt like his thousandth day in the United States, and nowhere closer to his goal.

Well, he did find out she was Alessandra Portillo, that's for sure. Now the entire world knew too.

He puffed out his cheeks and sighed. *No time to waste*, he thought, as he got up and headed out the door to go befriend a man who had just had his world collapse around him.

CHAPTER 33
BEN

Sunday Afternoon, October 26

Ben sat in the living room in stunned silence. Ricardo and Gabriela sat on the loveseat opposite him. Nico and Maria, thankfully, had enjoyed their personal tour of the police station and were now upstairs recreating what they saw.

"I feel like a dump truck has just backed into me," he finally said. "I thought I knew V better than anyone." He shook his head, gripping his mug of coffee as if it were the only thing between him and a full breakdown.

"She didn't want you to know. She didn't want to focus on the past," Gabriela responded in that comforting tone only a grandmother can achieve. "She worked so hard to put her previous life behind her that it was buried deep well before you came into the picture. Let me assure you, though, it was incredibly difficult for her to keep it from you."

"Thanks for saying that," Ben said. "But so much of understanding and truly knowing a person is seeing what fundamentally made them who they are. Now it turns out I don't know anything about that."

Gabriela turned and faced her husband. "Ricardo, what do you think is the strongest bond that keeps marriages together?"

"Shared experience," he answered, without hesitation.

"Exactly." She looked back at Ben. "No one ever knows all the details about their spouse before they met. What is most important is what you've done together. The children you've raised, the trips you've made, the memories you've created. That's what's important. Who you were when you met and how you grew, not who she might have been years before. Remember, you didn't meet her until long after she was done with all that."

Ben's face made it clear he wasn't convinced. "If you had told me yesterday that V shot those people, I wouldn't have believed you in a million years. But now ..." He gave an exaggerated shrug of his shoulders. "Her name isn't even what I thought it was!"

"Her name was her choice. It is the part of her that is most her. You don't get to choose your parents, you don't get to choose where and how you grow up, and you normally don't get to choose your name, but she *chose* this name," Gabriela said. "It's more hers than your name is yours."

"I guess I just have a lot of different emotions converging right now. I'm still frantic with worry about her, but now I feel betrayed and angry, but also ashamed that she never felt she could talk to me about her past. And how could she do all these things you say she did as a child? Kill people and... enjoy it?" Ben collapsed onto the couch.

"Do you want to know how she ended up in our family?" Ricardo asked.

Ricardo's question jarred Ben. Logically he knew there must be a story to it, but he still hadn't wrapped his mind around it all. He wasn't sure if he was ready, but if not now, when?

"It isn't our place to talk about her life before us, but we can tell you about how we ended up with such a wonderful daughter," Ricardo continued.

Ben felt tears coming into his eyes, and nodded as he wiped them away. "I've wanted to know stories like this ever since I met her. I would love it if you told me."

Gabriela settled into her seat. "It was twenty-three years ago, and Ricardo and I were both at the university in Guadalajara. You know these details I'm sure, since we both were teaching the same material we teach here in America. We were in the Center for Social Sciences & Humanities and lived in the Santa Teresita neighborhood, a 'foodie paradise' as it's sometimes called, about a thirty-minute walk away. We used to make that walk every morning and evening."

"We loved a little seafood restaurant on Calle Jesus Garcia, which we passed every day. We ate there at least once a week." She turned to Ricardo. "I can still remember exactly what we would always order," she said with a smile. "Piña Rellena de Mariscos. Pineapple stuffed with seafood." She gazed off, for a second lost in the memory.

"Anyway, one evening we decided to stop in and saw this young girl, a teenager, sitting against the wall right outside. Now, you know your father-in-law has a heart of gold, so he stopped and whispered to me that we should help her. We asked her if she needed food and she looked up with the fiercest eyes we'd ever seen. We didn't understand why then, but she was incredibly wary. She shook her head, so we went in and ate.

"While we ate, we kept thinking about her, seated right outside, so we ordered an extra piña rellena and brought it out to her after we were done. She stared at us, her expression bordering on paranoia, for what felt like forever before snatching the food and running off into Parque Alcalde nearby.

"We thought that was the end of it, but we saw her again two days later, this time near the aquarium on the north side of the park. We realized she must be homeless and living somewhere inside the park. The next weekend we went to the park and found her again, this time lying under a bench. It's hard to describe it—I'm sure you understand though—but she had this magnetism that stuck with us. We were desperate to help her. We convinced her to eat lunch with us—at that same seafood place of course—and tried to learn a bit more about her. She barely spoke for the longest time. She wouldn't even tell us her name. It wasn't until the end of the meal that we finally saw a little spark of emotion.

"We asked her if she had anywhere to go, or anyone we could contact on her behalf. She cleared her throat and averted her eyes, but we saw one tear escape and trickle down her cheek. She looked up at us and said the first complete sentence we had heard yet." Gabriela dabbed her eyes. "This precious young girl told us that her family had deserted her.

"We'd always wanted kids but it never worked out, so we asked her if she wanted to stay with us for a few days. Just trying to give her something to hold on to, something to stop her from hitting rock bottom. She agreed and we all walked home together. We said we needed to know what to call her, and she said she didn't want to be called her old name anymore. She said she wanted to be called Veronica." Gabriela sighed. "We later learned she had a fascination for old movies and loved Veronica Lake."

She chuckled. "That she saw herself in a femme fatale character might have been the first clue for us about her background. We let her have a key and told her she could come and go as she pleased. That was probably naive of us, but we felt so fulfilled helping her out, and she seemed to be coming out of her shell more and more each day. It was only two days later that we asked her to stay. We realized that we needed her almost as much as she needed us.

"All we knew about her in the beginning was that she was an abandoned child. We had no way of tracing her, nor would we have even known where to start. Ricardo and I worried about how to legally adopt her, and whether someone would come forward. We fretted about that for a while. Two months passed with no changes, and we decided to try to legalize our adoption. She was our child in all but name at that point. First we had to register as an official ward of the state, and she was placed in foster care. That broke our hearts, watching her be driven away. But we pressed forward with our adoption attempt, paid lots of money for a good lawyer, and eventually we succeeded. She was legally our daughter, Veronica Aguilar, with her own identification and passport. After that we figured out all the other details and entered her into school. We told our friends the truth—we had adopted a young homeless refugee. Whoever she had been before she came into our lives wasn't important anymore, and she was ours so that's all that mattered."

Ricardo nodded along. "Then, about a year later, we moved up here to the United States, and she got into college, went to grad school, got hired by Georgetown, met you, and now you know the rest," he said.

Ben sat there, glued to the couch. "I can't believe this. This is like something out of a movie. How could it be her life?" He shook his head and looked at his in-laws. "But you say that you've known about her past. How long have you known?"

Gabriela looked at Ricardo, prompting him to speak.

"It was probably about a month after she I and joined Gabriela here. She got her green card first, and then sponsored us and we followed at the end of that lengthy process. We were all together again, in our little apartment down in Williamsburg. We were about to go to bed, and we could see that she was working up the nerve to tell us something. She stopped us and asked us to sit down. She said she needed to tell us the truth. We knew, of course, that something must have happened that led to us finding her but had no idea the extent of it."

Ricardo looked across at Ben, his face a warning. "She's our daughter, Ben, and your wife, but there are still stories that are hers and hers alone. So, I'm only going to say the bare bones of what she told us. When we find her—and we will find her—then you can give her the opportunity to tell you more."

Ben nodded, understanding.

"She told us her real name was Alessandra Portillo, and that she was the runaway daughter of Yancey Portillo. She said that she used to do tasks for him and hinted at them involving violence. She held up her left hand and said that her pinky had been cut off by kidnappers after her father had decided not to negotiate or pay a ransom for her. She said that was what made her realize she was nothing but a pawn for him. She ran after that, and I still don't know how she made it all the way to Guadalajara."

"She told me her pinky had to be amputated because of a gardening accident as a kid," Ben said. "She said she was messing around in your garden and found the garden shears."

"Oh, Ben." Gabriela reached out her hand and grasped his. "We didn't even have a garden, but I think she was trying to tell you as much of the truth as she could. It was from garden shears, but not ours, and not an accident."

An uneasy silence descended. Ben had a million more questions but wasn't sure how to ask them. "I just want to see her," he finally sighed. He turned on the television and the three of them caught the tail end of the police press conference. He still couldn't fully wrap his mind around what he was seeing. His own wife's face, plastered across the television, with a warning not to approach if anyone saw her.

"Do you think she really could have done this?" Ben asked the question with no idea of his own answer anymore.

"No," Ricardo replied. "This isn't just me as a father saying that, either. I've watched her for over half of her life now, and I just don't see that as part of her anymore. I'm worried that Yancey has found her. That's what I think happened. He, or some henchman, attempted to take her, and somehow it went wrong and people died."

"Can I ask one more question?" Ben asked.

Ricardo nodded.

"Is her background why you two have always seemed so wary of me?"

"Oh, Ben," Gabriela said again. "That's exactly it."

"We've been so nervous that someone would find out," Ricardo added.

"I don't mean to make this about me, but you weren't wary because you didn't think I was the right person for her or anything like that, then?"

Ricardo stood up and walked across the living room. He beckoned for Ben to stand up. Ben got up and stood in front of Ricardo, wondering what was about to happen. Ricardo looked Ben up and down, gave a small nod, and pulled him in tight. Gabriela walked over and joined the hug.

Once they had extracted themselves, Ricardo said, "Ben, you are exactly the man we hoped our Veronica would find one day."

"You are perfect for her, and we are forever grateful that she found you," Gabriela said. "It's not your fault that the two of us have never been able to relax fully around you. We wouldn't have been able to relax around anyone. Decades of fearing our daughter's secret would come out has left us unable to trust anyone but ourselves."

"I felt like each time I saw you two was another audition," Ben said with a brief chuckle.

"Oh, it was. Don't you worry about that." Ricardo raised an eyebrow. "But only because of us, and our fear that her perfect life would come crashing down." He breathed a deep sigh. "The secret's out now, though, and it's up to us to stick together."

"Family is the most important thing. It always has been. And you're the son we never had but always wanted," Gabriela said.

———

Hours later, as Ben was in the kitchen making soup and sandwiches for dinner, his phone buzzed. He looked down and saw his mother's face looking up at him. *Oh Lord.*

"Hi, Mom."

"I told you. You didn't listen, but I told you that woman was trouble!"

CHAPTER 34
ZEKE

Sunday Evening, October 26

"This is the spot."

Zeke looked over to where Charles Wills was standing. He saw in the telltale flattening of the grass that Wills was right. The dark splotches erased any doubt.

They'd found where Miranda Belle was killed.

"Well, one part of this mystery has been solved," Brown said, standing next to Zeke, with Fahey on the other side. "It's up to you guys to confirm it, but I'm guessing that she was left here until someone moved her early this morning."

Zeke looked around at a yard he never imagined he'd set foot in. He knew of Robert E. Lee's boyhood home but had no interest in it. He'd never afford it, but even if he could, he would never live in the home of a former slaveholder. He had to admit, though, it was a spectacular house and gardens.

Now there would be another reason not to buy it. Who would want a house in which the previous owner was murdered?

"Two bullet holes in the side of the house, here and here." Brown pointed. "So the shots came from over by the wall. I bet our shooter scaled it before firing. Let me know when ballistics confirms that."

"What do you think happened?" he asked. "How is this connected to Rock Creek?"

Brown shook her head. "I don't know yet. If we're to assume that Ben Walsh is telling the truth about that phone call, it's got to be something, though."

"Can you believe going through everything that he's had this last week?" Zeke could not imagine what must be going through Walsh's mind. He knew they were only doing their jobs, but he had felt terrible watching Walsh's face fall as he learned the truth of his wife's past. He was thankful that his job didn't mean he had to be in the room telling Walsh. It was hard enough just watching through the one-way glass.

"I feel for him," Brown said.

Fahey snorted. "The two of you, such weenies you are."

"Weenies for having feelings like actual human beings?" Brown countered. "How dare we?"

"You really think the husband didn't know? That he had no idea at all? I don't buy that."

"Fahey, I know you've got this gruff façade you have to maintain, but you're taking it a bit too far. No one, not even you, could think that guy knew his wife was a former assassin. That'd be the most incredible acting job I've ever seen." Brown turned and rolled her eyes to Zeke.

"I still don't really understand, though," Zeke said. "Do we think that Veronica actually is behind all of this? Why would she kill those students, after all these years? It sounds like she'd carved out a decent life here."

"I don't, and I think I can speak for both of us in saying that," Brown said, nodding toward Fahey. "What's your thought, Fahey?"

"She did it. She did it all."

"Fahey, come on."

"All right, fine. I think there's a lot about her life here that we don't know and we're going to need to figure it out ASAP, and I think it's important we continue to warn the public about how dangerous she is."

"But…" Brown prodded.

"But," Fahey sighed. "I think it's far too coincidental that Yancey Portillo was spotted in the country. I think that he's the one pulling the strings here."

"But what did Miranda Belle have to do with it?" Zeke asked.

"Not a clue," Fahey said. "She was shot here on Friday night, a couple of days after the shooting by Peirce Mill. Miranda Belle was the babysitter for the Walsh children, so there's an obvious connection between them."

"It's a tricky one," Brown said. "Because if I had to guess right now, I'd say that Miranda got caught up in something she saw while at the Walsh household. But that doesn't necessarily jive with our other hypotheses."

"No, I think you've got a good idea there," Fahey agreed. "It also tells us exactly what our move should be, which is something we should have done by now anyway."

"Oh, yeah?"

"We need to search the Walsh house. And we need to do it as soon as we're done here."

CHAPTER 35
BEN

Sunday Evening, October 26

Ben hung up immediately. There was no reasoning with her, so what would the point be? His mother and father had not been an important part of his life for a long time now.

He and his younger brother Jared had lived through their nasty, eighteen-month-long divorce settlement. His father, the president of a Fortune 500 company, had affairs with interns, secretaries, and almost any woman over whom he exerted any power. When Ben's mother found out and filed for divorce, he tried to keep all the money. Ben and Jared were both in college at the time, Jared in his first semester. While Ben was preparing to graduate, already ready to move on with his life as an adult, Jared was still closely connected, and struggled mightily in school. Ben did his best to try to help him, but Jared dropped out after his freshman year. Ben never forgave his father.

Ben and his mother stayed on good terms, though, until Veronica entered his life. It was no easy thing to realize that his mother was racist. A few choice terms were thrown out when Veronica visited for the first time. What Ben originally tried to explain away as his mother's conservatism quickly became toxic.

Ben's announcement of his engagement to Veronica was met with a comment about how sad it was that Ben would not have "good little white babies." And that was that, as far as Ben was concerned.

The phone rang again. Ben looked down in anger, ready to explode, but realized it was not his mother calling him back.

"Hello," he said, trying to moderate his considerable heartbeat.

"Mr. Walsh, this is Detective Brown." Ben's heart sped right back up. "I'm sorry we have to do this to you. We have a warrant to search your house. We're setting up outside. Please come to the front door."

Ben sprang into action. He bounded into the living room, where Nico and Maria were sitting with Ricardo and Gabriela, all enjoying post-dinner mugs of hot chocolate. "Dad! Where's your hot chocolate?" Nico asked.

"Hey there, little man." Ben put on his best fake smile. "Can you and Maria go play in your room while I talk to Abuelo and Abuela?"

As they scurried off, Ben gave his in-laws a worried look. "What is it?" asked Ricardo.

"The police are here. They have a warrant to search the house." He slammed his hand on the arm of the couch, allowing his frustration to get the better of him. "I should've known they'd do this!"

"On a Sunday night?"

"I know, this is ridiculous."

"How about we take the kids out?"

"That'd be perfect, thanks a ton."

Ben watched as Nico and Maria came right back downstairs when called, and left the house with their grandparents, excited about the treat of a late-night donut from the local shop in north Old Town.

They were holding up remarkably well without their mother. But he would have to explain all of this to them eventually. He dreaded that conversation and just hoped that Veronica would be back before he had to have it.

Detectives Brown and Fahey, along with several police officers, descended upon his house. Detective Fahey said a stern hello and held up the warrant. As Ben stood by the door, he pushed his way inside and a dozen more followed.

It's not like they're going to find her hiding under the mattress, he thought. What's the point of having so many? And this level of aggression?

"Mr. Walsh, I appreciate you being gracious about this," Detective Brown said as Detective Fahey grumbled next to her. "I understand how hard this has been, and I just want you to hear from us that right now we do not suspect you were involved or had anything to do with this." The look that Detective Fahey shot at him made it clear that he was not on board with that assessment.

"Can your guys at least be careful with everything? I've seen this on TV where afterward it looked like the place was ransacked. The Alexandria cops that came by when I filed the missing persons report for Veronica this week were gentle."

"We'll be as careful as we can, but we need to be thorough. 'Gentle' is not an option for a homicide suspect." Detective Brown's attempt at reassurance fell flat as she moved past Ben into the foyer.

"And if you know something, it'd be a lot better for all of us if you told us now," Detective Fahey quipped.

"What could I possibly know that I haven't already told you?" Ben asked, his anger rising.

"Maybe how you and your wife planned this out. That'd be nice to hear." Detective Fahey shrugged.

"Knock it off!" Detective Brown turned back to face the two of them. "He knows you couldn't have been involved. He's just not a particularly kind person, is he?" She turned and pointedly stared at her partner.

"Whatever," Detective Fahey muttered as he moved into the kitchen.

"He just likes to play the gruff detective," Detective Brown said as she and Ben followed her partner into the kitchen. "Don't let him get under your skin. All he wants is the truth."

The two detectives leaned against the counter and watched as officers buzzed around. Ben stood next to the refrigerator and glared.

"Be careful with those pictures," Ben raised his voice, causing the officers in the living room to pause and glance back at him. "They're from our honeymoon!"

The officers turned back and continued their search as if they had not heard him.

"Wait, that's my computer, I need that!" Ben shot a desperate glance at Detective Brown as an officer carried his laptop toward the front door.

"We'll get it back to you as soon as possible. You have to let them do their job. It's only courtesy on my part that I didn't make you go outside while we do this."

Ben fell silent.

"Excuse me, sir." Ben looked around to see one of the officers holding a small Tory Burch purse. The two detectives watched expectantly. "Is this the purse that your wife had the day she went missing?"

Ben stared at the purse, studying it. "I recognize it, sure, but I don't think I can say for sure that it was that one, I'm sorry." He paused for a split second. "Wait, why do you ask?"

The officer turned and directed her answer to the nearby detectives. "We found this purse hidden, deep in the back of her closet."

"That doesn't mean anything." Ben jumped in.

"Inside it are several of her essentials, including her wallet and ID," the officer said.

Detective Brown's eyebrows raised. "I assume she had those with her, Ben?"

"Yes, of course," he said. "Wait, so what does this mean? She came back here?" His voice got higher as he became more incredulous. Neither detective answered. They looked at each other in unspoken agreement.

The search continued, as Ben flitted from room to room imploring the officers to be careful. Eventually, he gave up, and stood next to Detective Brown near the front door.

"Ok, let's wrap this up as soon as we can!" Detective Brown called out through the house to the remaining officers. She turned to Ben. "I thank you for your indulgence. We'll be in touch."

After the final officer had left, Ben stood in the kitchen waiting for his kids and in-laws to come back home. They arrived fifteen minutes later. Ben filled them in on the items that the police had taken.

"This is good news, Ben," Gabriela said. "This means that she came back home and hid her belongings. She must be on the run."

"I'm torn." Ben realized it was true as he said it. "You're right though, the most important thing is that this makes it more likely she's alive. But …"

"Her running makes her seem guilty," Ricardo finished Ben's thought.

"I don't understand why she wouldn't contact us, though," Ben said.

"But you do, Ben. If she's guilty, she wouldn't want us to be a part of it. If she's innocent then she's running scared and doesn't want us to be a part of it. Either way it doesn't involve us, and that's okay because we trust her, right?"

Ben looked out the window at the cloudless night sky. "Yeah, you're right. What now, though? What does it all mean?"

CHAPTER 36
BEN

Sunday Night, October 26

"Hey, Ben." Jeremy spoke into his phone. "How're you doing?"

"I don't even know anymore. I assume you saw the press conference?" Ben could hear the resignation in his own voice but made no attempt to hide it.

"Yeah, dude, that's just unbelievable. You really had no clue?"

"Not at all. Turns out I'm married to a former assassin who is now the lead suspect in a mass shooting. And on top of that, it looks like she must be the suspect in Miranda's death also." He couldn't believe he had almost forgotten about the events of last night and the early hours of this morning.

"Oh jeez, I didn't even think about that," Jeremy said. "But look, I need to talk to you about something."

"Yeah?"

"Look, did you see that I went on TV this morning and made a big plea to try to find V?"

"I did."

"I need to retract it. Well, at least the part about how she's an innocent victim. I absolutely believe that she did not kill any of those people. Seriously. But now with this story out there I'm going to take a huge hit if I don't get ahead of this."

Ben's heart fell. "What are you going to do?"

"I'm doing the rounds on the late shows in a few hours tonight saying basically what I just told you. I do mean it though. I'm one hundred percent sure she did not do this. It's just … my advisors are worried that my campaign will tank. My main competitors are already planning attacks on me for being friends with a murderer."

"No way."

"Come on, Ben, you know politics. I'm leading in every poll. They all know they need to take shots until something sticks."

"I can't even think about the politics of it right now, especially the idea that someone would use this as an attack."

"I know, and that's why the Congresswoman has covered for your absence. Hey, listen though, Nat and I talked, and we want to keep the reward out there. We can spin it for my benefit —the money is now there to try to help find a killer, something like that—but what's most important is finding her and I think an active reward will still help."

"I appreciate that."

"And Ben, please let me know as soon as you hear anything. I know I need to do all this stuff for politics, but whatever you need you tell me. I'll move heaven and earth to get her back."

"Thanks, Jeremy. You're a good friend." Ben hung up.

He knew, intellectually, why Jeremy had to do it, but he'd be lying if he said it didn't hurt.

Ben felt alone, more than he had since Veronica's disappearance. How could it only have been four and a half days? It had already felt like a lifetime.

He turned on the TV. He wasn't sure why he felt he needed to, but hearing people talk about his wife made him at least feel like there was still a connection. The last thing he was expecting was the name he heard come out of the broadcaster's mouth.

"We'll be right back with a recap of the bizarre turn in the

DC shooting case, and we'll hear from Kimberly McLanahan, the mother-in-law of the missing woman at the heart of it."

Ben snapped his head up. *You've got to be kidding*, he thought. He figured he had to stay on the channel now just to see what she said. Ever the opportunist, his mother.

The commercials ended, and the camera zoomed in dramatically on the seated anchor.

"Welcome back, thanks for sticking with us," he said in that practiced, cheerful voice all anchors learn.

"We have a dramatic update to the ongoing story of the mass shooting at Peirce Mill. We saw this morning that presidential candidate Jeremy Wiles gave a heartfelt plea for help in finding missing Georgetown University math professor Veronica Walsh, a close friend of his. His wife, international pop sensation Natalia Rochev, announced at the same time that they were prepared to give a reward for any information leading to her safe return. Now we take you to the press conference held by DC police only a few hours later."

The screen cut to Detective Fahey describing their findings. Ben realized he hadn't given any real thought to the fact that the name he knew his wife as was not her given name. Sure he'd talked to his in-laws about it, but he hadn't fully comprehended what it meant. He couldn't imagine her as an Alessandra. That, more than all the rest of this firehose of information dumped on him, felt the most galling. He knew there were parts of her childhood that he was unaware of, but he couldn't wrap his mind around the idea that she was an entirely different person for fourteen years.

The anchor returned. "To recap, Veronica Walsh, a well-liked mathematics professor, is actually Alessandra Portillo, the long-lost daughter of the legendary Salvadoran drug kingpin Yancey Portillo. She went missing after being kidnapped in San Salvador at age fourteen and had not been seen since. There were rumors that she was his mysterious assassin whose calling card was to cut off the victim's left pinky finger. Our sources confirm that Veronica was missing her own left pinky finger, thought to be retribution from the gang that kidnapped her."

"The police are confident that she was involved in the shooting, as well as the one last night at Jones Point Park that killed twenty-six-year-old Alexandria resident Miranda Belle. She is considered extremely dangerous, so if you do see her, do not approach but call the police immediately."

"Now, we have on the screen Kimberly McLanahan, the mother-in-law of Veronica, née Alessandra. Her son is Ben Walsh, the chief of staff to Massachusetts Congresswoman Chamique Moore. Ben Walsh has been married to Veronica for eight years and the couple has twin five-year-olds, Nicolas and Maria. Kimberly, thanks for joining us."

"Thank you for having me."

Ben couldn't believe it. There his mother was, seated in the study of his childhood house, facing a TV camera, dressed in an oversized sweater that just screamed 'kindly grandmother.'

"Let's start. You met Veronica for the first time when she and Ben were already established in Washington, is that right?"

"Yes, Ben moved to DC after he finished his master's degree at Harvard. Veronica actually lived in Boston at the same time, while she was getting some degree. I think they met at a party. That's where he would meet someone like her, in any case. They came and spent Thanksgiving with me, just a few months after they started dating."

Some degree, Ben fumed. Just a bachelors, masters, and Ph.D. from MIT.

"What were your impressions of her?"

"Honestly, the word that keeps coming to my mind is conniving. It always seemed like there was an angle to her, some way of using every situation to her benefit."

"That is quite a statement. Is it safe to assume your son did not share this viewpoint?"

"He did not. He was blinded by an exotic pretty face, I'm sad to say."

She had the gall to put her hand to her chest and sigh.

"But even you could not have seen this coming?" The anchor was impassive, just asking the questions and letting his mother's answers speak for themselves.

"No, but I can't say I'm surprised. I could tell she was a master manipulator. She had him wrapped around her finger and nothing I could say could convince him otherwise."

"Did you and Ben talk about your feelings?"

"Oh, yes. I voiced my opinion and, in return, he and Veronica, or Alessandra, or whatever her real name is, didn't invite me to my own son's wedding."

"When was the last time you saw your son and daughter-in-law?"

"It's been years. My son doesn't talk to me and hasn't let me meet my grandchildren because of my feelings about his wife, and I have to say I'm glad I've been vindicated."

"Do you hope that you'll be able to reconcile with Ben now?"

"I do. I hope that he now sees the error in his ways, and admits he was wrong. I'd love to host him and the kids for a holiday here in Boston, but it's entirely up to him."

Ben had enough and turned the TV off and threw the remote as hard as he could into the couch cushion. What was she thinking, going on a nightly news show like that? *That clip will be everywhere within an hour.* Then the country would all agree she was guilty, and he must be a sucker. What good would it do if he came out and refuted it? He watched live as the seed was planted; uprooting it would be very difficult now.

No way was he going to watch Jeremy tonight. No matter how well-meaning he said he would be.

CHAPTER 37
VERONICA

Sunday Night, October 26

Hiding away, expecting danger to follow every noise, a constant tension buzzing through my head. Heightened vigilance to the point of paranoia.

I had not felt these feelings in a long time. Funny how quickly it all came back, though. As if all these skills and feelings had been dormant just below the surface, ready to spring into action the instant they were needed.

Boy, were those skills ever needed these past few days. I thought about the growing list of feats since only Wednesday.

What hadn't I done?

It had been a stroke of genius to jump into the raging stream and let it carry me away from that murderous psychopath. Had I even consciously made the decision to do so? I couldn't remember thinking about it, I just did it.

When I was younger, I knew that my mind went on autopilot during tense, life or death, situations. My father always said that was why I was so good. My heart rate slowed at times when anyone else's would rise.

I looked around what I'd come to consider my spacious jail cell. As far as hideouts go, it was a five-star resort. When on the way from El

Salvador to Mexico I had hidden out in abandoned buildings that were just barely more luxurious than cardboard boxes. Not only did this place have basic amenities, it even had cable TV. Fourteen-year-old me would have been thrilled. There was about a week's worth of food in the pantry, which I knew I could stretch to two or three weeks if I needed to. Even the electricity was on, which I had been slightly concerned about.

What could I say? I had gotten used to a few more comforts the last two decades. I was a much different woman compared to the last time I was on the run. As a fourteen-year-old, I enjoyed the challenge and thrill of it. As an adult with a family and a life I missed immensely, that thrill was no more.

I wondered what Ben must be thinking. He was so pure-hearted. He'd be terrified that something happened to me and that he needed to find me to make it right. In truth, it wasn't out of the realms that he would find me, but I was certainly not expecting him to waltz in the door any minute.

It was better that way, though. The most important thing was to put the danger as far from him and Nico and Maria as possible.

Oh, how I ached to see them all again.

I'd never written down any of the stories from my childhood. I'd spent the past two plus decades trying my best to never think about them again. But sitting here in this hideaway, I had realized that it was time. If something happened to me, it was better that Ben knew why than to be left in the dark. I wasn't sure where to start. How do you even begin to encapsulate all I went through—all I did? I went back as far as I could remember. Funny that I couldn't remember anything before my father shot Angel. Therapists would have a field day with me.

I turned on the news each day, hoping to see that it was safe for me to come home again. But when I turned on the TV today, I saw something I never believed I would. I had gotten used to seeing my face on the news, but not like this, not with that name below it.

Alessandra Portillo.

A name and an identity I had worked hard to rid myself of. Turns out I hadn't needed to write those stories down anyway.

How did it get out? I was certain that secret would remain mine forever.

I realized as soon as I asked myself the question. My water bottle. Of course. They must have gotten my DNA, and, of course, my father was known. Still, impressive they put two and two together and actually made four.

Well, four and a half, give or take. I should have known they would immediately jump to the easiest conclusion.

That I was the killer. Here's someone who we believe has killed before. It must have been her!

The theory that I, a former assassin best known for my cunning and guile, even at such a tender age, would gun down five people so sloppily, was insulting. Honestly, that was the most outrageous part of it. That those kids weren't just poor, innocent, onlookers who accidentally came across a scuffle they should not have seen and paid for it with their lives.

I assumed the police would try to determine who would want to harm those kids. Maybe they'd find some feud and go down a rabbit hole, searching for clues and motives that did not exist. One kid had cheated on her boyfriend with another guy, who had a history of violence. Something like that.

Yet here we were. My name—my given name—on the national news. A national search for me. Details of my life broadcast to the country, things that I never even thought my husband would find out.

They must have talked to my parents. My adoptive parents. I hoped they would not get into any trouble. They brought a daughter into the United States with all the necessary forms and passports, but they must have known that I didn't come about those legally.

Their astonished faces when I showed up with the perfect Mexican passport. I think that was the first time they realized who they were dealing with. I didn't even use violence or a threat. Well, I might have implied a few things might happen to just a couple local government workers. But that was it. And the final time I thought about that life.

Not that I didn't have opportunities. I came close once in college. Some dumbass, entitled, frat boy smacked my ass at a party. If only he knew what I imagined doing next. The elbow to his ribs made my point, but I could've made it so his body was never found. The little prick actually asked his parents to press charges. He and I truly came from two disparate worlds.

Anyway, it wasn't my fault his ribs were so weak and two of them broke.

It's funny how the wild side doesn't ever go away, it just shrinks and becomes easier to hide. The rational, responsible side wins out over the years. By the time I met Ben, I considered myself Mexican, not Salvadoran. Up until this week I hadn't thought about my past life in years.

I sat and watched talking heads discuss my mental state. As if any of them could ever know or understand me. I would have to be more careful when I ventured outside now.

There was a way out though. My husband wasn't a trained assassin like me, but he was an incredibly capable man, even if he did not always know it.

He must have a million questions. I'd given a lot of thought over the years about what his response to my secret past would be. I never thought this was the way he'd find out. With me nowhere near him. No way to explain any of it. Not even a chance to simply say I'm sorry for the pain he must be going through and the betrayal he must feel.

A dark thought creeped into my mind. He would have every right to take the kids and leave if he wanted to. What defense would I have if he made that decision? Running to keep my family safe might have been the first step in losing them.

No. No point letting those thoughts in right now.

There was one way he could find me.

I hoped he was as clever as I believed him to be.

I hoped he still believed in me.

CHAPTER 38
BEN

Monday Morning, October 27

Ben sat on the back stoop, watching Nico and Maria draw on the stairs with large pieces of chalk. He tried to let himself relax and just appreciate the quiet morning with his kids. Veronica—he was not prepared to think of her as anything but that name—would have wanted him to continue to do so.

It was an odd feeling. His entire world had been turned upside down, and yet, he felt hopeful. There was a reason to believe that Veronica was still alive, hiding somewhere out there. That the reason was that she was potentially a mass murderer wasn't great, but he decided it was time to focus on optimism. Pessimism wouldn't get him any closer to finding her and would make the journey miserable.

So. Optimism it was. Veronica must have seen something, ran away, and was now hiding out, safe and sound, ready to come home as soon as she could.

A tall and slender man approached and stopped just outside the gate. Ben looked up at him expectantly. The Hispanic man staring back at him looked familiar.

"Are you Ben Walsh?"

"You must know if you've come around through this alley to my back gate to ask me." Ben surprised himself with how short he sounded. Maybe the attempted relaxing wasn't having the desired effect just yet.

"You're right, I do. I saw the story on the news and wanted to speak to you. I figured I was in the right place when I saw the reporters in front of your house." If Ben's abrupt tone had affected him, he showed no sign of it.

Ben waited.

"My name is Ademir. I wanted to find you because I am a refugee from El Salvador."

"Hold on," Ben said before he could continue, putting his hand up.

He turned to Nico and Maria. "How about you two go inside and see if Abuela will make you a snack?" They scurried up the stairs and into the house.

Ben looked back up at Ademir. "Go on."

"I ran away from El Salvador because of Yancey Portillo. I guess your wife did the same."

"You know Yancey Portillo?"

"Yes, better than I ever wished." Ademir sighed deeply. "He took everything from me."

Ben's curiosity won out over his caution.

"What did he do to you? I really don't know anything about him."

"I was a simple trader, trying to live a normal life in San Salvador. My parents, my brother and sisters, and I all worked together. Everything was fine until Yancey went to my oldest brother. I will not tell you the details, but he said that he wanted to start using our store as a front. We were doing good business and he wanted the money."

"I'm guessing your brother wasn't keen on that?"

"No, the opposite. He thought it was good business. Everyone in the family agreed but not me. So, we started working for Yancey Portillo. Our shop in front, his men in back, laundering money. One day, I got in an argument with his men. They acted friendly, but the next day, they set off firecrackers on my porch, almost burned my house down. They left a note that said they would burn me and my whole family alive if I ever was disrespectful again."

"Holy shit." Ben couldn't contain himself.

"What's worse is that I confronted the rest of my family about it. And not one of them stood by me. They blamed me for it. They said that I wanted to ruin the business. I was forced out of my country and my life by my own family, and I know that it was because of fear of what Yancey would do if they didn't get rid of me."

"Wow." Ben shook his head, marveling.

"I know, I couldn't believe it. So here I am, trying to make a new start, and now the news is talking about Yancey Portillo. I can't get away."

"I don't know what to make of all of this. I just want to find her. I just want to know she's safe."

"I understand. That's why I came. I remembered a conversation I heard between two of Yancey's men. They mentioned your wife."

Ben snapped to attention. "What did they say?"

"I only heard a little, but it sounded like they heard that there was a lead. Knowledge about where she was now. Yancey had never stopped looking for her."

"So you're saying that Yancey is the one behind all this?"

"I would not bet against it. And because of that I would like to help find her for you."

"Why would you want to do that?"

"To be honest, to feel closer to home. To feel like I'm doing something against the man who forced me to leave." He paused, and gave a rueful shake of his head. "Maybe because I still have hope left that my family will one day let me go home."

"What do you want to do?"

"I know about what he is like—I met him once. Maybe I can try to help figure out what happened? I just want to do some good."

"Tell you what, give me your number and I'll let you know. I really appreciate the info. Thanks for this."

"Not a problem. I think she's still alive. She's out there somewhere and you're going to find her."

With that, Ademir handed Ben a small piece of paper with a phone number on it, gave a short nod, and continued down the street.

CHAPTER 39
FRANCISCO

Monday Morning, October 27

L ess than an hour later, Ben was with Francisco again, this time in his own living room. As soon as he had gone back inside and told Gabriela and Ricardo about his new friend, they insisted he come back and talk to them.

Francisco had responded to Ben's text within seconds. He was at the door twenty minutes later, and so here they were, sitting together in Ben's living room like old pals.

"This is Ademir. He's a refugee from El Salvador and knows a lot about Yancey Portillo," Ben said to his in-laws.

Francisco once again thought about how easy it was for him to lie. *What a skill to have.* Some people learn the violin, or how to tango. Instead, his great skill, even more than making fellow humans disappear, was lying. Ademir was one of his favorite aliases. Much more interesting than Reynaldo. He saved Ademir for only the most important situations.

"Do you know why they are still looking for our daughter?" Ricardo asked. "Why search for her after all these years?" This was the reason they had asked Ben to call Francisco back. After he had told them about "Ademir," Gabriela wondered aloud what the endgame was. From Veronica's account, it wasn't like he had tried to get her back when she had been originally kidnapped, so why now? What would be the point of it? Did he want her back at his side, as the protégé he'd apparently always expected her to be, or did he want her dead?

The five murdered joggers pointed to the latter.

"That is a good question. I am sorry because I do not have an answer to that. I felt that something recent caused a... heightened tension," Francisco answered, thinking hard.

"I have another question," Gabriela said. "Can you tell me what you know about Yancey? I want to know more about what my daughter had to deal with as a child."

"I can do that—"

His response was cut off by a loud knock at the back door. Everyone jumped. Ben got up and headed for the door, heart pounding. He opened it, slowly. A man in a black oversized hoodie with the hood still up stood there.

"Hi, Ben."

"Jeremy? What are you doing here?"

"I just wanted to stop by and see how you all are doing. Is this a bad time?"

"No, it's just ... yeah, come on in." Ben opened the door and ushered Jeremy inside.

"Who is this?" Jeremy asked Ben under his breath as they entered the living room.

"Long story," Ben whispered back.

Ricardo and Gabriela glared at Ben. He gave them a small shrug, as if to ask what he was supposed to do.

Francisco watched on, looking at this other guest.

"No way." Francisco spoke before either of them had the chance to. "You're Jeremy Wiles. You're going to be the next president here."

Jeremy gave a deprecating chuckle. "I sure hope so! Who are you?"

Francisco, with the help of Ben, caught Jeremy up, leaving out the minor details that his name was not actually Ademir, and that most of what he had told Ben was completely made up on the spot. *I missed my calling. I could've been great at improv.*

"I was going to tell them about Yancey, or at least what I know of him," Francisco said to Jeremy.

Jeremy nodded. "If you don't mind me intruding, I'd like to hear too."

"You distanced yourself from our daughter last night on TV." Gabriela spoke up. "So I do mind."

"Gabriela, it's okay." Ben jumped in. "Jeremy called me before and told me about it. He had to, or else his opponents would take advantage. The important thing is that we know Jeremy wants to find Veronica, and the reward is still out there to try to help."

"I still don't like it."

"Gabriela, please," Ben said.

She huffed, but then gave a small nod.

Francisco began. "Okay, everyone who meets Yancey knows he is a gentleman. Only his closest friends see the other side of him. I heard two men at our store saying this. He lives with his entire organization in a..." he exaggerated struggling for the word. "A compound. No one can enter. People say he has lions and tigers inside. They even say there is a moat with crocodiles from Jamaica."

"Is that where my daughter grew up?" Gabriela interjected.

"I believe so. As far as I know, that's where Yancey has lived for many years."

"But you don't have any idea where Veronica might be?" Jeremy asked.

"No, I don't," Francisco conceded. "But I thought maybe my knowledge of Yancey could help you figure out where she is. I just want to help. I do have one story that I heard. Maybe you would find it illuminating?"

"Please, go ahead," Ricardo said.

"Did you know that she had an older brother, Kelvin?"

"Yes, but she said he died years ago."

"That is true. I was told that she was there. It was a family thing. The three, Yancey, Kelvin, and Alessandra, went out one night to attack a rival. But it was a trap. A sniper shot Kelvin. The story says that Alessandra hid in the car, and Yancey went out on his own. No one saw it, so I don't know if this is true, but what people said was that Yancey walked straight into the house where fourteen men were hiding. He was filled with rage and so, with only a machete, he killed them all. They all had guns, but they fired no shots. The police had never seen anything like it. Two detectives quit because it was the worst crime scene ever."

Francisco looked around the room at the faces staring back at him.

"That's the monster who my daughter escaped from." Gabriela squeezed her eyes shut.

"Why tell us that story?" Ricardo asked.

"I thought it would help explain. I'm sorry if it upset you." Francisco's face fell. "I just heard that maybe she ran away because of that. That it made her realize she wanted to leave. I thought you would want to know."

Again, just like with Miranda, make a misstep, correct it, and get welcomed in closer than you would have before.

"Right. So, we're all on the same page here, that we need to find Veronica," Jeremy jumped in. "Ademir, what are you doing now that you're in America?"

"Right now, I am working in a Salvadoran restaurant in Arlington. But I would like to apply to a business school and get an MBA."

"That's impressive," Gabriela remarked.

"I have always had big dreams, just like your daughter," Francisco responded.

"What do you mean?" Ben asked.

"I am sorry, I just assumed, because of what I have heard about her."

Ben gave Francisco a guarded look, but the answer placated him.

They continued to chat, and by the end of the afternoon Ben had introduced Nico and Maria to Francisco, and they had quickly bonded. Nico was thrilled to find that Francisco had never seen Thomas the Tank Engine, and dragged him around, describing every toy he had.

"I probably should head out," Jeremy eventually said. "My wife, and probably a few reporters, will be wondering where I am." He turned to Francisco. "It was a pleasure meeting you, and I sincerely hope you can help find Veronica."

Francisco nodded in agreement as he also got up to leave. "I will keep her in my thoughts," he said to the remaining room.

Jeremy and Francisco departed together out the back door. Jeremy pulled his hood back up to avoid the press stationed around the front and nodded to the two-man security staff who had been waiting in the back alley. They turned and headed to bring Jeremy's car around. After Jeremy and Francisco went down the steps, Francisco turned to walk away, but Jeremy grabbed his arm and pulled him back.

"I know who you really are," he hissed. "You work for Yancey."

"Why would you say that?"

"I don't buy this coincidence. My buddy in there may be too clouded by emotion to see it, but I can. You know too much. You're looking for her on his behalf, aren't you?"

"No, of course not. I just want to be helpful." Francisco pulled away. "I'm going home now. Goodbye."

"I'll be watching you."

CHAPTER 40
BEN

Tuesday Morning, October 28

"Daddy."

The first voice didn't penetrate Ben's dream.

"Daddy!"

The second voice had a bit more urgency. Ben groaned and rolled over. He opened one eyelid to see both his twins standing at the foot of his king bed, their heads barely poking over the footboard.

He ushered them over to his pillow. *They're still so small*, he thought. And far too young to have to deal with this. An unwelcome question popped into his head. What was V like at this age? Had she already learned how to kill people with her bare hands?

He had read as much as he could last night about Yancey and his organization, looking for every mention of an assassin or a daughter. By the time he finally fell asleep, he wasn't sure if he was married to a victim, a monster, or maybe both.

"What is it, Maria?"

"Where is mommy?"

Ben could feel his heart breaking.

"I know, honey. You two miss her, don't you?"

Nico looked down at his bare feet as he nodded alongside Maria. Ben took a deep breath and steeled himself.

"The truth is ... the truth is ..." he stammered out. He stopped and breathed a deep sigh.

Where is the manual for how to talk to kids about their mother's disappearance and subsequent surfacing of her secret past identity as an assassin?

"We don't know where your mother is right now, and your abuelos and I are worried she's in trouble."

"What kind of trouble, Dad?" Nico's eyes brimmed with tears.

"We don't know yet, Nico," Ben answered, thankful that was at least still true. "But we're all working our hardest to find her and make sure she's safe. She loves you very much and she'd want you both to remember that and be strong."

A single tear ran down Maria's cheek. Ben grabbed both his kids and held them close. "It's okay to be sad. You know what I do when I'm feeling sad?"

Neither child spoke. Maria let out a quiet sob.

"I come and see you two. I can't be sad when I'm around you guys. And that's what we all can do, okay? Whenever we're sad and worried about Mom, we all come together to help each other out, all right?" Ben nodded, encouraging as Nico forced a sad smile through his own puffy cheeks.

"And one more thing. Most important of all is that you two have each other. You're never alone because your twin is always there with you. Don't forget that." Ben gave them each a kiss on the top of the head. "Now, who wants to go downstairs and have some pancakes?"

While the kids sat and ate with their grandparents, Ben snuck back upstairs to the bedroom to get dressed.

He sat on the side of bed, halfway dressed, at a loss. It was almost a week since V disappeared, and in that time his marriage—and indeed his entire world—had been turned upside down. Yet each day previous, he'd woken up with an idea. Something to do, something to chase, some lead to find. An action, if only to keep himself from spiraling.

Yesterday he thought that Ademir might be the key, the one to give them the right clue, or maybe just background info, to lead them to her. Now he wasn't so sure. Not that Ademir was unwilling, but he only knew a bit about Yancey Portillo. It wasn't like he had been running with Yancey his whole life and had tons of stories to share.

What was the next step?

He opened the doors of Veronica's closet, and absentmindedly flipped through her clothes. She owned several dozen tops, although he wasn't in any position to judge considering the immense bulk in his half of the closet.

Ben wasn't sure what it was, but something made him search for a specific top he always liked. There wasn't anything inherently special about it—a yellow, striped tank top—but he always loved how it looked on her.

He flipped through the entire closet but could not find it. He wondered if it might be in the laundry, but he knew she had not worn it in months.

His thoughts running wild, Ben rushed over to Veronica's dresser, opening each drawer and closing it just as quickly. The clothes were all strewn around inside the drawers, evidence that the officers had picked through them. But there were clues Ben might see that they wouldn't have known to look for. When he came to her drawer of running clothes and athleisure he paused. There were several shirts and a few pairs of leggings missing.

Ben's mind continued to race, but his heart leapt.

Here it was. Clear evidence that not only did she stop at home at some point after she left campus, but that she took clothes with her.

She ran on purpose. That was now crystal clear to him.

The comprehension of this fact stopped Ben in his tracks.

Was this entire thing premeditated? Or did she get home and grab what she could as she left as quickly as possible?

A small white object that looked like a flower petal poked out just slightly from under one of her many Nike runner's tops. Ben reached in and pulled it out.

A white rose.

Ben's eyes almost leapt out of their sockets. He studied it. The petals were still fresh.

"Ricardo! Gabriela! I've found something!" Ben called as he grabbed the rose and sprinted out of the bedroom.

CHAPTER 41
BEN

Tuesday Morning, October 28

Ben and his in-laws stood over the kitchen table, looking down at the white rose Ben had placed on the table. Ricardo and Gabriela looked at Ben with dumbfounded expressions. Ben's face, in contrast, was ablaze, full of excitement and hope.

"You found a … rose?" Gabriela asked, raising an eyebrow.

"And it's supposed to mean something to us?" Ricardo added.

Several of the petals had fallen off while Ben ran downstairs. The stem was jagged, as if it had been torn from a bush.

"Yes. Absolutely yes," Ben was so excited he could barely get the words out. "All right, just bear with me. There's this band that V and I both got into, through a shared music station. They're called Blackmore's Night, formed by Ritchie Blackmore, who was in Deep Purple—you might have heard of that band— they were an English rock band from the sixties and seventies, and are still active today, but not with Blackmore anymore. So anyway, he and his wife Candice Night, they …" He trailed off, looking at his wife's parents, utter confusion written all over their faces.

"Okay, you don't need all this." He held his hands up and started again. "There's this song called 'Ghost of a Rose' that has a line in it where the singer says to think of her when you see a white rose."

He nodded as he saw understanding creep into their eyes.

He and Veronica loved the band, which he could best describe as folk rock. Their music sounded like what one would find at a renaissance festival, which is where they heard it first, in Annapolis. They both had been enamored with the song since hearing it playing over the speakers as they wandered through the festival.

"V and I would joke whenever this song came on that we'd leave white roses for each other if anything ever happened. Obviously, I never thought we actually would have to use it, but just look at it." He picked up the rose.

"This flower was ripped from some rosebush intentionally and left here, in a spot where only I would find it. No one else knows this. This is an inside joke between Veronica and me."

"I was worried that her license being here might have meant that someone else took it and broke in and left it as some attempt to frame her," Ricardo said. "But this looks for sure like it was her, and she's left you a message."

"What does it mean, though?" Gabriela asked.

"She put it there on purpose. I think that means she's okay." Ben couldn't tell for sure, but he was reasonably certain he was getting ahead of himself. Nevertheless, he felt a tremendous uplift in his spirit. Here it was, proof that his wife had deliberately placed a sign here for him.

Not only was she still alive, but she knew he was looking for her. She knew he'd see the message and understand it. He'd even managed to temporarily restrain that nagging question: What if she actually did kill those people?

"What do you think the timeline is, then?" Ricardo wondered out loud. "She was on campus until just after eleven Wednesday morning, and then it seems most likely that she ended up over in Rock Creek Park, presumably while running because her water bottle was there, too. But then her wallet and this rose show up back here. Maybe she dropped them off before she went toward Peirce Mill?"

"I get that, but why would she be all the way up there if she had come back to Alexandria first?" Ben asked. "If she were going on a run from here she would just go on the Mount Vernon Trail. I think this tells us that she came back here after whatever happened at Peirce Mill, and then hid her wallet and left this rose for me."

"That's an interesting point, actually," Gabriela jumped in. "I agree that seems like what she did. That means she wants to stay hidden. Which means she left of her own volition and is safe and in hiding."

"I think we need to make sure we're not letting the wish be the father to the thought, though." Ben vocalized his concern as he realized Gabriela had followed him down the rabbit hole and he felt he needed to make sure they both stepped back.

"Shakespeare?" Ricardo asked.

"Yes, sir." Ben smiled. "I've always loved that line."

They heard a knock on the door. Ricardo opened the door wide and shot a questioning look back at Ben. Ben shrugged an unspoken 'why not?'

"Come on in, Ademir!" Ben called.

CHAPTER 42
BEN

Tuesday Morning, October 28

"Ademir, not that we're ungrateful you want to help, but what do you think you can do?" Ricardo asked.

Ben, Ademir, Ricardo and Gabriela were seated in Ben's back patio, taking advantage of an unseasonably warm morning in the sun.

"To be honest, I do not know," Ademir conceded. "I have to say, I just wanted to talk to someone who knew a little bit about El Salvador. I have been very lonely since I arrived in the United States."

"It's okay," Ben said. "None of us really know what we can do, so we're not expecting you to have all the answers."

Ademir gave Ben an appreciative nod.

"It's just such a different feeling now, knowing that she ran on purpose," Ben continued. "I'm still so worried about her, but there's this new comfort, this feeling like she's got it all under control. Things don't feel as urgent anymore."

"Ben," Gabriela said, worry creeping into her voice. "I have to voice a fear of mine."

"What is it?"

"Well, the last time Veronica ran, she never went back. What if she's actually gone?"

Ben started a defiant response but paused before getting any words out. She had a point.

No, she couldn't actually be gone. Veronica had run away when she thought her father, her only remaining immediate family member, didn't care if she lived or died. It was a different situation now.

"She wouldn't leave me. She wouldn't leave Nico and Maria for good." Ben struck a far more authoritative tone than he might have just seconds earlier.

"I think he's right," Ricardo said. "I had that thought before, but I think this is different."

"One thing I realized. I think she must have known where she was going," Ben mentioned.

"Why do you think?" Ademir asked.

"Well, I don't know if this makes sense, but it seems to me like she took her clothes knowing her destination. I looked in our closet and there were no coats missing. I'd assume if she wasn't sure, she would have brought a coat. It is getting colder."

"That's an interesting point."

The four of them looked at each other, in turn, waiting for someone to carry the conversation further. Ademir excused himself to sneak inside to the bathroom. When no one else spoke up, Ben pulled out his phone and checked his email. Through the usual pile of junk messages, he noticed one email that stuck out.

A response from Dr. Flint.

Ben opened it and read as quickly as he could.

Nothing.

Gabriela saw Ben's look of disappointment. "What is it, Ben?"

"Oh, nothing. I just got an email from a colleague of V's and

I hoped it would say something useful. Remember how she got a call from Jacob Jordan the morning she disappeared?"

"Mm-hmm."

"Well, I was hoping to find some connection between her and Fermat's Last Theorem, because of that phrase Jacob kept saying, but her colleague basically said there's nothing there."

"Ah, that's too bad. But we knew that was likely the case since this is about her past."

"Yeah. I guess all it really does is confirm that Jacob Jordan really has lost it."

"Who is Jacob Jordan?" Ademir asked, coming down the three stairs from the back door to the patio.

"He's the young man who tried to kill the president last year," Ben replied. "He's the guy that Jeremy tackled. The incident that made him a celebrity."

"And your wife talked to him?"

"Yes. He had been her student, so she stayed in touch with him even after he went to jail."

"She did…" Ademir stopped. "I mean, she does sound like she became a thoughtful woman."

A loud buzz from Ben's phone spared Ademir more scrutiny. Ben looked down and read the news alert.

"What?" He couldn't believe his eyes.

"What is it, Ben?" Ricardo asked.

Ben read, slowly, not fully comprehending what he was reading. *"It's found! Isabella Stewart Gardner Museum announces the return of Vermeer's* The Concert, *the most valuable lost painting in the world. Who found it? None other than presidential candidate Jeremy Wiles."*

"Wait, Jeremy?" Ricardo was incredulous. "When did he have the time to do that?"

"I have no idea," Ben responded. "But I do know it's been an obsession of his for a long time. The article says there's going to be a press conference in a few minutes. Let's go inside and check it out."

———

"Jeremy, how did this happen?" Ben picked up Jeremy's call after the press conference was over. He walked outside into the back patio, leaving Ademir inside with his in-laws. "We watched the press conference, but they didn't tell how you found it."

"It's wild, isn't it? I'm sorry I didn't tell you earlier, I just figured you had a lot else to think about, so this would be an unwelcome distraction."

"Yeah, you're probably right. But tell me."

"Okay. I don't know if I mentioned him before, but I ended up in contact with a Dutch rare art dealer a while ago. It's a long story, but basically, I then reached back out to him, saying that I was looking for the art and would pay handsomely for him to search for it. He called me up a few days ago and delivered the Vermeer right to my campaign headquarters in Columbia Heights."

"That's absolutely unbelievable."

"I thought for sure it was a hoax. He's not exactly an upstanding citizen, but I got it authenticated before presenting it to the Gardner Museum."

"Who would've thought it? Those empty frames were such a big part of each of our childhoods."

"Yeah, but hey, enough about it for now, we'll have plenty of time for me to give you all the details. That's not why I called. Anything new on Veronica?" Jeremy asked.

"Sort of? I mean, yes and no."

"Go on."

"The police came here with a warrant and found V's purse with her wallet and ID in it—"

"Oh, shit," Jeremy cut in. "So, she went back home after whatever happened?"

"Yeah, hold on though, there's more. I looked through her

drawers afterward and realized that there are several articles of clothing missing. And even more, I found a freshly cut white rose in the bottom of one of her drawers."

"Blackmore's Night?"

"Wow, you immediately made that connection."

"You guys are constantly listening to them." Jeremy laughed. "So, this means she left of her own volition, and took enough clothes to hide out somewhere."

"Exactly. I have no idea where, though. It could be anywhere. I asked Ademir to come back over to see if he could help at all."

"You really think that's a good idea?"

"What would you have me do?" Ben asked.

"Anything that doesn't include a guy who you know absolutely nothing about."

Ben sighed. "He's the only one who actually knows anything about El Salvador and Yancey."

"But Ben, you know the American version of Veronica. That's the one who is hiding somewhere, not the Salvadoran version."

"This is all happening because of her past, though, so I'd be foolish to overlook it. All I know is that Ademir can help, and I'm not willing to pass up help, no matter what."

"Okay. Just ... be careful. I don't think he's a refugee, I think he's part of Yancey's organization sent here to find her."

"You know, I did think about that. But the more I consider that, the more it doesn't make sense to me. You'd assume this drug lord would send someone really good here. Why would that person be hanging around here? Wouldn't they be out doing whatever people like that do to find their target? I can't imagine they'd be so stuck they'd be looking to me for help finding her. He's also put his foot in his mouth a couple times, like telling that story about her brother. That doesn't mesh with what some criminal henchman would act like."

"I think that looking for you for help is exactly what they'd be doing, actually," Jeremy said. "Look, I'm not going to tell you what to do. She's your wife. I just want you to be wary of Ademir. Don't let him get too close."

CHAPTER 43
JEREMY

Tuesday Afternoon, October 28

I t was too bad that crime lords didn't keep public rosters. That would have been most helpful. Jeremy thought about how he could confirm his suspicion about Ademir. He didn't have a last name, or really any other knowledge. To tell the truth, he wasn't sure that first name was on the level, anyway.

He had plenty of friends in law enforcement. There wasn't as much overlap with the Secret Service and other branches as many would suspect, but Washington, DC, was an inherently small town, especially the central bubble in which the political world resided. But just saying there's a Hispanic man with a fake name might not be too much to go on.

Jeremy sat in his office, waiting for a representative from the National Fraternal Order of Police. He wouldn't be the one to talk to about this, and Jeremy was wondering why he even had this set up. It was an open secret the NFOP's endorsement was going to President Leishear. They weren't about to endorse a progressive candidate, no matter his background.

He could go tell the police in charge of the Peirce Mill shooting, say there's a potential suspect, but to what end? If this guy was connected like he thought, then there would be no evidence he was there. He'd likely have a set of forged documents ready, and it would end up just being a waste of everyone's time.

Besides, the main man was Yancey Portillo. He was the one to bring down. And Jeremy remembered a recent headline. A quick web search confirmed his memory was correct—Yancey Portillo had been seen in Miami not long ago.

He couldn't believe he hadn't put two and two together. Of course Yancey was in town. If the entire world had just learned of his long-lost daughter, then he for sure knew ahead of time.

What's the perfect way to solidify your status as the candidate who can keep America safe? How to one up stopping an assassination attempt?

Easy. Apprehend—or better yet, kill in a heroic shootout—the only man whose name rings out in this country like Escobar.

Ernest was his go-to for mundane campaign tasks, but this required a different touch. He picked up his phone and dialed.

"Mr. Wiles, how are you?" Colby McCormick's accent was a peculiar combination of his Scottish father and his Louisiana-born mother. Jeremy was reasonably sure he over-egged it just to make an impression, but who was he to judge someone for wanting attention?

"I'm splendid, Colby." Jeremy dove right in. "I've got a task for you, one more up your alley than the usual political humdrum."

"I'm all ears."

Colby was Jeremy's head of opposition research. He ran the team who found every detail of opposing candidates' lives and kept it all tucked away to be used on Jeremy's behalf whenever necessary. Sleazy and yet, ubiquitous in politics. Jeremy poached him from a corporate position where he was widely suspected of engaging in espionage. He jumped ship and joined Jeremy's campaign before any evidence could be found.

"I need you to find Yancey Portillo."

Colby's exhale was so loud Jeremy had to move his phone away from his ear.

"He's in town, and I need to know where he is."

"I mean, I guess? It's just... you know who he is right? Sorry, that's stupid of me, of course you do."

"You're not instilling confidence here, Colby."

"Look, sir, I'll do it. But I can't guarantee anything, except that I'm not physically getting anywhere near that guy."

"No guarantees needed. Just do your job and find me what you can. I'll do the rest." Jeremy hung up the phone and reclined in his chair.

He couldn't contain his smile. He could almost taste the presidency now. It was right there within his grasp.

CHAPTER 44
BEN

Wednesday Morning, October 29

"Good morning and a happy hump day to you all! It's now been one week since the shooting in Rock Creek Park and sources say the authorities are no closer to finding main suspect Alessandra Portillo. To recap ..." Ben turned the radio down. He didn't want Nico or Maria coming down the stairs and hearing that first thing in the morning. He glanced to his right where Ademir nodded in agreement.

Ricardo looked up from the kitchen table and nodded his own silent affirmation over the fold of his newspaper.

"Thanks for letting me come this morning," Ademir said. "I did mean it about being lonely."

"It's no problem. Plus, anyone who brings Duck Donuts is welcome here any day." Ben was starting to wonder if Jeremy was right. Ademir was acting clingy, and Ben couldn't tell if he truly was that lonely, or if maybe he was seeking information. Ben understood Jeremy's concern, but he just didn't see it, and he had his own need for information.

Gabriela took a sip of her coffee and beckoned Ben over to join her in the living room.

"Ben. We need to chat about something."

"What is it?"

"We think we're going to have to go back home soon."

Ben stared, mouth agape. He never considered his in-laws would leave before Veronica was back safe.

"I know what you're thinking, but we're not giving up on finding her. Not in the slightest, okay? But we need to go back to our house, our students, our lives, so that the life Veronica's left is here for her to return to. You get that, right?"

"I just assumed you'd stay here until she came home," Ben's voice was barely over a whisper.

"That was what we planned too, Ben, but things change. Even if it happens exactly as we hope, there's still going to be a lot of fallout to deal with. I think you need to prepare yourself for that. And I think the best way is for us to head back to Williamsburg."

"What about the kids?"

"They're stronger than you give them credit for Ben, they'll understand."

"Logistically, I can't go out and search and have them with me the whole time."

"Ben," Ricardo joined in. "I think you need to recognize that you're not going to find her just by searching around. Whatever may have happened at Peirce Mill—and I know we all believe she didn't kill anyone—she is an incredibly capable woman. She puts you to shame on that front. Hell, she puts us all to shame."

"It just feels like if we try to go back to normal life that it means we've given up on her."

"We all know that's not the case, though. Look, the silver lining about the police thinking she's the shooter is that they for sure aren't giving up. If anything, they're going to be ramping up their efforts to find her."

"I just don't know what I'm going to do without you two around."

"What's the Walsh family motto?" Ricardo's abrupt question made Ben jerk his head up toward him.

"Oh. I know what you're getting at," Ben responded, shaking his head. "*Transfixus, sed non mortuus.* Transfixed, but not dead."

"A weird one, I've always thought, but I'd say it's appropriate here. You, me, Gabriela, all of us are in a tough spot. But we're not dead, and Veronica is somewhere out there, also not dead. So, we're all going to continue on, okay?"

"Yeah, well, there's a reason I got the crest rather than the motto tattooed on my arm."

"Yes, and I know you're very proud of your family, even if you all don't get along. But even more than that, the family crest on your arm means never giving up."

"Oh, my God. The crest."

"What?"

"You're right." Ben jumped up. "Oh. My. God."

Ben ran out of the kitchen and grabbed his phone from the arm of the couch.

Ricardo exchanged confused looks with Ademir.

Ben ignored his father-in-law and ran upstairs. He scrolled through his contacts until he found the name he was looking for.

"Hello?" A female voice answered after a single ring.

"She's at your river house, isn't she?" Ben asked.

A long pause followed.

Ben could feel his heart pounding through his chest. Sweat beaded on his brow. The seconds dragged on, each one an eternity.

"Yes."

CHAPTER 45
BEN

Wednesday Morning, October 29

"I found her!" Ben bolted back into the kitchen. "I know where she is!"

A barrage of questions met him as Gabriela and Ricardo bolted upright in unison.

He barreled right past them and toward the front door. "I figured out her clue! We can go find her!"

"Which clue?" Ricardo asked.

Ben turned around, stood in the entryway. "The white rose. I should have known it had multiple meanings. Veronica really is brilliant." He shook his head in admiration, and a broad smile spread over his face.

Ben continued, "The white rose was the symbol of the House of York."

Ricardo nodded, but Ben could tell he didn't know the connection Ben had just made.

"When you mentioned the family crest it made me remember that the white rose has a lot more meaning than just our own little one, based on that Blackmore's Night song. The obvious one is the House of York. We don't have any connection to York, Pennsylvania, but we do to Yorktown, Virginia. She and

I went on a short vacation to Yorktown a few summers ago and stayed at her friend's empty house right near the battlefield. We had so much fun that we've discussed several times since then about setting up an annual trip, maybe even looking into getting a summer house down there. That friend who owns the house we stayed in is who I just called. She confirmed that Veronica is there."

"My goodness. We've found her," Gabriela breathed. "Our poor girl. All she wanted to do was get away from her past life."

"Ben, go. Go now," Ricardo said. "We'll look after Nico and Maria. It's less than three hours from here. I know it's still only nine in the morning now, but if you find her and it's too late to come back home, here's the key to our house." He handed Ben a familiar old house key.

"Ben?"

Ben turned around and realized in his excitement that he had completely forgotten that Ademir was there.

"May I come with you?"

Ben didn't know what he was expecting, but it was not that. "I'm sorry?"

"I just think ..." Ademir kept going before Ben had a chance to respond further. "You might need another person, and just in case anything goes bad."

Ben thought for a second. He realized he had absolutely no idea what he was headed toward. He had this silly notion in his head that he would just turn up at the door and Veronica would be there and they would come home and all would be okay. But that couldn't be the case, or else why wasn't she home already?

A further worrying thought crept into his head. He had spent so much brain power in the last three days convincing himself that Veronica could not be the killer the police and media were describing her to be that he had almost forgotten the inevitable follow-up. If he truly believed she wasn't the killer, then he also believed that someone else out there had killed at least five, and probably six, people.

Where has that person been this whole time? What if that person confronted Ben? What if they had already found Veronica?

He knew that Yancey Portillo was somewhere nearby, and for a second wondered if going to find Veronica was playing directly into Yancey's hands. But how could he find out? The only ones who knew were his in-laws, and Ademir, a man who seemed to have just as much reason to hate Yancey as Ben did.

Jeremy's voice popped into his head, warning about Ademir. Ben realized that he'd already said the name of the town out loud. *Better to keep him near me, just in case,* he thought.

"Yes. You can come along. I want to hear more about El Salvador and Yancey Portillo so you can tell me while we drive." He hesitated. "The one thing, though, is that I want it to just be me when I get there. Is that okay with you?"

"Of course," Ademir responded.

"Perfect. Then let's do this."

———

As they drove down Richmond Highway toward the Capitol Beltway, Ben pulled out his phone.

"I need to tell my best friend," he said to Ademir, who simply nodded from the passenger seat.

"Ben, what's up?" Jeremy's voice was surprisingly calm, Ben thought, before realizing that of course it had no reason not to be right now.

"I just wanted to let you know. We know where Veronica is. She's hiding at a friend's house in Yorktown and I'm headed that way now."

"Holy shit, that's amazing. How did you find out?"

"I found a clue she left me inside a drawer. I called her friend Jennie. Do you know her?"

"Her running buddy?"

"Yea, she's the one at the Hungarian Embassy. Anyway, I called her, and she confirmed that Veronica is hiding there."

"This is unbelievable news. You'll let me know as soon as you find out anything, right?"

"I can't promise I'll call you before I call her parents." Ben laughed. He felt a surge of joy for the first time since V went missing. After all the stress and worry, he was now on the move. Not waiting. Not hoping. Getting out and actually finding her.

"I mean, I guess that's reasonable ..." Jeremy trailed off and Ben could feel him smiling on the other end of the line. He glanced over and saw Ademir smiling broadly too, his fingers going a mile a minute on his own phone.

Everything felt right. Soon it would all be over.

Ben hung up, shared a determined nod with Ademir, and accelerated into traffic.

CHAPTER 46
BEN

"We're getting close," Ben said as they drove on Route 64 east of Richmond. The drive had been mostly silent since they got onto I-95 at Springfield and headed south, except for a few intermittent comments from Ademir about Ben's slow pace. Ben had thought he wanted Ademir along to talk more, but he soon recognized that he did not want any distractions. Ademir did not seem to mind. He had kept his head buried in his phone the entire time.

"Got a question for you, Ademir."

"Yes?"

"You said you'd be useful if we run into any trouble. Do you have experience with that?" Ben asked.

"Yes," Ademir said with a sly grin. "I was a troublemaker as a child. I was in lots of fights and got beaten up a lot. My sister teaches judo so she taught me how to use it. Things went a lot better for me after that."

He pulled out an object from his pocket. "I also always carry one of these."

"Is that a knife?" Ben allowed himself a quick glance.

"It is. A six-inch folding knife."

"You've had that in my house, near my children?"

"Yes, of course. Is that a problem?"

"Don't do it again. I don't want weapons around my kids." Ben turned and glared at Ademir.

"It's less deadly than any knife in your kitchen, though. Hey, the road!" he said as Ben drifted over the rumble strips.

Ben corrected but continued facing Ademir. "Those are for a purpose. Your knife is not for any legal use."

"That makes no sense."

Ben let out an exasperated sigh. "You wouldn't understand."

Another silence descended upon the car, this time much more uneasy than the first. Ben thought about Ademir's answers. Jeremy's warning was now lodged at the front of his mind. That Ademir was an accomplished street fighter who carried a large knife around certainly made it seem more likely that Jeremy was right.

Ben suddenly steered the car off the highway onto the exit for the rest area that they had almost passed. Ademir finally looked up, a confused expression spreading across his face.

"I'm sorry," Ben said as he pulled to a stop at the far end of the parking lot. "I don't know you. I can't take you to my wife."

Ademir stared at Ben, stone-faced. He raised his right eyebrow as he spoke. "What changed your mind?"

"What changed my mind? Maybe that giant knife you pulled out, for starters." Ben cast his gaze to Ademir's pocket. "And maybe it's just that I've been a fucking idiot, willing to listen to whatever you had to say because I was blinded by the hope you'd help find my wife. But did you? No. You just came and hung around our house, positioning yourself perfectly to be here when *I* found her."

Ademir remained frustratingly impassive. "Okay, if that is what you believe,"

Ben pursed his lips. "Why are you not fighting this?"

"How can I?" Ademir raised his hands, palms forward. "But tell me this, if I am working for evil, why do I not fight harder?

If I accept, that should convince you I am with you. I will explain. You leave me here, and then you pick me up when you come back. I am happy to stay. If I needed to know where your wife is, would I say that?"

"I don't know, but I have to be alone." Ben sighed. "Look, if I'm just being too cautious, and you are just here to help, then I will sincerely apologize when all this is over, I swear."

Ademir shrugged and gave a single nod.

"I have your phone number, so I will call you as soon as everything is safe, okay? I really am sorry, I just have to protect her now." Ben cringed as he spoke. Every bit of his personality screamed at him to let Ademir stay, to trust him, but Ben knew he was doing the right thing.

Ben watched as Ademir opened the passenger door and hopped out of the car. He leaned down by the front wheel to retrieve his dropped phone, before straightening up, giving a small salute, and walking toward the vending machines.

Ben pulled away, remorse and relief sparring inside his brain.

As he passed the exit for Colonial Williamsburg and the College of William & Mary, and turned onto the Colonial Parkway, he touched the dashboard to make one final call. The navigation system alerted him that this was the fastest route, due to an accident on I-64 eastbound. He loved driving on the parkway by the scenic York River each time he and Veronica were here. *Must be a good omen to be directed onto it*, he thought.

"Hi, Ben," Jennie's voice came out of the speakers just as Ben thought his call was going to voicemail.

"Jennie, how are you?" he asked, more out of habit than curiosity.

"I'm out on a run right now, actually. What's up?"

"I'm on my way to get Veronica. Can you give me the exact address?"

"It's 223 Nelson Road. When you drive into Yorktown on Water Street, turn right onto Ballard right before you get to the beach access. If you see the beach, you've gone too far. Follow that as it curves around near the battlefield and you'll eventually turn left onto Nelson just before the Coast Guard Training Center."

"Perfect, thanks!"

"No problem. If that's all …?"

"Wait," Ben quickly said. "Can I ask … how did she contact you about the house? Where did you see her?"

"All I know is that she showed up outside the Hungarian Embassy—"

"When was that?"

"It was early afternoon, I think. I had eaten lunch. I could tell something was going on, but she had this almost eerie calm about her. She said she needed to get away quickly and she needed somewhere no one would find her. I gave her the key to the house, and she thanked me and took off."

"And that was all?"

"She texted me that night to say she had reached the place."

"Wait, that night?" Ben was getting a clearer sense of the timeline. "But how did she get down to Yorktown? Our car was still at home."

"I think she said something about having cash and taking taxis, but I don't know for sure."

"And you didn't tell me or anyone else, this whole time?"

"I'm sorry about that, Ben. I really am. But she made me swear to not say a word. I didn't know what she was involved in, but I could tell it was serious and she was scared."

"Even after you heard about the shooting?"

"There was something about the way she asked for my help. I just knew I needed to stay quiet."

"Okay, thanks for this info, Jennie. Seriously, thank you so much for helping her."

"You're welcome. I hope you find her there safe."

CHAPTER 47
FRANCISCO

That's why you always have a backup plan.

It was all going along almost too easily. Francisco couldn't believe that Ben had agreed to let him ride down with him.

The original plan for Ben to lead Francisco to Alessandra wasn't meant to be *that* literal. Francisco thought for a moment he needn't have even planted the bug and tracking device in the front wheel well.

He watched cars whiz by as he leaned against a tree by the vending machines. Single men and women, couples holding hands, and families with children all went right past him without even a glance. He was very good at looking like he belonged somewhere. No one ever saw him and wondered what he was doing, or thought he looked out of place.

Every couple seconds, he checked his phone, watching the blue dot continue down the road. Ben wasn't going to get rid of him that easily. He wasn't built for this. Francisco wondered what would happen to him now. He'd been given a glimpse into a world he was much better off not knowing. A world that's hard to squeeze back into the box once it's out, roaming freely in your mind.

Beep! Beep!

A dingy gray Honda Accord pulled up, and Francisco hustled over to the passenger side door. He pulled it open and dropped into the seat, swinging the door shut behind him in one continuous motion.

"How long?" Yancey did not waste time with small talk.

"About five minutes." Francisco held up his phone. "He's a weirdly slow driver, we'll beat him to the house easily."

"And you have the address?"

"Loud and clear." Francisco relayed what he'd heard from Ben's call with Jennie.

"It's time, then." Yancey met Francisco's eyes and gave a curt nod. "Time to do what should have been done decades ago. I've been waiting a very long time."

CHAPTER 48
VERONICA

Wednesday Afternoon, October 29

This house would be a great place to live. A riverfront property, a nice big porch, lots of windows. A quiet town in a wonderful part of Virginia. I wondered if maybe Jennie would be willing to sell it when she was sent to the next country to serve. On the other hand, she couldn't stop talking about how she would eventually retire to this pretty place. I couldn't blame her.

Jennie.

She turned out to be a better friend than I could ever have imagined.

Would I have done for her what she did for me? I wanted to say yes, but I could not say for certain. When—well, I guess if—this all ended, I would have to figure out some way to repay her.

I showed up at her work, drenched to the bone, asking for help and shelter, and she didn't even hesitate. I didn't even explain why I was soaking wet!

I was lucky. Even with everything else, I'm not sure what would have happened if it hadn't rained the entire night before. Rock Creek was still raging. I was able to jump in the water and let it take me downstream. If it hadn't been, I wouldn't have been able to escape so quickly.

The second lucky part about Rock Creek being so high was that I was able to climb out just before the pedestrian footbridge only about five hundred feet downstream. I was close enough that I was able to just sneak back through all the chaos to the Hungarian Embassy right by Peirce Mill.

The police hadn't arrived yet, but a crowd of runners was growing. I already knew those bodies on the ground were not getting up. It was a gruesome scene. I'd know.

It took a bit of convincing to get the security to call Jennie and ask her to come down. I was shocked they acquiesced at all. I did exaggerate my visible distress, though. A young woman in distress can convince security of just about anything.

Jennie gave me quite a look when she eventually arrived at the front entrance.

"Veronica? What is going on?" She stared, mouth agape at what I had to admit was a startling view.

"This is going to be a crazy request, and I'm sorry in advance, but is there any chance you'd lend me your river house?" I had asked, trying to project as much calm as humanly possible, like this was just some old request, no big deal.

"Now? Why?" she asked, completely befuddled.

"Look, I need to go somewhere no one will find me. It's a wild ask, I know, but can I hide out at that house for a few days?"

Jennie blinked. I could see the wheels spinning as she tried to bring herself to ask the dozens of questions that probably came to her head at once.

"I'll explain everything, I swear, but right now all I can say is that there's danger and I need to keep it as far away from my family as possible." I tried to get her to understand while saying as little as I could manage.

She sighed. I could see in her eyes that she had already decided to agree. "Okay, here you go." She pulled out her massive set of keys and shimmied off a small bronze one. "I don't understand. How are you going to get there?"

I gave my best casual shrug. I'd learned through years of experience that portraying confidence is one of the easiest ways to conjure up confidence. Or, to put it another way: 'fake it 'till you make it' actually works. "Taxis," I said, like it was the most obvious thing in the world.

It was partly true. After I left her, swearing her to secrecy, I took a taxi back home, avoiding the questioning glances of the driver along the way.

When I got home, the first thing I did was pull up a floorboard in the back of our bedroom closet. I pulled out my go-bag and grabbed from my stack of passports the Costa Rican one, a credit card associated with that name that I'd created years ago, and with five thousand dollars in cash. I powered on my burner phone. I never believed I would ever have to use this stash. I always assumed it would stay hidden until long after I was gone. Someone in the future would find it and have quite a mystery on their hands.

Benita Barrantes. I couldn't see myself as a Benita, and definitely not a person with an alliterative name. Exactly why I had chosen such a name for this passport.

I secured the board back down, grabbed some extra clothes from my dresser, and headed downstairs, but not before leaving the small white rose, hidden away where only Ben would find it.

I called an Uber using my new name and had it drive me down to Mount Vernon. From there, I got a Lyft to Fredericksburg. I took a taxi from Fredericksburg to Richmond's Main Street Amtrak Station and then hopped on a train down to Williamsburg. I went by my parents' house and looked through the window. I came so close to knocking on their door.

I figured my trail had long been obscured, so it was safe enough to get another taxi and have it drop me off at Yorktown Beach. I walked the last couple miles of my journey to my new safehouse.

There were no grocery stores within walking distance, so I was again lucky in that Jennie kept the house stocked with nonperishables. I ordered delivery when I needed, taking care to always request contactless drop offs.

The rest of the time I just tried to relax. There were plenty of books and movies, and the television had Netflix and Amazon Prime, so I had more to binge than I could possibly get through. There were a lot of shows I needed to catch up on. Nico or Maria always had something they wanted to watch so I rarely got time to watch the shows I wanted anymore.

It turns out Breaking Bad *really is as good as everyone told me years ago. Some of it was a little close to home, but after decades out of the life, I could take it in stride. I watched an entire season each night. What a finale.*

The Great British Baking Show *is what really got me through each day, though. Heartwarming and cheerful, it was exactly what I needed, and served as a balance to my nightly* Breaking Bad *routine. I wrote down a lot of tips and ideas I'd like to try out for Ben and Nico and Maria.*

No matter what happened, I just hoped they would be proud of their mother. That they'd know that the truest version of me is who I am when I'm around them. The past might have come back up, but I chose not to let my past define me. Yes, who I am is partly based on who I was, but I took that past and made the best out of it. I became empathetic, believed in second chances, and realized that while the most important thing in life is family, you get to decide who that family is.

Knock.

I heard the noise but wouldn't let myself acknowledge it at first. I wasn't waiting on any delivery and hadn't made any friends down here.

Knock.

The second time, I knew it was real. I scrambled down the stairs and, using an old trick I'd learned, put a book over the peephole. That way if someone was on the outside waiting to see it go cloudy before shooting through it, they would miss and reveal themself. One of those survival skills people with normal childhoods don't learn, and those who do learn never forget.

No shot came.

I stood there for a second, deciding the best way to respond.

That decision was taken away from me, though, when the visitor broke right through the locked door.

CHAPTER 49
VERONICA

"You thought you could get away from me?" the man thundered. "You really think there's anywhere I wouldn't be able to find you?"

I stumbled backward, trying to get some distance.

"Wait, stop!" I cried.

"Clever, hiding away here. It made it hard to find you, that's for sure."

I straightened up, feeling defiant. For a second there, I'd forgotten who I was. "And how exactly did you find me?"

He laughed. A cruel, emotionless laugh.

"Your own husband," he sneered. "He led me straight here. He didn't even realize he was doing it. You didn't marry a smart man, do you realize that?"

"Not smart? Then how come you, with all your resources, couldn't find me, but he could?" I shot back.

In response he reached down and pulled out a Glock G19. "I know better now. I'm not going to underestimate you and let you get away like last time."

He raised the gun, glaring at me as I stood in the doorway to the kitchen. "I know you can run, but you can't outrun this."

I had spent my entire early life expecting death around every corner. What was that Avon Barksdale line about death? Another classic TV show. I memorized it as soon as I watched that episode because I felt that deep in my bones. "You only got to fuck up once... Be a little slow, be a little late, just once. How you ain't gonna never be slow? Never be late? That's life."

There was nowhere to run now. I hadn't reacted quickly enough. Maybe this was it, my time. A little slow, or a little late. That's all it took.

I glanced backward.

I backed further into the kitchen. A butter knife sat on the counter, just out of reach. Not the most useful weapon for most, but I'd done more with less before.

A lot of men could attest to that. They wouldn't though, because they're all dead. And I'm still alive.

I took another deliberate step backward. It was now within my reach. I just needed a distraction, something to take his mind away for a split second.

A car door outside slammed. Perfect timing. I'd have to thank that person later.

He swiveled to check outside the window.

In one move, I grabbed the knife and flung it with one flick of my wrist. As soon as I released the knife I dove around the corner into the dining room. I heard a thunk but could not dare look. I waited in silence for what felt like an age.

A patronizing chuckle eventually came from the entryway.

"Nice try."

He stepped into view.

"I think you'll owe your friend for that chunk you took out of the wall." He clucked his tongue. "You almost got me. But I told you I wouldn't underestimate you this time."

I heard a second car door slam. No wayward glance this time. He'd learned his lesson. No matter who they were, or how much they knew about me, I was always underestimated the first time. I did my utmost to ensure there was no second time.

He stood in front of me, his gun just out of my reach. I could see right into the barrel. Here it was.

A calm, almost relieved, feeling washed over me. I wasn't supposed to live this long. I wasn't supposed to do this much with my life. I'd already done more in my life than I ever dreamed I would.

I just hoped my kids would understand. Their mother wasn't a saint, but she tried her hardest and loved them very much. At least I was leaving them in the most capable hands I could. Ben would take care of them.

I shut my eyes.

BANG.

CHAPTER 50
BEN

Ben drove up Ballard Street, workshopping his first line he'd say when she opened the door. "Hi" just didn't seem to cut it.

His thoughts kept going back to Ademir, though. Why had he been texting so much? Who was he talking to? Why was he willing to drive all this way just to hang around and then drive back? Now that he really thought about it, that made no sense to him unless Ademir was lying about his involvement.

Why couldn't these thoughts have settled in his mind three hours ago? He could've had a nice drive down on his own, instead of now fretting about what Ademir was up to.

He tried to push those thoughts away. They weren't helpful right now. He was on the verge of seeing Veronica again. He had been so excited, but now that he was almost there, he felt farther away than ever. He wasn't even sure if he knew this woman who had been his wife for nine years.

No, these thoughts weren't any better.

Where were the happy thoughts? The excited thoughts?

Ben turned on the radio. At least maybe that would help distract him, get him out of his own head. Natalia Rochev's new song came over the airwaves. He wondered what Jeremy was doing right now, now that they were so close to the end. He could rescind the reward, go back to normal. Or would he lean in on her being a murderer? What was in store for them after he did find her? Would they convict her of this shooting, or maybe send her back to El Salvador for what she did as a criminal? What if rescuing her was the last time Ben would ever see her? A tiny thought sprouted in the dark corner of his mind. What if life became easier?

He sighed and turned the radio off. Nothing except arriving at Jennie's house was going to keep him from spiraling.

Ben approached the Coast Guard Training Center and took a left just before the entrance, as instructed. He followed the curve of Nelson Road until he reached the cul-de-sac.

This is it.

He pulled up in front of the house and got out of the car. He looked around, taking it all in. The area had the calm and peaceful quiet of a vacation destination. No one came down this street unless they absolutely had a reason. Ben realized he was procrastinating now. In his mind Veronica would fling open the door and welcome him happily. But what if that wasn't the case? What if she didn't want him to be there? There was a reason she was hiding, staying away from him and the rest of her family.

Wait.

Why did that car in his peripheral vision look so familiar? Ben turned and peered at the car, parked a couple houses down from Jennie's.

Ben watched, astonished, as Jeremy climbed out of the driver seat. Jeremy saw him looking and gave a cheerful wave and headed his way.

"What are you doing here?" Ben asked.

"You thought I'd let my best friend walk into a potentially dangerous situation without me by his side?" Jeremy scoffed, feigning hurt. "When you told me you knew where she was, I sat at home for five minutes before realizing I needed to be down here with you. I'm a much faster driver than you, so I got down here before you but didn't know the address! I've been driving around this little town trying to find some sort of clue until I saw your car down on Water Street, and then I just followed you here. You didn't see me pull in behind you?"

"No, I must have been really concentrating."

"Is this the place?"

"Yep, this one right ahead. You know you didn't have to do this, though?"

"Yeah. Look, I feel really bad about this whole ordeal and how I amplified Veronica's case, which didn't help once her background came out. I felt I owe it to you, and to her, to help out now."

Ben smiled. Having his best friend here pushed all the negative thoughts from before out of his mind. Things were all going to be okay now.

"Let's go find my wife," he said and walked ahead of Jeremy up to the front door.

Ben jogged up the steps ahead of Jeremy, skipping every other one. He could feel his heart thumping.

Ben got to the front door and stopped, taken aback. He turned to Jeremy with a startled look.

"Look at the door. It's splintered and broken around the handle." Ben felt his heart go into overdrive, propelled by a very different emotion than minutes before. He fiddled with the doorknob. The door swung open.

"Oh, shit," Jeremy whispered.

"Veronica! Veronica! Are you here?" Ben shouted as he nervously stepped through the threshold. He glanced left and saw a butter knife stuck in the wall next to the door, its blade buried up to the hilt.

"What the hell?"

Ben rushed into the house. When he got into the kitchen he

gasped. A foot lay on the floor, connected to a leg stretching out of the kitchen and into the dining room.

Ben turned the corner, and, upon seeing the full scene, paralysis took over. He couldn't move, could barely breathe. His mind tried its best not to comprehend what he saw. His head felt foggy and his vision started to close in on his pupils.

Veronica lay face down, a large pool of blood continuing to grow bigger and bigger around her head.

"Veronica! Oh, my God, what the—" He broke off when a flash of movement caught his eye. A man holding a gun opened the back door and took off.

"I'm on him!" Jeremy leapt past Ben and ran toward the door. He pulled out his gun and fired at the retreating figure. Ben saw the man stumble as he was hit, but the man kept running and Jeremy chased him out into the yard. He finally broke out of his paralysis and crouched down next to his prostrate wife. He flipped her over onto her back as gently as he could.

"Jeremy, stop! Wait!" Ben's heart found a reason to continue beating. "She has a pulse! I need your help now!" Each weak heartbeat pumped more blood out into the surrounding pool.

Ben dialed 9-1-1 as he ripped off his jacket and used it to apply pressure to the bullet hole in her neck. "Jeremy! Where are you?" Ben looked out toward the back door but saw no sign of his friend. It didn't matter to Ben whether Jeremy caught the guy right now. Nothing mattered to Ben except Veronica. The seconds dragged on as Ben looked back and forth from the door to Veronica's supine body. He didn't want to look at his wife, lying on the floor clinging to life, but he couldn't keep his eyes away.

Jeremy finally came running back. "I'm sorry. I wanted to get him. Did you see who that was?" He panted as he knelt down next to Ben.

"No," Ben responded, distracted.

"That was Yancey Portillo! He was right there!"

"That doesn't matter right now! They'll get him. We need to save her, though!"

"What do you need?"

"Just help put pressure here!" Ben nodded his head in the direction of Veronica's neck. He looked down at her and tried his best to keep his creeping thoughts out of his mind. He wondered if he'd be able to ask her all the questions he'd amassed in the past week. But more importantly, he wondered if he would ever be able to look her in the eyes again, or if she'd be able to tuck their kids into bed once more.

An agonizing ten minutes passed as Veronica's pulse grew weaker until Ben could barely feel it under the jacket he held wrapped around her neck, covering the entry and exit wounds. To try to keep himself sane, he looked around and tried to picture what had happened.

He guessed the shot had come from the kitchen and she had been just inside the dining room. He noticed the edge of the dining room table was smeared with blood. Maneuvering his right hand so he could keep pressure on her wounds, he used his left hand to shift her head and found an inch-long gash on the back of her head.

"Oh fuck. She must have hit her head on the table when she fell," he said out loud, more for his own sake than Jeremy's. He pulled a sleeve of his jacket around her head, a futile attempt to stop the bleeding, and shot a frantic look back toward the front door. *Where is that ambulance?*

"Jeremy, help!"

"What?"

"She has a cut on the back of her head. Stop that bleeding." Ben could hear the strain in his voice. He had taken a first aid class before—all of Congresswoman Moore's staff did it together—but he didn't believe he'd have to use any of that knowledge. The most he really had planned for was the occasional scratch that Nico or Maria would run inside with. He couldn't believe the amount of blood that had come out of her entry and exit wounds, even after he'd attempted to stop the bleeding with his jacket.

Ben could have sworn entire civilizations rose and fell in the time it took for the ambulance to arrive, but finally he heard the sirens outside. Ben and Jeremy lifted Veronica in their arms and carried her out and down the front stairs. They waited at the sidewalk the final few minutes until the ambulance pulled up. Two EMTs jumped out and pulled up a gurney. Ben and Jeremy placed Veronica on it as gently as possible.

"Is this where she was shot?" the younger EMT asked.

"No, inside, but we thought it'd be tricky to get a gurney up the stairs, so we wanted to be as ready as possible," Ben answered.

The two EMTs shared a concerned glance but didn't question further.

"Can I ride along?" Ben pleaded.

The older EMT shook her head. "Let us do our jobs. We need to move as fast as possible. Follow right behind." She gave him a conciliatory look that did nothing to soften her words.

"Okay." Ben took a deep breath.

He squeezed his wife's hand and let it go, hoping against hope that it wasn't the last interaction they would ever have.

CHAPTER 51
BEN
TWO WEEKS LATER

Wednesday Morning, November 12

Ben gently laid the flowers down next to the gravestone in St. Paul's Cemetery. He swallowed a sob, told himself he was going to keep it together. It had been a good funeral. People always described funerals like that, as if that somehow would matter to the dead. No one ever said a funeral was bad. No one said it was great. It was always just good.

He looked over his shoulder and saw Jeremy approaching. That man really knew how to fill out a suit, Ben thought. He looked like a million bucks. Well, that is what having enough money you could literally spend a million bucks on a single outfit could do for a person.

"It was a good funeral," Jeremy said, stopping to stand next to Ben. "I think she would have been proud of it."

Good.

Again, with that sentiment. Wouldn't she have been prouder to actually get to know the impact she had, however fleeting, on people in her life while she was still alive? Why do people have to wait until someone is gone to extol their virtues openly?

"It's just gut-wrenchingly sad," Ben said, pointing one by

one at the four adjacent gravestones. "But I kind of think it makes sense for her to be buried here, so close to The Female Stranger. That's sort of what she was, isn't it? A mysterious woman who comes to Alexandria and is shrouded in death, who then dies before anyone really gets to know who she is. You could argue she's a modern version of that old story."

Despite his best efforts, Ben could feel the tears start to roll down his cheeks. It was just so unfair. A family member lives to old age and dies of natural causes, and we can understand it and process it. But an incredible woman who had been through so much already, cut down in her prime, with so much more to live and give to the world? It was too much for his brain to bear. There would be no rationalizing this.

"Mysterious woman, shrouded in death. You might have a point," Jeremy conceded.

"It's cliché to say, but at least she's with her family now. Miranda is with her family now." He repeated it to convince himself. "The Belles are all back together. I'm trying to tell myself there's some comfort in that."

An hour after Miranda's funeral, Ben had pulled back into the visitor's parking lot at Inova Alexandria Hospital and parked in the same spot he had the last twelve days, ever since he was told staying overnight was doing no one any good. He walked into the hospital, nodded at the nurses he had come to recognize, and slipped into the room with which he had become so familiar.

No changes.

Veronica lay, unresponsive, just as she had since she was first brought to this room. She had been flown back to her home hospital two days after her emergency surgery at Bon Secours Mary Immaculate Hospital in Newport News. She looked better, Ben thought, but maybe that was just wishful thinking. Her health didn't seem to be hanging from a cliff edge now that she was no longer intubated.

Here he was, day fourteen, settling in for another long day

of waiting, hoping, and praying that his wife would come out of her coma.

The doctors and nurses who were a constant presence the first few days now flitted in and out less often. They worked in almost complete silence now, coming in to check vitals, test things that must be important but that Ben had no knowledge of, and nod or grimace accordingly. Most of all, they kept encouraging Ben that they each believed Veronica would wake up.

"It's in her hands now, Ben," the surgeon had told him after the operation. "Only she can decide when she's ready."

Veronica's parents visited the hospital every day, coordinating with Ben so that someone would be at the hospital at all hours. They wanted Veronica to have a friendly face when she woke up, trading off being at Veronica's side and taking care of Nico and Maria at home.

No sign of Yancey Portillo, though. He had not been seen since. A police manhunt was still ongoing, but no one was particularly optimistic. A man like that knew how to hide.

The door opened. Ben looked up to see Jeremy enter the room. He, too, had been visiting every day. He gave Ben a solemn nod and sat down in the chair opposite his.

"You know, you probably could have just driven over with me," Ben said.

"You're right, but I can't stay too long today, so I thought it was better to drive myself."

"More campaigning?"

"It never stops. Hey, I know I've thanked you already, and it's not at all important relative to Veronica's health, but I really appreciate you giving that interview and telling the journalist about how I winged Portillo." Jeremy gave a sad smile and shook his head. "No one's going to catch me in the primary now."

"Honestly I didn't even mean to do it," Ben smiled back. "I just answered her questions truthfully."

"Where do you think he is now?"

"If he's smart, and by all accounts he is, I bet he's back in El Salvador now." Ben sighed. "I just want to know why. Why did he try to kill her? Why was that the first step?"

"I think neither you nor I are well suited to understanding the minds of maniacal mass murderers." Jeremy shrugged. "I'm so pissed at myself, though. I should've been able to take him down with the one shot I got off. Everything would be better if he were dead."

"I just keep coming back to one question. How did he find Veronica? It took her leaving a clue only I'd recognize for me to find her, and there's no way Yancey would have known anything about Jennie's river house on his own."

"You know my thoughts," Jeremy responded. "And I'd even go as far as saying it's obvious. I know you grew this weird quick attachment to him, but what do we know about Ademir?"

He didn't give Ben time to respond.

"He shows up randomly, knowing a lot of details about Portillo, is there when you figure out she's in Yorktown, listens in when you get the exact address, and is consistently on his phone. And that's just before it happened. Since then he's been conspicuously absent, wouldn't you say?"

"He's texted me a bunch of times to check on how she is," Ben argued. "I mean, I did leave him on the side of the road in a small town in a country he doesn't know well, so it was nice that he understood, at least."

"That's literally the least he could do," Jeremy scoffed. "I don't know what the connection is, but I'd be willing to bet a lot of money that Ademir is connected to Portillo."

Ben was ready to continue his rebuttal, unconvincing as it was, but the door swung open again and in strode Dr. Ilhan Gundogan, Veronica's primary doctor since her return to Alexandria.

"Good morning, Mr. Walsh. Morning, Mr. Wiles," he said with a kind smile. Ben had immediately taken to him. He was hunched over, with a mop of white hair, a stern gaze, and a wicked sense of humor. "No change in her status overnight."

He checked the dressing on her wounds and gave a short nod. "The good news is that her neck continues to heal. Like I have told you before, she's very lucky her spine was not hit. That isn't to say this is going to be an easy recovery. Regardless of when she wakes up, it will take a long time for her to get back to some semblance of normalcy."

"I know I ask this every time I see you," Ben started. "But you do believe that she will wake up, right?"

"Indeed."

Ben liked asking him that question. There was a surety of response that put his nervous mind at ease. "But no hypothesis on when?"

Dr. Gundogan shook his head. He paused as he exited, turning around. "I will say this. To have even survived to the hospital was remarkable. I wouldn't bet against her."

CHAPTER 52
BEN

Thursday Morning, November 13

Ben stopped when he reached the small section of the cemetery that now held the entire Belle family. He gazed, moving slowly from headstone to headstone, trying again not to be overcome by the overwhelming sadness of it all. An entire family, gone far too soon. Her funeral had been so small. He worried no one would make the effort to remember her, so he told himself he'd visit her grave each morning before going to the hospital to be with Veronica.

Ben leaned down and lifted the bouquet of flowers lying in front of Miranda's grave back up. He stood still, trying to hold in his emotions. He hadn't even known her that well, and yet somehow she'd ended up connected. What did Yancey gain by killing her? He just couldn't understand why she had to die. That feeling of guilt constricted his gut every time he thought about it. He had to admit to himself that was at least part of why he was here.

To Ben, there was something peaceful about cemeteries. Normally he enjoyed walking through them, searching for stories and families. In a cemetery there was no stress, no strife, none of the worries of the world of the living. Most of Alexandria's cemeteries were on the same plot of land in southwest Old Town, a little way off the beaten trail. Many days Ben would be the only living soul present.

Today would not be one of those days.

In a place as quiet as a cemetery, it was hard to sneak up on someone without being heard. And yet, as Ben turned around, he recognized the tall, thin man leaning up against a tree only ten yards behind him.

"Ademir?" Ben asked, trying to disguise the surprise in his voice.

Ademir stepped out from behind the tree. "Hi, Ben."

"What are you doing here?"

"We need to talk," Ademir responded. "Come with me." He turned around and started walking away.

"No. I'm visiting a friend's grave, I don't want to leave," Ben said.

Ademir turned around and pierced Ben with a stare that made it clear he was not willing to engage in a dialogue. Ben scrambled to catch up and they walked in silence to the entrance to Alexandria National Cemetery. Ademir sat down on the top of the steps next to the giant American flag.

"Sit," he said. Ben sat down next to him, squeezed in a little too close for comfort on the narrow stairs.

"Okay, what is this about?"

"Did you know that I knew Miranda, too?"

That was not what Ben was expecting. He looked at Ademir, confused. "What do you mean?"

"She and I went on a date the night she died."

"Wait, hold on, what? You and Miranda were dating?"

Ademir shook his head. "I'm not sure one date counts as dating."

Ben was starting to get frustrated. "Okay, but what are we talking about here? Did you come just to talk about Miranda?"

"I did not come here simply to talk about Miranda, beautiful as she was."

Ben waited as Ademir sat silently. He could see him trying to work out in his head what he wanted to say.

"I haven't been entirely honest with you," Ademir said.

Ben had a pretty good idea of what was coming next. He'd owe Jeremy an apology.

"Yancey Portillo didn't co-opt my entire family, and I'm not a refugee."

Ben nodded, trying to reason if he was more furious at Ademir or at himself for believing that bullshit the first time.

Ademir gave him a wry smile. "You started to have some doubts didn't you? In the car ride down to Yorktown?"

"I did think it was weird that you were texting nonstop."

"Well, you can probably guess what I'm about to say."

"That you helped the man who tried to kill my wife, absolutely." Ben stood up. "Tell me where he is or I'm calling the police right now."

Ademir rolled his eyes. "If you do know who I am, or at least who I'm associated with, you probably have a decent guess at what I can do. Sit back down."

Ben hesitated.

"Do you need me to spell it out?"

Ben sat back down.

"Now, let me continue," Ademir said, his calm voice only serving to infuriate Ben further. "My name is Francisco Orellana. I am Yancey Portillo's main enforcer, among other roles. I was raised within the organization, and yes, I was sent here to find out if the rumors about Alex were true. She was a few years older than me, but we grew up together. She was the most incredible person I've ever known, besides maybe Yancey himself. If she had stayed in San Salvador, I have no doubt that she would have been in line to be his replacement, especially after her brother Kelvin died."

"Your English is much better than you let on." Ben realized what else was jarring about the conversation.

Francisco replied with a derisive snort. "My English is probably better than yours. Anyway, Kelvin died, the way I told you before"

"Was Kelvin her only brother?"

"You really know nothing about her childhood, do you?" He paused, looking at Ben with contempt. "Yes. She was the second, the baby. Kelvin was her older brother. He was being groomed for command one day but was killed in a raid gone wrong. You know this already. If Alex running away broke Yancey's heart, Kelvin's death certainly provided the fissures."

"Why are you telling me this?"

"Because Yancey did not shoot Alex. He would not shoot his own daughter."

"Oh, come on. You expect me to believe that? I saw him!"

Francisco nodded. "You did. He was there, because I was passing on all the info you got as soon as you had it. But—"

"Oh, fuck me." Ben knew it to be true, but hearing it out loud caused a shudder to run through Ben's entire body. "I really did lead him straight to her."

"Let me finish," Francisco admonished. "I have been following Alex for weeks. I finally was able to get proof that it was her when I saw her missing pinky. At that point, I had already sent word to Yancey that I was ninety-nine percent sure, and so he came to America too, although I did not know it at the time. He does not want to kill her. The thing he wants most in life is to have her back."

"But how did you know to come look for her in the first place?"

"Yancey has never stopped looking. He had no idea where she was until recently. I don't know what it was, but he heard something, and sent me here to find out more. I was told to find a young Georgetown math professor who could have been Alex. Your country is not so great with diversity, so it wasn't hard. I followed her home. I set up in Old Town Alexandria to be close to her and her family. A lot of rooftop surveillance."

"You watched us from a nearby rooftop?" Ben was horrified. He felt his stomach drop.

"Oh, yes. It's not hard. Piece of advice, you don't always pull your bedroom curtains closed the whole way and I think you might want to."

Ben felt his face get red. "You—"

Francisco silenced Ben with a glare.

"I followed you to work a couple days, I watched your kids go to school, I kept track of it all. That's how I knew who Miranda was, too."

"I don't think that's possible. We didn't see you that whole time?"

"I could follow you from five yards behind and you'd never know I was there. Alex was the only one I was worried about. She might've been able to recognize me, so I stayed hidden. I eventually was able to catch a glimpse of her missing pinky finger as she closed the blinds one night. A Georgetown math professor with a missing pinky? The intel all added up. So, like I said, I called Yancey and told him. My role was done, unless I was needed for an extraction to get Alex back home."

Ben considered this new information. "I think you believe this is true, but I don't at all believe that Yancey somehow just happened to be there in Yorktown after someone else shot her. That makes no sense."

"I was passing on info from you. So of course he was there."

"And it just so happens that someone else was there too and he's the one who shot my wife? I do not buy this at all."

"Would you like to hear it from the man himself?"

"He's here?"

"Sure. Not in the cemetery, but he's in the area." Francisco's lips formed a mischievous grin. "I bet he'd even like to meet his son-in-law."

"I'm not his son-in-law. Veronica's parents are Gabriela and Ricardo Aguilar. Parents who actually raised her and cared about her."

"You think he didn't care about her?" Francisco's eyes were daggers. "You think her mother didn't care about her before she died? You don't know shit about the life she led or the people in it. I came here to tell you that we've been looking for your wife because Yancey misses her, and if you don't want to believe that he wasn't involved in her shooting then that's on you."

Francisco stood up, tossed a scrap of paper toward Ben, and walked away.

Ben watched as he left, then picked up the paper. It had a Washington, DC, phone number on it, with the letters "YP" scrawled below.

Ben put it in his pocket and walked home.

CHAPTER 53
BEN

Thursday Morning, November 13

Yancey Portillo was waiting for the call. "Meet me at Belle Haven Park. I'll be seated at one of the picnic tables. You'll know who I am. If you bring the police, I'll see them coming and you won't like what I'll do next," he hung up before waiting for a response.

Thirty minutes later, Ben parked in the narrow lot and walked over, alone, to the picnic table nearest the water.

Ben had always liked the park. There wasn't much to it, just some picnic tables and the Mount Vernon Trail running right through it, but the view of the Potomac River was tremendous. Just south of the Woodrow Wilson Bridge, the view included all of National Harbor across the river, and if he looked south, he could see the corner of Fort Washington peeking out. This time he had absolutely no interest in it, though.

He sat across from the man he now knew must be Yancey Portillo. It was surreal to see him in the flesh after all he had heard about him.

Yancey Portillo was well into his sixties, but you wouldn't know it. He wore a dark linen suit, with a white tee shirt underneath, and loafers on his bare feet. Although he wasn't wearing a sling, Ben could see him favoring his left shoulder.

"Ben. It's very nice to meet you," Yancey said with a smile.

"Your guy, Ademir, or Francisco, or whatever his real name is, tells me you didn't shoot my wife," Ben said, brushing right past the pleasantries. "I want to hear it from you."

"Right to the point. I can appreciate that. His real name is Francisco. I told him not to lie to you anymore. How is she doing?"

"Nope. I'm not here to answer your questions. Convince me that I made the right decision by not bringing the police."

Yancey smiled. "I find it charming that you think bringing the police would do anything. And I knew you wouldn't be able to hold back, despite how angry Francisco said you had been. Your need to know would outweigh all else. But I'll go ahead, because you and I have something in common. We both love your wife, even if you know her by a different name. Now, you, no doubt, know that she disappeared after she was taken at age fourteen. Do you know why she ran?"

"Because you wouldn't negotiate to get her back," Ben said.

"Yes. I only recently learned from the news that this was the case. That hour-long special last week on her and me was quite something, don't you think? Must-see TV, I'd say."

"I haven't watched it."

"Really?"

"A special report about how my wife is a mass murderer who killed in the past and may have recently picked up the habit again? Absolutely not."

"Hmm." Yancey raised an eyebrow. "You are a strange man. Anyway, the first thing is, that's not actually what happened. Yes, I told her kidnappers that it did not matter what they did. But not because I do not love my daughter. It had nothing to do with my daughter. Simply put, if I had shown weakness there it would have been the end of me, of us, of our entire organiza-tion. I made a choice, not knowing that my daughter would hear my words, and I've regretted it ever since. Did you know we found those men, likely only a few hours after Alessandra got away from them? We tried to find her. I had my best people searching and we came close several times. We knew she made it to Mexico, but that was where we lost the trail. I never imagined she would let herself be adopted, so I never looked. I don't want to say I'd given up hope, but I had not heard of a decent lead in a long time."

"But then somehow you did," Ben interrupted.

"I did. That's an interesting story on its own. An intriguing source, I must say. We can discuss that later."

"So then you sent Francisco here. What's his story?"

"Ah, Francisco. Incredibly skilled in hand-to-hand fighting, probably the best liar I've ever known. A good man. I like that he chose to use the name Ademir. He only uses that name for his most important assignments. It was the name of his grandfather."

"I don't really care, and those don't sound like the qualities of a good man."

"To each his own." Yancey lifted his hand in an imaginary toast.

"Okay, so you sent him here."

"Yes. He followed your wife for weeks, learning everything he could, trying to determine if it was really Alessandra. His first clue was that she had gloves on every time he saw her outside. Even though it was cold, it wasn't that cold. Then he contacted me and said he suspected it was her and I made my way here. I left my number two in charge back home."

"I don't understand. How could we have not seen him?" Ben asked.

"Of course you didn't see him," Yancey said, a mirth in his eyes. "You really don't understand the sort of people you're interacting with now, do you? Francisco could follow your every move for a decade, and you'd never know his presence. You know the only person who would be able to tell?"

"Veronica?"

"*Alessandra*. The Alessandra I knew could spot a tail before they even began tailing her."

"So why didn't she see him then?"

"It sounds like she hasn't used those skills in a long time."

"This is all fascinating, but where you lose me is when Veronica—*not Alessandra*—disappears after someone, you or Francisco, I'm guessing, shoots five people at Peirce Mill."

Yancey steepled his fingers. "That, my son, is where I also am lost."

"Don't call me son."

Yancey shrugged. "I do not know any more than you do about what happened at Peirce Mill. I was in Washington, yes, but I was not a factor there."

"Okay, then Francisco did it."

"No. He called me soon after. By that time, he had confirmed that she was indeed my daughter, so had not been following her every move anymore. His role was over. He was simply staying, should I need any assistance."

"Assistance with the extraction, as he called it?"

"Of course. With bringing her home."

"She would not have gone with you willingly. She wouldn't leave the life she has."

"I see that now. But that matters not. So there we were, in the same position as you. Neither Francisco, nor I, is familiar with this area, although I have been here far more times than your FBI knows, so I determined our best chance was to follow you. I instructed Francisco to get close to you. I imagine he told quite a tale. Like I said, an exemplary liar."

"He said you threatened to kill his whole family. And to burn him alive."

"Ah, yes. An incredibly effective threat, I must say. Though strangely not as effective as threatening to cut off an appendage. It might be the immediacy of that one that does it," Yancey said, as if describing his favorite child-rearing methods.

"I need to be less trusting," Ben said. "I was convinced he was an ally when he first showed up."

"Yes, yes you do. I, frankly, am astonished you showed up here without some backup."

Ben looked straight at Yancey, taken aback.

Yancey chuckled. "Were you going to pretend you did? That wouldn't have gone well. It's obvious for a man like me to see that you're here on your own. No one else I deal with would come alone. Although, in your defense, Francisco was acting as an ally. You and he had the same goal, to find her safe. If the actions mirror your own, then the words are of secondary importance."

"Tell me, then. What happened in Yorktown?"

"As soon as you discovered my daughter's clue and realized she was in Yorktown, Francisco texted me and I headed out immediately. I then followed you, and picked him up right after you dropped him off. You really are a very slow driver. We went straight to the area. I'm quite sure we passed you along the way. We parked in front of Moore House and then ran behind it to Nelson Road and the back of the house. I crept up to the back door to look inside and I saw Alex lying there on the floor. The door was unlocked so I went right in. I had only just knelt down next to her when I heard you and your friend come through the front door. I knew you'd get her help, so I ran off, but your friend shot me as I was fleeing."

Yancey looked at his right arm and grimaced. "No matter how tough you are, bullets still do a lot of damage. I ran and hid in the trunk of my car, a trick I learned a long time ago. No one looks inside the trunk when they're looking for someone they know to be alive and alone. I eventually slipped out and drove off. And now here we are."

Ben stood up and turned toward the water. If this were true, he could not make any sense of what happened.

"This sounds convincing, but I also know that you're someone who could make anything sound convincing."

"Let me ask you, then," Yancey said as he stood up and followed Ben over to the water. "Why would I try to kill her? And what would I or Francisco have been doing at Peirce Mill?"

"I don't know. You tried to convince her to leave with you, but she wouldn't, and you got angry?"

Yancey gave a nod of concession. "Fair enough, that's at least a reasonable case you make. But let me ask you another question, then. What have you been told of my prowess?"

"What does that matter?"

"It matters because no one has ever stopped me before. I'm sure you've heard the stories. Someday, somewhere, I'll come up against someone better than me. It might be time itself that wins. But it would not be my daughter, rusty from a lifetime spent away from it all."

He turned and started walking back toward the parking lot.

"I'll leave you with this. I had a tail as soon as I arrived. A sloppy, amateurish attempt that was borderline insulting, but a tail, nonetheless. Who could have found out her secret past? Who do you know who has the resources to contact me once they have found out? Because someone wanted me to come here. You need to have a long think about that, and once you do, there's where you'll find your shooter."

Ben's heart thudded. He didn't fully understand it, but things started settling in his mind.

And he did not like what was bubbling up to the surface.

CHAPTER 54
VERONICA

Thursday Afternoon, November 13

A m I dead? I can't be dead. Everything hurts too much. And why does my throat feel like it's on fire?

I had a lot of muddled thoughts when I first woke up. It was probably only a few seconds, but it felt like ages until I fully realized where I was. I finally remembered my last memory—the gun going off, and the thump as it hit my neck because I'd jerked my head at the last second.

It took all my strength to drag my eyelids open. No sooner had I completed that task did they come right back down. I had run marathons, chased, beaten, and been beaten by rival drug dealers, yet never felt anything like the strain of physical exertion it took to simply keep my eyes open.

The next time I succeeded in doing so, I actually kept them open long enough to see my mother standing over my bed. My heart swelled. No matter the situation, no matter what age, seeing your mother always makes life better.

Well, I guess not in my husband's case. Exception to every rule.

"Mama," I tried to make a sound but I'm not sure any noise actually came out of my mouth. Her eyes grew wide. She couldn't hear me

but could see that I was awake. The tears started to flow. My own tears flowed in response.

She called out to my papa, and he came sprinting in. I watched them hug. They touched my face, my arms, my shoulders. They kissed my forehead over and over.

"We have to call Ben now!" Mama exclaimed. I tried to talk but still could not. I attempted to mime a pen and paper. After several minutes they finally recognized what I was doing and got me something to write with.

"Did they catch him?" I scrawled, in barely legible handwriting.

Papa's face fell. "No. Yancey got away. I'm sorry, V."

I grabbed my paper and frantically scribbled "NO!" as quickly as possible. Papa looked at me, confused.

"What do you mean?"

"Get … Ben … now!" I managed to croak.

———

I tried to stay awake until Ben arrived but failed miserably. I only lasted a few more minutes before falling back asleep. Just long enough for my parents to fill me in with a rough summary of the last few weeks. When I woke up again, he was seated at my bedside and Mama and Papa were gone.

This time it was my turn to cry first. I saw how my husband looked at me, the mixture of fear and relief in his eyes, and once again the tears flowed. I was pleased to see that Ben quickly started crying too.

He came over to the side of the bed and leaned in, giving me the gentlest of hugs. I clung to him as hard as I could.

When I was growing up, I thought I could do anything. I didn't believe there was a single thing beyond my capacity. The one thing that I never expected, though, was to be comforted by anyone, let alone that another person's presence would just make everything feel like it was going to be okay. But I'm a grown woman now, and seeing my husband, my wonderful, sweet husband, standing over me, I felt secure. Wherever I might be, even in a hospital bed hooked up to God knows how many machines, I felt the most myself when Ben was next to me.

But first, I needed to make sure he knew. When I looked deep into his eyes, past the happiness, the relief, and the love, I could see it. He had an idea of what I was about to say.

"Ben ..." I said.

"It's okay," he quickly responded. "I know, and it's all okay."

"No, not about me. You have it wrong. Everyone has it wrong!"

Ben gave me a sad smile, and nodded once as I continued, struggling to push the words out, my throat still tight, voice gargling.

"Yancey had nothing to do with this. It wasn't him. It was Jeremy!"

Ben squeezed his eyes shut, then slowly opened them again. I could tell that this was a hammer blow, even though I got the sense he knew it was coming.

"Go on. Please," he said, barely above a whisper.

"You know I've never fully understood what made Jacob Jordan do what he did, right?"

Ben opened his eyes. "Yeah."

"Well, I finally pieced something together. It was Miranda who helped, actually. She told me that she thought she recognized him from something."

"Wait. She told you she recognized Jacob, and that was important?"

"Yes."

"Oh no. No, no, no." Ben put his face in his hands. When he looked back up, his face was ashen. "I think I told Jeremy that she recognized Jacob. It was just an offhand comment."

My poor husband. Life would change for him. Becoming acquainted with death was something that happened to all of us at some point, but knowing death as if it were a close personal friend, that was something else entirely. Miranda's death wasn't his fault, of course, but he would carry that with him regardless. Some things you don't shake.

I tried to give him my best sympathetic look, tricky to do when ninety-nine percent of your body is screaming at you whenever you move.

"Ben. Look at me. This is incredibly important for you to understand." *He looked directly at me, his face now completely white.* "It isn't your fault. Jeremy did this. Not you."

"But why?"

"Miranda realized that the reason she recognized Jacob was from the worst moment of her life. He was the man who was driving the car that caused the accident that killed her family. She told me she saw his face as he passed their car, right before he tried to switch lanes with them in his blind spot."

"Wow. So, Jacob was the culprit of the hit and run? But why didn't she tell me that? She still just said she couldn't place him."

"She wasn't entirely sure, so I don't think she was ready to say it out loud to anyone but me. He left the scene. The police are still looking for answers a year later, but I know the truth."

"So what are you saying, then?"

"You know that I've been convinced there was something more going on with Jacob's assassination attempt. Once Miranda told me that she thought Jacob had driven the car, I wondered if maybe someone else could have known and blackmailed him into doing the shooting."

"But he would go to jail anyway after he assassinates a president. Why would he go for that?"

"I thought about that too. It must have been much more of a threat than just turning him in."

"What does this have to do with Jeremy, though?"

"Something he said recently. Remember how he would go to see a movie every Saturday night?"

"Yes …?" *Ben wasn't yet following.*

"That means he must have been at the Regal in Potomac Yard the same night that Jacob caused the accident that killed the Belle family, right there by Potomac Yard."

"Sure, I guess so, but the chances that he saw anything would be really small, wouldn't they?"

"Yes, but the chance that he was there in the vicinity and then just happened to also be there when Jacob attempted the assassination?"

I could see the wheels turning. Ben lifted his eyebrows. "Okay, that would be pretty coincidental."

"So that's been on my mind for the last few weeks, but it was still pretty flimsy. The final piece was when I talked to Jacob on the phone last week. It was fresh on my mind because of that front page Washington Post article, the 'in memoriam' piece on the anniversary of the Belle family's crash."

Ben gave me a concerned look. "Babe, you've been in a coma. That was over three weeks ago now."

"You're kidding."

"No, you were shot two and a half weeks ago."

"Well, that explains why my entire body is screaming at me."

"So, that Wednesday. Was that right before you sent me that cryptic text?"

"Yes. As you know, he barely ever says much. Mostly I call just to try to give him the opportunity to talk. This time I asked him straight up if Jeremy Wiles was blackmailing him. He said, 'The proof didn't fit in the margin.'"

"That's what he said to me."

"You talked to him?" Maybe my husband was a good detective after all. I was not expecting him to have gotten that far.

"Yes, I went to your office and saw Dr. Flint and he told me you ran out quickly around eleven. You had the Washington Post front page up on your computer, but it had reloaded to the current day's version, so I couldn't tell if you had seen something on there. I looked at our Verizon and saw you had made two calls. One to the prison and one to…" He trailed off. "One to Jeremy. I confronted him about that call and he said it was just you calling about planning my birthday."

I shook my head. "Nope, not at all. We'll get to that, though. First," I went on, "the cryptic message Jacob said. He knew he couldn't just tell me. Calls are monitored. So he said something I'd understand. Do you know what he was referencing?"

"Fermat's Last Theorem."

That brought a smile to my face. "So you do listen when I go on about math history?"

"I might have picked up a thing or two along the way." He shrugged, his face giving nothing away.

"Do you know who finally solved it?"

He shook his head.

"An English mathematician, who was at Princeton at the time. He solved the Taniyama conjecture and as a corollary, proved Fermat's Last Theorem to be true. His name is Andrew Wiles."

"Wiles, as in Jeremy Wiles?"

"Not actually related, but yes. Jacob was saying yes to my question about Jeremy, but in a way that he knew only I would understand."

"And then you called Jeremy right after," Ben said, nodding.

"Mm-hmm. I called him and said I knew. I knew that he forced Jacob to attempt to assassinate the president, but then stopped him at the last second." I paused. "I still don't understand why, though."

"So, it was Jeremy at Peirce Mill? How did you and he both end up—"

Ben stopped and looked down. His phone was vibrating in his pocket. He pulled it out and his eyes grew big.

"It's Jeremy," he whispered.

CHAPTER 55
BEN

Thursday Afternoon, November 13

"Hey Jeremy, what's up?" Ben hoped his voice didn't sound as weak as it felt.

"Ben, are you with Veronica?"

"Does it matter where I am?" He got a poke from Veronica with an exasperated look.

"*Act normal!*" she mouthed.

"I mean, I guess not. I just wanted to hear how she was doing."

"She's good. She woke up this morning but still can't communicate."

"Oh, wow! That's amazing news! Look, I have my rally today, but I'm going to come by as soon as I can after."

Ben glanced at Veronica and raised his eyebrows. "He's coming here this evening," he whispered.

"Great. I'll probably have the kids," he replied to Jeremy.

"Hey, Ben, one other thing. I know this is crazy to ask, but are you gonna be at the rally?"

Ben thought for a second. It probably wouldn't hurt to keep an eye on him. "I'll see. It's going to depend on Veronica, though."

"Sounds good, man. I'll make sure you're on the VIP list, so come on around back when you get there."

Ben ended the call.

"What do you think?" he asked Veronica. "He wants me to come to his rally this afternoon and said he was going to come visit you tonight."

"Well, that means if we don't stop him by tonight, he'll kill me," she said matter-of-factly.

"Wow, you were really nonchalant in saying that," Ben said.

She shrugged. "I don't want to die, of course. But I spent most of my childhood expecting death at any moment. It's ingrained in me now."

"We're going to need to talk about all of that." Ben sighed. He had gotten so caught up in Jeremy's guilt that he had forgotten about his wife's own past as a killer.

She nodded. "Yes, but not right now."

"You're right. You were telling me that you called Jeremy."

"I did. I told him that I knew the truth from Jacob Jordan, that I was going for my daily run at lunch, and that if he wanted to talk, he should meet me at Peirce Mill. I figured the final piece of the proof would be if he showed up."

Veronica took a deep breath, summoning up the energy to continue. Ben watched in silence.

"He was standing at the southeast door, closest to the trail. He had a dark jacket on and a beanie pulled down low. He pulled a gun on me as soon as I got there and said, 'Hello, Alessandra.'"

Ben recoiled. He knew what Jeremy had done, but hearing that his best friend used his wife's original name still caused his blood to run cold.

"He might be skilled," she shrugged. "But I'm better. I started to get him to talk. He confirmed that he had seen Jacob in the SUV driving away from the scene. He didn't tell me how he figured out who he was, though.

"Jeremy was just starting to tell me why he blackmailed him, when a group of runners came up the path. He glanced at them for a second, and it gave me a chance. I've still got the skills I used to have. I did a little double move and snatched his beanie off while kicking the gun from his hand, and ran toward the water.

"The first runner saw what was going on and ran toward Jeremy trying to stop him." She shook her head. "Wrong place, wrong time. Wrong shooter, too. Anyone else probably would have run away at that point, but Jeremy is a public figure already. He had a lot to lose if anyone saw him pointing a gun at a woman. Which is what I was hoping for when I pulled his hat off. I just thought he'd run at that point, though. Instead, he grabbed his gun off the ground and shot the runner in the head. I saw that just before I jumped into the water. I heard four more gunshots and knew they weren't at me so I assumed he must have shot the other witnesses too."

"He's a well-known figure," Ben repeated, as if saying it himself would confirm the truth. "So any of them could have recognized him."

"Exactly. So I swam downstream, staying underwater as much as I could, then circled back and called Jennie."

"Why didn't you just come home, though? Or tell the police? Or tell me, even?"

"I know you're probably upset about that, but I need you to believe me. I didn't want to put you or Nico or Maria in danger. Jeremy needed to think that you knew nothing. The best way to do that was to disappear for a while. I figured I'd stay hidden while I worked out a plan. But I wanted you to know I was okay, which is why I left that white rose. I assume you found it?"

"I did, after several days, though. It took a couple more days before I realized it wasn't just from Blackmore's Night but also a clue about Yorktown."

"I wondered if you'd get that," she grinned, before quickly grimacing from the pain. "So, you made it to Yorktown, then? I think it's my turn to ask some questions."

"I did, yes. But I think I messed things up …"

"How so?"

Ben felt his face redden. He hadn't had a chance to fully comprehend his role in Veronica being shot. He gulped air, trying and failing to catch his breath.

"Ben, are you okay?"

"I … I was the one who told Jeremy where you were. He had been so helpful looking for you. I just wanted him to know." Ben felt red hot. "He and I were the ones who found you in the house, together. He was in his car outside the house when I got there. Yancey was in the house, with a gun. Jeremy tried to shoot him as he ran away. With all we learned about Yancey beforehand, how could we do anything but assume he was the one who shot you?"

"Yancey was in Yorktown too?"

"Okay, so here's the thing. I think I might have accidentally brought all the parties with me. How could I have been so naive?" He paused. "Do you know a Francisco Orellana?"

Veronica's jaw dropped. "Francisco Orellana. Wow. I have not heard that name in a long time. He and I were tight back in San Salvador. He idolized me and tried his best to hide it." She smiled at the memory. "Is he here?"

"He's apparently been here for weeks now. Yancey sent him to find out if the rumor that you were here was true. He then called Yancey to come once he knew it was you."

Ben knew he'd been taking a risk, letting Ademir come to Yorktown with him, but he had not once considered that it was unsafe to tell Jeremy where he was headed. He wondered if Yancey's involvement stopped Jeremy. He hoped that was at least the case so he didn't have to feel so guilty.

"He's been tailing me?" Veronica groaned. "How did I not spot him? He must have gotten good."

"After you disappeared, he approached me and said he was a refugee and that he wanted to help. He said his name was Ademir. He and I ended up driving to Yorktown together, and he kept Yancey in the know the whole way."

"So what you're saying is that you unwittingly brought my drug lord birth father and your psycho killer best friend to my hiding place?" She shook her head, smiling. "My own husband, the sweet, innocent guy I married, caught up in the middle of all of this. I'd laugh if it didn't hurt so much."

"I bet." Ben paused. "I bet Jeremy meant to kill Yancey because it'd all be over if he did. He thought you were dead, and with Yancey dead he'd be in the clear. He'd have been able to tell the world Yancey was behind it all. I thought he was just trying to be protective."

"Definitely not being protective. He broke down my door. He told me he had underestimated me the first time and wouldn't do it again. I tried to hit him with a butter knife I grabbed, but it must have missed."

"That butter knife that was buried all the way to the hilt! You threw that?"

"I did." She winked. "Now that you know my secret past, there's a thing or two I can show you. But maybe not just yet." Veronica closed her eyes and laid her head back.

She's in better spirits than I am, Ben marveled. *She's been through more in the last weeks than anyone should have to go through in a lifetime, she's just woken up from a coma, and yet she's laughing and joking about it.* While here he was, sitting at her bedside, an emotional wreck, still trying to pick up the pieces of his life scattered all over the floor.

"I don't understand, though. If Jeremy shot you, then how did he end up back outside when I pulled up to the house in Yorktown. I parked, and then he got out of his car just after," Ben said.

"Not sure I'm the one who can answer that, babe." Veronica didn't open her eyes but managed a wry smile.

Ben stood up. It was clear what he needed to do now. Veronica would be able to do it. She'd handled situations that made this look like child's play. Now it was his turn.

CHAPTER 56
BEN

Thursday Night, November 13

Ben stood just inside a classroom at Wakefield High School in Arlington. He could hear Jeremy's voice booming out from the gymnasium, thanking his supporters for all their hard work. He had no interest in getting any closer, though. He had no interest in anything Jeremy said except for one thing. He needed to know exactly why he shot Veronica. Which was why he was here, waiting for Jeremy to come offstage.

Ben reached into his pocket and felt the knife there. Turns out when an internationally known drug lord and his homicidal sidekick are on your side, you get some better weapons than the average person can find. Francisco promised Ben this knife was the sharpest he had, before launching into a story to prove it that Ben absolutely did not need to hear and would show up in a nightmare in the future.

Bypassing security was a nice perk of being on the VIP list. He wasn't sure what his plan was, but he felt a fury he'd never known before.

Jeremy came off stage to rapturous applause. He walked with a spring in his step, a man with the world at his feet.

He almost walked right past Ben, standing in the entrance to the classroom.

"Jeremy," Ben said as sternly as he could.

"Ben! I didn't know if you'd actually make it." Jeremy turned and walked over to Ben. "You guys all go ahead, we're just going to chat for a second," he said to his campaign manager and two security staff, who continued down the hall.

Ben ushered Jeremy into the classroom and shut the door behind him.

"Is that really necessary?" Jeremy asked.

Ben stared straight at Jeremy. In a calm voice he hadn't known he could muster, he asked, "Why did you shoot my wife?"

"Excuse me? You and I were both there. We saw Portillo do it."

"No." Ben kept his voice steady. "I know what happened. I know it all, Jeremy. And now you're going to explain it to me."

"Look, I don't know what you're talking about Ben. This is ridiculous." Jeremy shook his head, exasperated.

"Oh, is it? I could have a chat with all those reporters lined up outside about it instead."

Jeremy looked down and sighed. He looked back up. His eyes flared, and Ben saw a side of his friend he had never seen before.

"Your fucking wife. Everything would have been fine if your fucking wife hadn't meddled in someone else's business. She woke up and talked, didn't she?" Jeremy's anger continued to boil, his cheeks and forehead reddening.

Ben stood, silently watching, waiting for Jeremy to continue.

"So. What do you want?"

"Tell me why you blackmailed Jacob Jordan."

"Jacob." Jeremy laughed without humor. "What a perfect patsy. Who else knows?"

Ben knew this question was coming. Jeremy needed to know

if he could still contain it. "Too many people, Jeremy. Too many people have died over this already."

Jeremy gave a big sigh. "All right. I wanted to be the president. You and I talked for so long in grad school about this. There was no way I'd ever actually make it to the presidency from where I started, so I needed to make something happen. Any possible way, I've probably thought of it already, and realized it wouldn't work. And then there was Jacob Jordan. A solution plopped right down into my lap.

"I was in the parking lot at Regal Potomac Yard, parked as far away as possible from the building, like you know I like to do. I heard the Belles' car go off the road and saw the SUV fly by after. I memorized the license plate, thinking I would just call the police and let them know. But I didn't. I looked him up instead. I found his name and then found out he had a math degree. I don't know how it came to me but instantly I had the idea. Every Secret Service member has had a fantasy of stopping an assassination attempt. And here was a guy who gave me serious Unabomber vibes."

"Just because he had a math degree?"

"Sure. Sue me, plenty of people think that about mathematicians. So, I went and visited his home. I broke in and waited for him in his living room. He came home and I told him I knew what he had done, and I would tell the police unless he did exactly as I said. You know that little shit tried to negotiate with me? He said he was clearly valuable to me, and so I'd have to offer more. I got pissed off and alluded to some things I could do to certain appendages of his. Weirdly, that didn't work. So, I had to up it and tell him I'd kill his family, slowly, with him watching, and then kill him. That worked much better. Although I did tell him I had a powerful co-conspirator who would kill him and his parents if something were to happen to me. Just to make sure."

"Jesus Christ." Did bad guys all have the same manual? Ben knew this wasn't the time to dwell on the specifics, but the fact that Jeremy and Yancey both mentioned threatening appendages stuck out to him.

"I planned it meticulously. It had to be a big enough event to get national attention, and I had to be off work so I could make sure that I was in the right place. I got the gun past security by distracting my friends who were working the event. I handed it off to him in the crowd after wiping it down and then stood and waited. He had no idea I was planning to stop him.

"It happened perfectly. Jacob did enough damage that the whole country noticed, and I became the hero. Only problem then was whether he would hold his tongue in prison. I couldn't believe just how well he did. I assumed he would make up some story, not that he wouldn't speak at all.

"I knew I needed to build my celebrity organically after that. I stayed in the public consciousness but not so much that people got tired of me. So then once the primary was in full swing and no Democrat was pulling away from the rest, I knew this was my moment to jump in. You know the rest."

"This is psychotic. You killed people to become president."

"Oh, come on, Ben. You think I'm the first? Everyone who has ever become president has adopted policies that will kill people, mostly Brown and Black people, and only because they want power. I'm worse because I killed a few people to get there? I'll make the world better, and you know it. Give me a break."

"You murdered people!"

"If you think that killing a few people to make sure we have four to eight years of prosperity, rather than another four years of that man in office waging a war on poor people, isn't an acceptable tradeoff, then I don't know what to tell you."

"But what about Veronica?"

"I heard that she kept speaking to Jacob in prison, so I had to keep tabs. I can't say I was surprised when she called me saying she knew what had happened. So I went to meet with her, to see what she wanted to keep quiet."

"You thought she'd take some bribe?" Ben scoffed. "You don't know her at all if you thought that."

"Coming from a guy who didn't even know his wife was a missing notorious assassin? That's hardly an insult."

Ben had to admit, he did have a point there. It stung. "She said you called her Alessandra. How did you know?"

"Like I said, I kept tabs on her. She did a decent enough job of hiding that missing pinky finger, claiming she was a germophobe with those gloves always on, but once I found out about that, it wasn't too hard. I was Secret Service, Ben. You don't think I learned all there was to learn about Yancey Portillo? I've known of his missing daughter for years."

"You alerted Yancey Portillo," Ben realized the missing piece of the puzzle. "You needed something to distract from your involvement. But you did this before she even found out about you? And how did you even get to him?"

"Let's just say I was proactive. And it turned out to be a great idea, so I feel vindicated. As for the how." Jeremy grinned. "Nothing like killing two birds with one stone, there. The very same man who found me the Vermeer is the man who got me a line to Yancey Portillo, although I never told him who I was. Apparently, Yancey and I share an interest in the Dutch masters. It's almost like I meticulously planned it all out. I even had Yancey followed once I knew he was in town." He smirked and gave an exaggerated shrug that made it clear to Ben that it was all part of his plan.

Ben felt his fists tighten. It took all his restraint to not charge at Jeremy. "But you screwed up. Twice. You had two chances to kill Veronica and you couldn't do it either time. You know why? Because she's better than you ever will be."

"She got lucky that Yancey showed up before I could finish her off," Jeremy snapped. "And then you and your in-laws just wouldn't leave her hospital room. I'd hardly call that skill."

"Hold up. You were there but Yancey stopped you?"

"Yancey came in the back door, probably because he heard

the gunshot. He never saw me, and I ran out the front door. I may be skilled, but I was not about to get into it with a guy like that. I got in the car and waited for you to show up, which I correctly assumed would only be a matter of minutes."

"Then you followed me back in, knowing that he'd be there," Ben finally understood the timeline. "Regardless, V figured it out, she evaded you, and she got the truth out, so I'm not sure she'll care if you think that wasn't skill."

"All right, then. I bet she'll care if I shoot you right now, though." Jeremy leaned down and pulled a handgun out of his ankle holster.

"You wouldn't do that."

"Oh yea? Why not?"

"Because there's no reason to do so. You're already going down for this."

"No," Jeremy replied, shaking his head with a wry smile. "That's a bluff. Only you and Veronica know. Once I get rid of you, I'll go take care of her. Then we'll be back to normal."

"And how would you explain this? You shot your best friend for no reason?" Ben's tone remained defiant, but he started to worry. Jeremy had easily seen through his bluff.

"You think I don't see the giant pocket knife you're hiding there? Again, I was Secret Service, don't make me laugh. Here's my friend, who everyone knows has his own political aspirations, worn down by the events of the past few weeks. He gets angry that he's not the one who's going to be president and, in his diminished mental state, attacks me with a knife—a knife that I'm going to guess is not, strictly speaking, legal." Jeremy looked straight at Ben and held his hands up with his palms facing out. "What was I to do? It was self-defense. And then poor Veronica, just when things were looking better, took a turn for the worse. An absolutely tragic tale, but not my problem."

Ben tried to regulate his breathing. His heart was racing, and he could feel sweat dripping down his back.

"Pull out your knife," Jeremy said, using what Ben realized

must be his practiced presidential voice. Ben could tell he was losing the upper hand. "Pull out your knife, or I'll shoot you in the leg and then pull it out myself."

Ben took his knife out and flicked it open. "I hear Veronica almost got you with a knife much more dull than this one."

Jeremy laughed and shrugged. "She almost did. That was one of the most impressive things I've ever seen." He raised his gun. "But I'm sorry, Ben. I didn't want it to end this way. You brought this on yourself."

"Wait!"

"I'm not here for some 'any last words' bullshit, Ben."

"Did you actually have a co-conspirator?"

Jeremy looked at Ben for a second, his tongue flitting back and forth across his lips. "Ah, what the hell? I'll tell you. It won't matter anyway. Who has the most to gain if I win?"

"I don't know."

"Think, Ben."

"Umm." Ben was finding it hard to think about anything other than the gun pointed at him. Then it clicked. "Oh. No, that can't be."

Jeremy smiled. "I always knew you were smart. Yes, my powerful co-conspirator was the Chief Justice of the United States, Bart Marsden."

Ben gasped.

Jeremy nodded, smiling. "That's right. An aging Supreme Court justice looking at another four years of a president from the opposition party potentially replacing him? No one had a chance against Leishear, and Marsden didn't think he'd last long enough for another Democratic president. I'd heard rumors—who hasn't?—that he was on the verge of retiring, so I got on his calendar and laid out my plan to become the next president. I left out that I expected Jacob to actually kill at least one of them up on stage, just in case he got squeamish. I have to say I expected to have to convince him more than I needed to."

He shrugged. "I guess he was desperate. Anyway, it's not

like he actually would've gone after Jacob if something happened to me, but the powerful ally aspect definitely helped convince him to pull off the assassination. Now, that powerful ally needs me to win, which brings me back to you."

"So he wasn't a conspirator at all." Ben rolled his eyes. "You always gave yourself too much credit. That's just a guy hoping you'd win, who was willing to look the other way as to how you did it. You made up the powerful ally role. Marsden wouldn't have done shit to Jacob."

"Maybe." Jeremy smiled. "And maybe now is the time to find out just how much he'd do for me. I think I'll put in a call later tonight."

"Why Miranda? Why did you have to kill her?" Ben blurted out.

Jeremy shook his head dismissively. "You know the answer. You're just hoping I'll tell you that it wasn't because I heard from you. You want to die with a clean conscience. Let me take away the uncertainty. I had no idea that Miranda knew anything about Jacob Jordan until you told me she thought she recognized him. I couldn't take a chance that she'd put it together." He smiled at Ben and licked his front top teeth, his eyes menacing. "If you hadn't told me, she'd still be alive today."

"Why Jones Point?"

"Why not? It's dark out there, and secluded enough that I knew no one else would stumble upon her before you got there. No one was going to find her in her own backyard, so I could take a day thinking about the best spot."

My own best friend, Ben thought. After all the worry about an international drug lord and killer, the true threat was the man he thought he knew best. *I hope Veronica understands why I tried this.*

Ben watched as Jeremy lifted the gun. Time slowed. He never believed that people had their lives flash before their eyes, but a string of memories were running on a loop through his brain. Graduating from college, meeting Veronica, the twins being born. A good life. Not a long one, but a good one.

Jeremy looked in Ben's eyes. "No more talking now. Goodbye."

The door flew open.

"Drop the gun now!" Detective Brown burst through the door. Jeremy started to turn the gun toward her. Halfway, he paused.

"Don't even think about it!" shouted Detective Fahey, his large frame taking up the entire doorway. Jeremy dropped the gun and put his hands above his head.

"Ben, you okay?" asked Detective Brown.

"I'm good," Ben breathed out. "Your timing was impeccable. Maybe next time you could come a bit earlier though?" He took a couple more deep breaths.

Detective Brown winked at him and held up her recording device, the complement to the one next to the knife in Ben's pocket. "We heard everything. It's over for him."

Ben looked back at Jeremy.

"You think you're so smart, so much better than everyone, and you needed me to know it," he said, adrenaline coursing through him. "Think about that while you spend the rest of your life in prison. Your hubris took over and you had to explain yourself. You're not even going to be notorious. You're no villain, you're no hero, and you're going to go down in history as a failure."

CHAPTER 57
VERONICA

Friday Morning, November 14

My parents and husband sat together beside the bed in my hospital room. The bed was upright, in a sitting position. I'd managed to keep my head up well enough that I could manage sitting up. The four of us watched the anchor on the news describing the list of charges against Jeremy Wiles. And those were only the crimes that the FBI felt confident enough to indict on.

"I never was sure about that guy," Mama said. "I feel vindicated."

"You have to admit," I said. "It was a clever plan. I can appreciate the craft he put into it."

"Veronica, really?" Papa asked.

"You can appreciate it because you've done something similar?" Ben asked.

"Ben! Not the time." Mama gave him a warning look.

"No, Mama, it's okay," I said. "I'm ready to talk about it. What do you want to ask me, Ben?"

"Do you miss it?"

"There are parts I miss, sure. But overall, no. My new life is the best thing I've ever accomplished." I could see Ben watching my eyes when I spoke. He always said they twinkled when I was happy. "Why is that your first question?"

"I know Yancey wanted you back. I guess I just got a little worried that maybe you'd want to go."

"No, of course not. I'd never go back."

Ben took a deep breath. "Honestly, it's a huge relief to hear you say that. It's been gnawing at me." He gave me a pained look. "Can I ask a really intrusive question? I really don't want to know but I also think I have to know."

"Go ahead." I could see him trying to summon up the courage to ask the question I knew was coming.

"Have you really killed people?"

"Ben, do you really want to know the answer to that?"

"Yes. No. I don't know. Please." He grimaced.

"Okay," I sighed. "The easy answer is yes, and the follow-up answer is no, I don't know how many people I've killed. I was just a kid doing her father's bidding, taking out rivals and other bad guys. I wasn't keeping score."

Ben's eyes got wide and his jaw dropped. "You … you don't know?"

"It's a lot, Ben."

"And every single one of them was justified and done expertly." A voice came from the hallway.

We all looked to the door for the source.

Yancey Portillo strode in with the easy saunter of a man who knew he was always in charge. His right arm was still in a sling and the jacket arm hung empty.

"Holy Heavens," Gabriela said. "You're Yancey Portillo."

"That I am." He smiled. "And this is my long-lost daughter." He held his one good arm out, palm up, in my direction.

"I'm not your daughter any longer," I hissed. "You made that very clear long ago."

"Alex—"

"That's not my name," I said, each word ice cold.

"Will you let me talk?" Yancey asked, his voice the same even and calm tone. "I evaded a lot of security to get into this room."

"What do you want? Why have you been looking for me?"

"Isn't it obvious? I've been looking for you every single day since you disappeared." Yancey looked down, a show of emotion so out of character that even I was taken aback. "You were the best part of my life."

"But ... I heard you. You told those kidnappers that it didn't matter what happened to me. Look at this!" I raised my hand, showing my missing pinky. "This is because of you!"

"I know," he said, his voice lowered to just above a whisper.

I had never heard my birth father talk like this. I turned to my parents and husband. "Can we have the room, please?"

Ben shot a worried look at me.

"It'll be okay, just wait right outside," I said.

Yancey held up his right shoulder. "Don't worry. Your friend, the wannabe president, has rendered me much less capable, even if I did wish to harm my daughter."

Once they were outside, Yancey spoke. "I played it wrong. I thought that my reputation alone would keep them from touching you. I didn't think for a second they'd actually do it. Do you know where your pinky is now? Did you know that I found it?"

I exploded. "All I wanted was your approval. All I cared about was living up to your standard. Do you know what you did to me? You destroyed me when you chose your business over me. You did more damage than those kidnappers ever could have."

"Alessandra." He put up his hand to stop my incoming protest about my real name. "I'm very, very sorry. The thing is that I treated you too much like my number two and not enough like my daughter."

"I loved being your number two! I loved being the only one who held the same level of respect as the great Yancey Portillo. But I also needed you to care about me."

"May I tell you something I've never been able to tell anyone?" he asked, his face giving away that he was unsure what my answer would be.

"I don't see why not," I said, exasperated.

"I was never the same after Kelvin died. I cried every night for years. I'd already lost your mother and then I lost my son. Because of that I tried to wall off my emotions for you. You were all I had left. I kept you at arm's distance for fear of losing you. And that is what eventually lost you." Tears came to his eyes.

I sat silently, staring at the man who raised me for fourteen years. I had never seen anything like this from him. This was a man who got rid of someone when I was young just because he cried in front of him. That was after the man's brother had been killed. He told me it was a life lesson. Emotion gets you nowhere.

"I brought you and Kelvin along that terrible night, because I loved the idea of the family being together. All of us working together, especially after your mother died. That's what got Kelvin killed. You have to understand I didn't want you to be part of any of this anymore."

"Then why did you let me?"

Yancey chuckled. "I think for a while you were too young to realize how extraordinary you were. I couldn't stop you because you were incredible. You remember when you dropped in on all of us to say you'd killed Maynor?"

"I do."

"You should have heard the discussion after you left. I've never seen them so stunned. Look, in any profession, when you witness greatness, it's a transcendent experience. Honestly, that's why I didn't stop you. Who would stop Shakespeare after his first play? Lebron James after his first year in the league? So that's what happened. I got scared of losing you after Kelvin died, but I also wanted to nurture your talent. I tried to keep emotion out of it because I would never have been able to handle it if something happened to you. I won't say anything in particular, just in case these walls have ears, but you wouldn't believe the fate that befell those two men who kidnapped you." He took a deep breath and swallowed down what I guessed must have been a sob. "Sorry, I know I'm just rambling now, but I need you to know all of this."

To my surprise, I felt tears start to run down my face.

"I've spent all these years convincing myself that you were a terrible father. That you didn't care about me." My voice broke and I looked away. "I thought if you really cared you would have found me. I kept running because I assumed you were chasing. Once I got to Mexico and I hadn't heard anything, I figured you must not be looking."

"Do you remember when you were in Quetzaltenango?" Yancey flashed a rueful smile, clearly reminiscing.

"Yes. That was as far as the taxi driver from Escuintla would take me when I offered him my knife."

"That taxi driver, his name was Dani, right?"

"How do you—you found him?" I had wondered for years just how close he came to catching up to me. I thought that was a question that would forever remain unanswered.

"You stayed in a grimy little hotel there. I got there a few hours later in the morning that you left. I was too late. No one had any idea where you'd gone and that's where we lost you. I didn't think you'd let yourself be adopted so I only ever looked for single women that fit your description, not a family. That knife you bartered to get a ride from him, that was your special one, wasn't it?"

"It was. It was my dearest possession, the one thing that made me feel like me. Once that was gone, I knew there was no turning back." There wasn't anything inherently special about the knife. It was a simple folding knife, a black hilt with a six-inch blade. But Kelvin had given it to me, just weeks before he was killed. I knew in my heart that all of my actions should have been his, so keeping the knife made me feel as if a part of Kelvin were still alive. When I was down to nothing, that sleazy taxi driver Dani said he'd only give me a ride if I gave him the knife. Well, he suggested a couple other possibilities that I was absolutely not going to allow. I thought there was something symbolic about it. Kelvin helping me one last time.

Yancey reached into his breast pocket and pulled out a folding knife. He set it down gently in my lap.

"Oh my God. This is it. You found it?"

"I got it from Dani, probably only hours after you gave it to him. I've been carrying it with me ever since, waiting for this moment. I *didn't know if it would ever come, but I wanted to be ready. It's yours, and now I can finally return it to you."*

I reached out and held it in my hands. I took a deep breath and breathed out, a slow and deliberate exhale. "This is a lot to take in."

Yancey nodded. "For me too." Neither of us had believed we'd ever see each other again.

He looked down at me, his long-lost daughter. "So … what now?"

CHAPTER 58
BEN
ONE MONTH LATER

Saturday Evening, December 13

Ben helped Veronica out of the car and held her hand as she walked, each step slow and unsteady. Her other hand was held by Maria, with Nico alongside. Every stair was its own journey. When they reached the front door, Ben moved in front of Veronica. He opened the door wide.

"Welcome home, babe," he said with a wide smile. A loud cheer came from inside the house. Veronica stepped over the threshold and looked across at her welcoming party. Her parents, Gabriela and Ricardo, beaming. Jennie, the friend who turned out to be so much more than just that, with Dominik Puskás next to her. Dan Flint, her closest friend and confidante on campus, and several other colleagues. And, oddly, Natalia Rochev.

"I'll explain later," Ben whispered.

The food and red wine flowed. After a while, Ben started moving around the room, handing everyone a flute of Möet.

"Looks like you all have the right beverage now," he said after completing his rounds. "So I'd like to offer a toast to a woman for whom words can only do a disservice. I'll try my best, though.

"She brought down a conspiracy that would have irreparably changed American politics, and, by proxy, all of America. She survived not one, but two, attempted assassinations. Yes, I'm using that term, assassination, because God knows she's practically a legendary figure at this point. In the midst of running for her, and her family's, lives, she had the wherewithal to plant clues to help us catch up, and, when all else failed, she still would not give up. She never gave up, and let's not forget the most important part. This started because she was the only person in this country not willing to give up on Jacob Jordan. We've learned a lot about her skill set recently, but none of it could possibly compare to her heart, and her compassion, and her empathy. For all those reasons, for a million more I could name, and for being back home, safe, where she belongs, I want us all to raise our glasses and toast my wife, Veronica Walsh. Cheers!"

Ben looked at his wife, seated on the couch wiping tears away. "*I love you,*" he mouthed. He turned back to the crowd. "And now, dessert!"

"Ben." He turned around. He hadn't noticed Natalia walk up behind him, munching on one of his famous Congo bars.

"Hey, Nat. How are you doing?" He pursed his lips. Bad question. How could she be doing?

"I'm just trying to get through each day right now." She shrugged. "You?"

"Same. It's all much better now that V is able to come home, though. I just ..." Ben lost the words. What could he say that encompassed the loss of her husband in such a way?

Natalia nodded. "I've been getting that a lot. It's okay. No one knows what to say. How should they? There's no guidebook for what to do when it turns out your husband blackmailed a man into attempting to assassinate the president only so he can save the day and then run for president himself, and in doing so kill at least six more people to try to keep his secret."

"If you find that guidebook, or a version for your best friend who attempted not once, but twice, to kill your wife, you'll let me know?"

Natalia chuckled ruefully. "You and I understand each other the most, I think. The wife and the best friend."

Ben nodded. "The betrayal. It stings."

"I know. I was sure he was on the side of the angels. He was so sincere about how much he wanted to fix the country. I was drawn to that idealism."

"I think that's how he rationalized it too. That it was all part of the greater good." Ben knew he should be furious at Jeremy for all that he had done, but he couldn't bring himself to keep up the anger. Every time he thought about his former best friend, the only feeling he could muster was sadness.

Jeremy's plea date was coming up, and it was assumed he would plead guilty. With that plea, he'd get life without parole and, barring the movie that would inevitably be made, slip from the public consciousness and be lost to history.

"You know, I think he almost told me," Natalia said.

"What do you mean?"

"I got this sense for a while that he was excited but holding something under the surface, like there was this extra excitement he wanted to tell but couldn't. Then, on the night he must have been out moving Miranda's body—ugh, I can't believe I'm saying that out loud—he started talking to me about the Supreme Court Justice."

Ben's jaw dropped. He stared at her.

"Jeremy told me he had gotten a secret email from Marsden, telling him he would retire if Jeremy won." She shook her head. "I think he wanted to tell me, but couldn't give away his secret, so just pretended like Marsden emailed him out of the blue. He then told me that Marsden told him to delete the email and that he'd disavow it if Jeremy said anything publicly. He must have been making that up as he went. He just wanted to tell someone about his Supreme Court plan."

Congress had begun impeachment proceedings for Justice Marsden, but he was claiming both ignorance and innocence. With the Senate split, it was likely he would see no true repercussions.

Natalia looked Ben square in the eyes. "I'm so sorry, Ben, I should have asked more questions, done something more to figure it out, but then you called about the body you found, and then we learned all that stuff about Veronica, and it just slipped my mind."

"I don't blame you, Nat," Ben said and put his hand on her shoulder. "The two of us were both blind when it came to him."

"I think we might need each other," Natalia said. "To get through this. I don't know how I'm supposed to be mentally ready to start my tour next week. I told my manager I wasn't sure I could go through with it, but he made the point that my fans need to see me. They need to be convinced I'm still the singer they all love."

"We'll help each other out, don't worry," Ben responded. "Let me know when you're in the area. You have my number. Use it whenever." He paused and laughed. "Never thought I'd be saying that to a pop star."

"To a friend, Ben." Natalia raised her glass and turned away.

————

The party carried on until late in the evening. It was almost midnight when Congresswoman Moore finally called it a night, and only Veronica's parents remained.

"We're going to go upstairs and check on Nico and Maria," Ricardo said with a mischievous smile. "I bet they're only pretending to be asleep."

"Finally," Ben said after they went up the stairs. "Back home. Me and you together."

A knock on the door broke his momentary peace. Ben jerked his head toward Veronica.

"Seriously?" he asked.

She shook her head, bewildered.

A second knock.

Ben and Veronica looked at each other. Veronica saw the worry in Ben's eyes.

"It can't be. Jeremy's locked away. The threat is over. It's okay, Ben."

"Okay, I'll get it."

Ben peeked through the peephole and saw Francisco standing outside. He opened the door and let him in.

"Oh my God! Francisco!" Veronica exclaimed. He walked over and gave her a kiss on the cheek. "I didn't think I'd ever see you again."

"I can't believe it, either," Francisco said. "The weeks I spent here without being able to even walk by you in the street were really difficult!"

"I heard you tailed me, and I didn't even notice." Veronica laughed. "Did you get good, or did I get bad?"

"I'd like to think I got good." Francisco smiled.

"Well, it's just fantastic to see you."

"That's actually why I'm here." Francisco looked at both Ben and Veronica. "I came to tell you that I'm going to be here for a while longer."

"What do you mean?"

"Now that your name is out there, we think there's a chance you could be in danger from any number of rivals of ours, most notably Osmin Mejia, who we know is hiding out in the United States. I'm staying here to make sure that doesn't happen."

"Are you going to be watching us from rooftops?" Ben asked, a nervous expression on his face.

Francisco laughed. "Oh, nothing like that. We don't think

there's any immediate threat, so my job here will be more about making inroads with the diaspora and information gathering. I'll most likely start with the leader of MS-13. We don't like them at all, but they respect the Portillo name, so I'll get an audience. I figure if Yancey could get an entire organization to disband with a quiet word to their leader, I can at least make some progress here with these guys." He hesitated and then looked at Veronica. "I'm not supposed to tell you this, but I'm also here as an intermediary. If your father wants to get in touch with you, he'll relay the message through me, so I figure I should extend the courtesy to you, too. Any time you want to talk to your father, you tell me. I don't know exactly how your discussion in the hospital went, but he's happier than I've seen him in decades."

He nodded toward Ben. "Your husband has my number. I hope I get to spend some more time with you and learn about the adult version of you. I've spent a lot of time imagining what you might be like."

"I never thought I'd get to see how you grew up, either," Veronica said. "Promise me you won't be spying on us for Yancey, though. Tell me you're not just going to pass anything we say right back to him."

"I promise. I wouldn't do that."

"Then I'm glad you're staying around." Veronica smiled.

Francisco gave Veronica a gentle hug and gave Ben a deferential nod. "I'll leave you guys to it." He left as quickly as he had come.

"Wow. I mean. Just, wow." Veronica couldn't find the words. "This is unbelievable."

Ben took her hand in his. "I guess there's gonna be a new normal around here. Whatever comes next, I'm just glad we're going to take it on together. But right now, how about we head upstairs and see exactly what fun your parents are having with Nico and Maria?"

EPILOGUE

JACOB

Three Months Later

Jacob Jordan smiled as he stood outside the Foggy Bottom Metro Station. He had been planning his escape from Red Onion when he had been transferred to a mental hospital back in Washington, DC, instead. Upon arriving there, he learned that Jeremy Wiles had confessed, that his role as a patsy had been confirmed, and that, although his conviction had not been overturned, he was going to be moved out of his supermax. There was the unfortunate case of Jeremy having witnessed him run the Belle family off the road, but the state decided it best to keep him out of a bona fide prison.

While he was proud of how his escape plans had come along, new plans in his new location would be much easier. There was a great deal of sympathy for him among the staff, who clearly believed he was not well enough to have a grasp of what he did. They were not particularly careful either, and he had his escape planned out within a week of arriving.

Jacob waited several weeks until the uproar had died down. He continued to remain completely silent. Then one evening at dinner, he simply slipped away out of sight, put a single guard in a sleeper hold, and snuck off into the night. In the thirty minutes it took them to notice he was gone, he stole a Honda Accord from the lot, drove it to Union Station, parked in long-term parking, and snuck down to the bottom floor and the metro station. The few dollars in cash he found in the car got him a one-time use metro card, and he disappeared into the crowd on the other side of the turnstiles.

Ever since the first contact from Jeremy, he realized he would need to cultivate a persona. He knew he was in a bind and had read about the Unabomber while in college, so he knew people would fall for the "brilliant mathematician but mentally lacking" routine. He knew he would be able to play it too. There would be worry, and a search, but no manhunt.

Easiest way to convince everyone you're a patsy is to act like a patsy. He even changed his voice when Ben Walsh called, just to keep up the ruse. Now he was free, and fairly certain no one was going to pull up trees looking for him.

The sun had gone down over Washington, DC, hours ago but the streets were still abuzz when he stepped out of the metro. He looked on as sharply dressed men and women walked up and down 23rd Street, streaming out of the Department of State, the Institute of Peace, and the other government and nonprofit organizations housed in the area. Undergrads from George Washington University, in a far different—but for their purpose, no less important—dress code, hopped into rideshares and made their way to whatever Friday night excitement was in store. Street musicians provided the night's melody, a cacophony of trumpets and drums.

There was a safe feeling in the air, an assurance that the horrors of the past months were behind them. The man responsible for all the deaths was rightfully behind bars, where he could not hurt anyone anymore.

Almost all the deaths.

It was ironic, Jacob thought, that Jeremy's entire plan, including using him as the patsy, was only initiated after he caught a glimpse of step one of Jacob's own plans. The only one who had at all wondered if there was something more going on was his old professor, Dr. Walsh. Boy did she turn out to have a backstory. She had asked him point blank, the first time they talked after he was arrested. She knew that this was not him, could not have been what he did. After all, he was far too clever to pull an assassination attempt with no escape plan.

She did not even begin to fathom the real truth, though. The truth that, if Jeremy had known, could have made Jacob's short stint in prison much more complicated.

The truth that the accident, the one that killed almost the entire Belle family, was not what it seemed. It was not the act of a distracted and ill mind, tragically not seeing the car in the cruising lane before it was too late.

He had seen the car.

He had known exactly who was in it.

And he had known exactly what he was doing.

He executed his plan perfectly. The one snag was Jeremy Wiles. He knew there was a small chance someone might have seen his car and it was a risk he had been willing to take. He didn't think it'd be someone with the ambition of Jeremy, though. The fact that Jeremy's unnamed co-conspirator turned out to be none other than the Chief Justice of the United States was more than even Jacob's mind had imagined. When Jeremy threatened him first, he figured he'd pretend to go along with it, and then kill Jeremy as soon as he had a chance, before the planned assassination day. Even though Jeremy didn't let it slip, it was obvious to Jacob that his plan was to thwart the assassination to gain notoriety.

The co-conspirator became an issue. Jeremy was smart, Jacob had to give him credit for that. He recognized the weak spot in his threat, and the added threat of what would be done to Jacob and his family should anything happen to Jeremy was just enough to force Jacob to see it through. Everyone has a weak spot.

He sat down on a bench in Washington Circle and took

stock. The death of the final Belle family member while he was in prison was a bonus he had not counted on. He mentally crossed Miranda Belle off his list and moved on to the next victim.

The Belle family was simply the first domino to fall. There were many more remaining. They would fall in time. Being arrested for the most high-profile murder of the decade had not been his intention, and he was now behind schedule. Maybe that was a blessing in disguise, though. Now it was time to take it slow and do it right. He would wait, he would plan.

Jacob smiled again, and looked around, taking in the sights and sounds of the city. The sights and sounds of freedom.

These people had seen nothing yet.

THANK YOU FOR READING RUN

We hope you enjoyed it as much as we enjoyed bringing it to you. We just wanted to take a moment to encourage you to review the book. Follow this link: Run to be directed to the book's Amazon product page to leave your review.

Every review helps further the author's reach and, ultimately, helps them continue writing fantastic books for us all to enjoy.

———

For more information on Matthew Becker's books, check out his website: www.matthewbeckerbooks.com.

———

Want to discuss our books with other readers and even the authors? Join our Discord server today and be a part of the Aethon community.

Facebook | Instagram | Twitter | Website

You can also join our non-spam mailing list by visiting www.subscribepage.com/AethonReadersGroup and never miss out on future releases. You'll also receive three full books completely Free as our thanks to you.

Looking for more great thrillers?

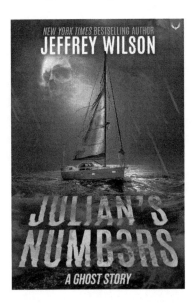

Lost at sea, can Julian save all he loves from the ghostly stowaways trapped aboard with him?

Julian wants more than anything to be like every other kid—skateboard, hang out with friends, have sleepovers, and tease his little brother and sister. But Julian has a special gift, one which, to him, feels more of a curse.

In his dreams, he is visited by spirits who tell him things—sometimes very important things.

He has called these "tell-you" dreams since he was little, and he knows now to keep them secret, ever since one such dream came true when the little Mendes girl down the street was murdered in her basement.

But now, Julian will need the ghosts from his dreams more than ever. Voices have given him the winning lottery numbers and he and his family are setting out on a family sailing vacation on their new sailboat, *Julian's Numbers*.

The dreams are warning him of an evil that will capture his mother and put his entire family—and maybe much more—at risk. He will need to listen to his ghosts if he is to have any chance of stopping the growing evil aboard their yacht and save his family from certain death…

THE SHINING meets DEAD CALM in this supernatural horror ghost thriller from the mind of Jeff Wilson, New York Times bestselling author of the TIER ONE and THE SHEPHERDS Series and now Tom Clancy's JACK RYAN Series.

GET JULIAN'S NUMBERS NOW!

———

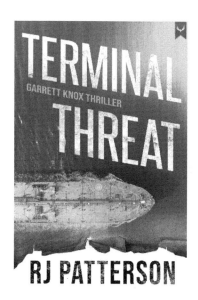

In a daring act of piracy, Yemeni terrorists have not only seized a special oil tanker but they've also captured a high-value asset.

With President Lewis desperate to save his biggest donor's assets and protect his deepest secret, he orders Director of National Intelligence Camille Banks to deploy her secret team to recover the asset.

Garrett Knox, along with his hand-picked team members of elite operatives, must attempt the impossible: infiltrate the treacherous Yemeni mountains and bring the asset home alive. Battling hostile terrain and relentless attacks, Knox and company close in on their target only to have the tables flipped on them as a far deadlier plot emerges.

The terrorists offer a chilling ultimatum—the asset in exchange for a notorious bombmaker in U.S. custody. With time running out and the world watching, Knox and his team embark on a pulse-pounding mission to retrieve the bombmaker.

But when a shocking betrayal threatens everything, Knox must make an unthinkable choice to save Rico and save the president.

From the Oval Office to the explosive climax, Terminal Threat is a non-stop thrill ride packed with jaw-dropping twists. As a sinister conspiracy tightens its grip, will Knox's team prevail, or will the President's dark secrets destroy them all? The clock is ticking in this electrifying novel by R.J. Patterson.

*This action thriller is perfect for fans of Tom Clancy's **Jack Ryan**, Vince Flynn's **Mitch Rapp**, Robert Ludlum's **Jason Bourne** or Stephen Hunter's **Bob Lee Swagger**!*

GET TERMINAL THREAT NOW!

———

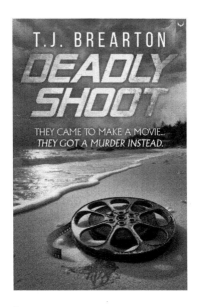

THEY CAME TO MAKE A MOVIE...
THEY GOT A MURDER INSTEAD.

Mack Banner hasn't made a movie in fifteen years. He's been laying low, raising his daughter, hoping not to be recognized.

When a hot young screenwriter writes a script for him to star in, he's drawn out of hiding to a remote island off the coast of Maine where part of the film will shoot.

Only, the screenwriter, on location for some last-minute rewrites, is suddenly missing. And as the crew spreads out to search for her, a storm brews on the horizon.

Soon they'll be trapped, and people are starting to turn up dead...

Part Agatha Christie, part action thriller, DEADLY SHOOT by bestseller TJ Brearton will have you on the edge of your seat figuring out "who done it" as Mack races to keep his friends and loved ones safe and to stop a brutal killer before it's too late.

Perfect for fans of Shari Lapena's AN UNWANTED GUEST,

Alex Michaelides's THE FURY, and lovers of all things psychological murder mystery thrillers!

GET DEADLY SHOOT NOW!

———

For all our Thriller books, visit our website.

ACKNOWLEDGMENTS

Thank you to the whole Aethon Books crew for all your work, from the first manuscript read all the way through publication.

Thank you to my agent Gina Panettieri, and the Talcott Notch team, for taking me on and being a constant source of wisdom and expertise.

Thank you to my dad and siblings, for years of listening to me talk about ideas and encouraging every single one of them. Especially my twin brother Tim, whose opinion is the litmus test for any piece of my writing.

Thank you to my sister-in-law Emily, for being a constant source of enthusiasm and support.

Thanks to all of you who helped answer questions, read early versions, or acted as sounding boards, including but not limited to Daniel Harrington, Cole Gessner, Yolián Amaro-Rivera, and Kelsey Moreland.

Thank you to Sarah Pekkanen, for your support and kindness in helping to mentor a new writer.

Of course, thank you to my wife, Sarah, for a million things including being a wonderful example of a badass woman who does have it all. I'm sorry I made Veronica so murdery–I swear that part wasn't a reflection of you!

Finally, to anyone who downloaded or picked up this book. There are more good thrillers out here than you could ever get through, so I thank you for choosing mine.

ABOUT THE AUTHOR

MATTHEW BECKER is a mathematician, and formerly worked as part of the national Covid-19 response. He has a doctorate in applied mathematics from the University of Maryland, College Park, and is published in the Bulletin of Mathematical Biology. Matthew currently lives with his wife, a U.S. diplomat, and their two children in Tashkent, Uzbekistan. Run is his first novel.